GEORGE'S LAIR

GEORGE'S LAIR

John Bayley

Duckworth

First published in 1996 by
Gerald Duckworth & Co. Ltd.
The Old Piano Factory
48 Hoxton Square, London N1 6PB
Tel: 0171 729 5986
Fax: 0171 729 0015

A catalogue record for this book is available
from the British Library

ISBN 0 7156 2747 3

Typeset by Ray Davies
Printed in Great Britain by
Redwood Books Ltd, Trowbridge

Contents

CHAPTER 1

The Bower

'My Darling, however did you find it?'

The young man she had addressed did not reply. He was on his knees on the cluttered stone floor, pulling at a bulky object tightly encased in a covering that looked like waxed linen or plastic. It clung and crackled as he unwrapped it, revealing dark metal.

'I took this one out to play with,' he said at last. 'The rest are still in the box. No, take it with both hands, Dulcie. Feel the balance of it.'

She did her best to obey. She cradled the object awkwardly, not wishing to seem afraid that grease would get on her clothes. Her soft pop eyes gazed at him with their usual look of boundless affection, as if she wanted to hold only him, not this hard and heavy child.

But she was accustomed to obey. Loving him as she did, she could not help sometimes having a strained look of love when their eyes met. Yet the strain she was under when they were together was made joyful by the total ease he seemed to feel with her. The way he loved her seemed as pure as selfishness. It delighted her unfailingly, and made her deeply thankful. As long as he behaved as he did she knew he was happy with her. And when they were together like this she could feel sure he would never leave her.

Now with an effort she knelt down beside him on the dank floor. It was like playing children, but her joints were not like those of a child. Nor were they were those of a young man. She adjusted a fascinated look on her big features, over her more natural expression of placatory good will.

He was telling her about the mechanism of the gun that he had peeled out of its dark skin of wrapping.

'Gas-operated. You know what that means, Dulcie, don't you?'

Dulcie was not her name. It was the pet name he sometimes used, because, as he told her, she reminded him of the heroine in a novel he had once found himself reading, by some woman author or other. George had a sort of reading habit, though he was unselective. The novel had been left in the bedside drawer of a hotel room in Leeds. There was this paperback under the Gideon bible, and George, who had been sleepless that night, had read it absently into the small hours.

He had been drinking whisky, which he disliked doing, with a businessman his father had sent him up to contact – a builder like his father. Until he managed to escape to bed he had found it a depressing evening, and the novel, read through an insomniac hangover – he was not used to whisky – had unexpectedly cheered and comforted him. He finished it, which he rarely did with anything he read, and he was sorry afterwards that he had not taken it away.

If he could have remembered what it was called he would have given it to Dulcie. She would have loved it for his sake, though she was not a great reader. But she loved him to call her his Dulcie.

Her real name was Martha. Or Mrs Alexander Grey.

Now she tried without much success to look knowing and intelligent, as well as fascinated and excited.

'Gas-operated,' she repeated obediently.

'Yes. That means some of the energy from the cartridge when it goes off behind the bullet is tapped from the top of the barrel into this cylinder and works the mechanism which gives automatic fire. About six hundred rounds a minute, Of course that's theoretical, because the operator fires it in bursts, four or five at a time, and the mag holds thirty rounds. You can fire the whole lot off in about three seconds, if you fancy; but it would just be a waste.'

'Just be a waste,' parroted Martha. She supposed it would. She continued to hold the thing in her arms, wishing George would take it back, as if he were its mother, and she an outsider unaccustomed to babies. But she could see he was pleased that she was holding it.

8

Although she worshipped everything that he did, and wanted to do when he was with her, she couldn't help but be a bit appalled by this new aspect of their ecstatically secret relationship. She had only been seven when the war ended, but she had been terrified by everything to do with it. She remembered the hysterical note of the air raid sirens, and her mother making her look up to see a buzzbomb flying over, grumbling horribly to itself like a mad old man in the park, and then suddenly silent before plunging down somewhere, on to some house or group of people. She remembered the distant sound of the explosion, and how she had cried and buried her face in her mother's ARP overalls.

She had indeed been a timid little girl, though always anxious to please. Her brusque father, who was in a Highland regiment, had instructed her to revere the British army, especially the allied and independent Scots forces; and it was he who wanted her christened Martha. Martha Mackay had a good military sound about it. Her mother had wanted to call her Blanche, which was now her second name. But since she was only a girl, and her mother, if she had to have a child then at all, had wanted a son, her father got his way. (He had wanted a son too.)

But the name Martha was obviously hers: it suited her. She could hear her mother calling it out impatiently now, as she used to sit among the coats in the cloak-room downstairs, a refuge she had first taken to when the Air Raid warning went and there were distant bomb explosions. Her busy mother never paid the air raids any attention.

She didn't pay her daughter a great deal either. She might have had a son if her husband had not been killed at the Anzio landings. As it was, she was left in 1944 with Martha, who missed her father very much but never said anything about it. Neither did her mother, except for the odd reference to Daddy, made with a dry eye and a casual voice. But, to do her mother justice, she had soon set about the easy task of making friends with the willing little girl; and by the time Martha went to boarding school (her mother had a bit of money of her own) they lived quite happily together.

Then her mother met and married a middle-aged man who

had marked her down at a dinner party. He was a barrister; divorced, with no children, fifty plus.

Martha's mother, still barely out of her twenties, had always had a penchant for middle-aged men. It may possibly have been sharpened by her brief impulsive marriage to Lieutenant Mackay, who was the same age as herself. That had been very much a wartime affair.

Always a biddable and adjustable child, Martha obediently liked her stepfather from the start. But she was soon aware that he didn't greatly care for her, or consider her much more than a small drawback in the new scheme of things. Perhaps he resented his new wife's money going to pay her school fees, although her absence for much of the year could only have been a bonus to him. Her mother got in the habit of smiling at her apologetically during the holidays, and giving her a swift hug when they were on their own, which did not seem very often.

Then her mother had another child, a boy, and when she was home from school Martha threw herself into worship of the newcomer with all the abandonment she could manage. She changed its nappies assiduously, and was better at this and other aspects of nursery care than her mother, who sometimes told her friends with a little laugh that she really had the most obliging of daughters, who in time would make some nice man such a good wife. Martha was obliging too, when, at the age of nineteen, an older colleague of her stepfather's seduced her. It was a one-off thing and both of them kept absolutely quiet about it. (So did Martha's mother, who was the colleague's part-time mistress.) Not very long after that a rather younger man, also a friend of her stepfather's, proposed to Martha. She accepted of course.

Martha was tall, although fortunately her new husband, Alexander Grey, was slightly taller. Big as she was, she had grown quite pretty, in spite of her large features. Her mother, and to do him justice her stepfather too, made unstinting arrangements for the wedding to be a success.

Alexander Grey, who was quite high up in oil, already had a big house not far from London, in an area that seemed rural, but was not quite the country. Like her stepfather he had been previously married and divorced, and had no children. After some years of disappointment Martha had two in quick succession, Penelope and Benjamin.

Martha greatly enjoyed being married and having a family: it was the culmination of her urge to oblige the human race for accepting her existence.

Not only did she feel she was happy but she liked her husband, who went in for being a husband in the same spirit in which Martha threw herself into being a wife, although naturally he had to work at it less hard than she did.

Martha soon came to be aware that her husband continued to love his first wife, and to see her surreptitiously. No doubt he still went to bed with her, if he took her with him to hotels during his trips on business. That precaution, in fact, might not have been necessary, though Martha was hardly to realise it, for Alexander's real interest was not so much in his former wife as in her new husband.

Martha came to know this too, or some of it; and so far from unsettling her the knowledge was in some curious way a comfort. It meant that she wasn't bearing the burden of marriage quite alone. She felt she had not one but two invisible co-workers. Although Martha was so obliging and so conscientious – such a good person in fact – she remained weak and unsure inside herself, craving the kind of reassurance which the conventions of her new life in prosperous metroland did not give her.

And no doubt would not have wanted to give her. Metroland was in its own quiet way sadistic; it liked to keep on the hop those who had no nerve of their own. And the place was still formal, even when the sixties were well under way. Martha came to know people but made no friends. Not that she had much time for any at first. They had a nanny for the children, who kept her busy.

Her husband's relations with his other family, whatever they were, gave a background of secret warmth, of invisible stability, to the world she had to live in, a world in which her own unconfidence never seemed to find a friendly response. She thought of her predecessor, Fiona, fighting the same battle as herself, at Haywards Heath. No doubt she was quite mistaken about Fiona having to fight any sort of battle; even though she

11

was fairly sure about Alexander's continued relations both with Fiona and with Nigel, her young husband. Could she have done so, but she couldn't, she would like to have asked Alexander how his other family was getting on, and whether there were any little ones as yet.

After the first two no more little ones came for her, although she took it for granted she would have liked a bigger family.

'Ally', as she sometimes called him – he had confided his childhood nickname in a tender moment when they were court-ing – had never suggested that he loved her for herself alone, and she found this honesty endearing. Even before he proposed he used to tell her how much he looked forward to a family. And indeed Ally, as the children too addressed him instead of Daddy, seemed at least in that persona a most endearing man: a sterling chap, if a trifle ponderous. His was a solemnity Martha learned to repose upon: there was something owlish about it, at intimate moments, which always melted her.

And she felt proud of the area where they lived. She loved the big house in Gallions Way. At the end of its drive was a curly and carefully dishevelled roadway, never properly made up, which ran in loops all over the extended acreage of what had once been a forest.

From time to time this road dropped off handsome rural residences in a variety of styles, with drives, even quite long ones, of their own. Gardens were ample in size, but the old forest trees had been mostly cut down and replaced by ornamentals – cherry and whitebeam, mountain ash and silver birches.

In their own spacious grounds a giant old crab-apple tree of the original wood had been retained as a feature. Over the years Martha had become attached to this arboreal relic. With the children at school and her husband at his office she used to take a cushion on warm days and sit in its comfortable crotch, a few feet from the ground. She never did this with the family at home. She thought of it as her tree house.

The Greys had their friends of course even if Martha herself had none; and relations with these had become comfortably formalised. A few in for drinks; occasionally a bigger drinks party. Dinner for dinner; and sometimes a barbecue, which Martha privately loathed. As they grew up the children made

12

their own arrangements; sometimes the parents of their friends became friends with the elder Greys, sometimes not. For the holidays every year Martha braced herself with an effort. Holidaymaking was the most demanding and draining occupation she knew, and she looked forward gratefully to being back in Prentice Wood (the houses were apt to have such names) after an exacting fortnight, sometimes three weeks, in Scotland or Cornwall, or in Greece or Spain.

The children grew more impatient with her as they grew up, though continuing to treat her with offhand affection. Like their father, they seemed good at getting on. It was as a trio that they came, in a not too unkindly spirit, to regard Martha as an apt to be clueless outsider. She was sometimes aware of not fitting into her own family, but even that status reassured her in some way. And she was easily reassured.

As time went on she saw less of her husband. By that time too she had no means of knowing whether his relations with his former wife, and her once new husband, still existed, or whether he had found someone else. She and Alexander continued to get along very well, for he retained his sterling qualities without effort, and they bedded in more solidly from year to year. He took increasingly little notice of Martha, which she did not mind; indeed she was mildly thankful.

Her husband did not strike his acquaintance as leading any sort of double life; he was not in the least secretive. It was Martha, in her own unemphatic way, who began insensibly to develop all the instincts of secrecy, although she had nothing at first to be secretive about.

And then she had. She fell in love.

It had never happened to her before, in her adult life. Once it had happened at school, when she was twelve; and she remembered that now, while awkwardly holding the heavy gun and gazing into George's face. The loved one then had shown her things – clothes, cosmetics, jazz magazines – in the same offhand but important way. Louise Bruce had been her name. A very fair girl, with long hair down her back. Not much less than forty years ago.

George knew she was not attending to what he told her. But he knew, too, that she was understanding everything in her own

13

way, taking it in simply by looking at him. It was so easy to talk to Martha, and with speech so miraculously agreeable it seemed a part of speech to take the gun from her arms, and to begin kissing her.

*

George Pusey was just twenty-five, and had no particular job. He had helped in his father's business from time to time, but at the moment he was doing nothing, because his father was bankrupt.

Pusey *père* had been quite a successful speculative builder. As a young man he had helped build some of the quality housing estates which had nibbled away what was once a wide wooded area around the village, for in itself it was hardly a town.

This extensive woodland had originally been preserved and keepered by a single large landowner, a nobleman. But after the war the forest, which had barely survived intact through the twenties and thirties, the era of garden cities and of a new rural metroland, had at last succumbed to wholesale development. No more beech glades, with their great deep drifts of fallen leaves, and rosy clouds of willowherb, and slim straight ash in the coppices. Tasteful gardens, tasteful ruddy tiled roofs and gables, remorselessly took over. By the time Alexander Grey had brought his new wife there, the prosperous householders of the Earlwood estate were already second generation, and beginning to be third.

Mr Pusey senior had also known a good deal of prosperity in his time. George was his only child, a fact which had grieved his mother, for like Martha she would have loved a big family. She came from farming stock in Bedfordshire, and Jim Pusey had met her there on an occasion when he had gone to see about bricks. They were a choice and speckly kind, suited to the high quality requirements of his new clients, and their houses.

Anne, still in her teens, had taken to him at once, and George had been born soon after they were married. But there had been complications; she had been told that she could not, or at least should not, become pregnant again. To this advice she paid no attention. But the specialists had been right, and the miscarriage and haemorrhage that followed a new pregnancy had nearly killed her. She had not been quite the same after that. A big rosy-faced woman with prominent eyes and a naturally hearty manner, she was miscast as any sort of invalid. She knew it too; and her good-heartedness became obsessive, lavishing the love which was her natural capital; less on her husband and on George than on a whole tribe of deprived persons, of either sex, whom she picked up in the course of more general do-gooding.

So George never felt close to his mother. Sometimes when he was young, she would bring a disturbed boy or girl home to play with him. He hated that, although his natural politeness disguised the fact; and he knew how wounded and how contemptuous his mother would be were he to reveal how much these underprivileged children repelled him, and how his sense of privacy shrank from them. Even as a child he was resignedly aware of the extent to which his mother was liked locally, as well as respected. Insofar as there could be such figures in such a well-off private milieu, she had become madonna and matriarch of the Earlwood community. She was also its social conscience, though she held no political views.

George became lonelier as he grew up, but he had never felt lonely as a child. Escaping the hangers-on of various ages whom his mother had often had about the house, he would vanish into the surrounding country, which was not really country at all, though clefts and enclaves still possessed a natural wildness long since forfeited in more rural but also more industrialised farming landscapes. Real country would have had no interest and no charms for young George. But close to the Earlwood estate were some quite large properties of which he made himself discreetly free. At the back of houses a great deal grander than that of his own family, with names like King's Keep and Castle Hill, there had been planted miniature but dense plantations of ornamental fir, carefully designed to dull traffic noise, and to hide the property away from the new motorway and the main roads.

Secret fastnesses and small invisible nests could be made in these, unbeknownst to distantly busy owners, who spent the day in offices and most weekends on the golf-course. Once landscaped none of these extensive domains were in the true

15

sense occupied; and it would never have occurred to the owners, as it might have done in real country, to try to keep the public out. There was no public around the place; and barbed wire or notices would have not been in keeping with the locality.

It was not long before George graduated to the more spacious hunting ground of a still private park, whose derelict defences were eminently penetrable by a determined twelve-year-old. The big house at its centre had become in succession a business school, a religious centre, and a hostel for unmarried mothers. Its grounds were filled with Victorian shrubberies, growing more densely luxurious and neglected year by year.

Young George was himself at school, but he continued to possess his own secret places in the locality, whose charm for him, during his holidays, did not diminish. Puberty enhanced it. He had daydreams of strange women, found wandering solitarily in his haunts, holding some plucked leaf or flower in their slim fingers. His secret rounds, precise and punctual as those of a fox, were entranced by these visions. Sometimes they poured a tale of sorrow and estrangement in his ears, caressed and kissed him, and told him that his understanding had sweetened for ever their desolate lives.

Such fancies mingled harmoniously with the umbrageous nooks he had grown so fond of; and they went just as well with his growing expertise in the names of things: the plants, the trees and shrubs. He loved all the exotic and neglected flora encountered on his rambles; and the birds too: softly twittering little families of long-tails in the high fir-tops, green yaffles, and the more exotic woodpeckers in their black and red and white.

Meanwhile the family business was doing well, and his parents encouraged George to try for university. He got there with surprisingly little trouble; but he found the business of being a student both over-demanding and unrewarding. He had no peer group; he still made no friends. He studied history, which had been his best subject at school, but he only really cared for dates, personalities and battles, or details about armour and archery. That was not the way it was taught now, and he was expected to interest himself in social and economic trends which

16

held no appeal. Exam results were most indifferent: indeed he only just scraped a degree.

His attitude to other student activities was similarly negative. He did not fall in love, nor did he try to cajole any of the busy and self-possessed young women who bustled about the college to go to bed with him. It seemed so obviously not worth trying, for all the emancipation which was supposed to have entered the world of students and sex a dozen or so years earlier. He took no hard drugs, and when he was persuaded at a party to try a joint he felt no effects from it. Others, particularly the women students, seemed effortlessly to meet social and academic challenges for which he himself had no stomach at all. His teachers tried to buck him up, but George's demeanour remained unhelpful; he failed to buck up: and he was soon written off in that quarter too.

In the vacations he was equally unenterprising. He did not hitchhike to Nepal or join relief expeditions to Africa; nor did he find jobs in cafés or on construction sites. He would have been prepared to help his father more, but Pusey senior was preoccupied with a long-running business crisis, and was thankful only that George, unlike many students, did not overspend his grant or expect his parents to finance him. George lived at home during the holidays: the sole extent to which he constituted a burden.

That was just as well, because by the time he left university his father's business was in trouble. The elder Pusey had none of the patriarch's temperament or instincts. He did not in the least care whether or not his son followed him into the firm; and indeed he assumed, so far as he had time to consider the matter at all, that if George did not exactly better himself he would at least do something different. He was possessive about his self-made business, and about his workpeople: his family he saw as a different lot, living in a world apart. He was a thoroughly sound-natured man, and tolerant – even meek – about the problems of the new genteel status which his wife's activities had imposed upon their original prosperity, and which she quite unconsciously carried off so well.

Those little difficulties had never bothered him much, and

now they were to bother him no longer. A week after he had to give up, and was declared bankrupt, his wife died.

George could not pretend to himself that the event deeply grieved him; but he sorrowed for his father, and still more for his own security at home. He saw now how much home had meant to him: too much, no doubt; for the sense of defensiveness it had cherished in him had repelled all the usual normalities of growing up and going out into the world.

Fortunately, as his father recovered from his bereavement, he seemed to find yet more unacceptable any sign of maturity in his offspring. Misfortune had paralysed not only his once considerable powers of work and will but left him unable to accept from what was left of his family anything but the happily docile dependence with which George had unknowingly flattered him in the days of his success.

Mr Pusey missed his wife all the more from the fact that they had for years been strangers to each other, strangers joined amicably together in the cosy interdependence of married habit. He had always tolerated, if sometimes with mild exasperation, his wife's shelter and nurture of the lamest of lame ducks; and sometimes of ducks who seemed less lame than cunning. Now he sorely missed not these hangers-on themselves – they had all vanished away at the death of their benefactress, and at the news of her husband's bankruptcy – but that need for forbearance his wife's disposition and way of life had, with equal mildness, imposed on him.

George welcomed the disappearance of the odd characters who had come to be helped by his mother, and who had often stayed in the house. He saw that his father felt guilty towards him; and he himself felt, in consequence as it seemed, not so much sorrow for his parent as a rush of filial warmth. His father may have considered, and for good reason, that he had let his son down badly; and yet George did not take that view at all. His mother, he knew, had never even been told about her husband's financial worries. It was the kind of thing that would have meant nothing to her; and though she was never personally extravagant she had always spent money unthinkingly on her lame ducks and good causes. She had died without knowing of the change that had come upon them; and her husband could at least take satisfaction from the knowledge that his own misfortune had in no way hastened his wife's death.

It was a source of satisfaction to George that it was to him, and not to his mother, that his father had spoken; it was to him that his father had naturally turned in his trouble. Not that he thought his own son could do anything about it, nor had he expected him to try; rather it was George's own qualities of inertia that were to become such an unexpected comfort to George's parent. He sensed obscurely that his son was grateful for the bankruptcy, rather than shocked or worried about it. In fact George felt released by proxy. Here was a licence to be seriously irresponsible in his own negative way. He was empowered in a need not to get on with his own life.

George had always failed to grasp, no doubt, what was going on in the 'real world' of the young. There was no saving oddity about him, except his natural talent for regression. Had he collected old colour supplements, or learned how to make period instruments, he would have acquired a recognisable persona. People would have said 'Oh, and George Pusey does such-and-such.' He might have grown a beard or sported a Welsh crook. Anything like that would have placed him. And yet nothing did. He was up to nothing. And if he had been up to something no one would have noticed.

His father's bad luck or bad management made George begin to grow younger, not older. It freed him, for example, to re-explore, more cautiously than in the past, his old secret nooks among the tailored boscage at the edge of the larger grounds. The curious unbeing of these wholly secluded though definitely non-rural spots still seemed to welcome his wish for non-performance. He felt more at home in them than ever. Their abandonment, their lack of function, held for him an undiminished force.

And then, quite by chance, he made a real discovery. Nothing negative about it at all. Soon after that, since big events sometimes go in pairs, he met Martha.

*

She had been strolling on a side-road of the big estate, making for one of the carefully maintained rights-of-way, and wondering, as she often did on her little walks, if she might get a dog. She didn't think her husband would mind, or at least not mind much.

Martha and George exchanged one of those comely little greetings which, among the local residents, who did not happen to have met, were the proper sign of communal good will. George took a quick shy look back at her and found she was doing the same thing at him. Both hastened to resume their way, as if they had taken no notice of each other. There had been nothing coy about Martha's glance over her shoulder, but after she had seen him looking back at her she blushed slightly as she strode on towards her chosen footpath.

By pure chance they met again a week or so later. A kind man who had once employed Mr Pusey, and who felt he ought to be compassionate about the business difficulties, invited father and son to their quite grand house for a drinks party.

The Greys, living nearby in a house almost equally grand, were there. Martha and George were introduced, and were able to get going almost at once by remembering that they had already met, or at least exchanged a greeting when out walking. 'Walking' in this area was a perfectly reputable activity; one that could be indulged in by persons in retirement, or temporarily at leisure. George and Martha's respective age groups could thus be said to have something honourably in common.

After only a moment or two Martha's daughter Penelope, now getting on for thirty, and home for once for the weekend – she had a flat in London and worked at a merchant bank – came over to remind her mother that they mustn't stay long: they were due at the Lloyd-Harris barbecue over at Chalfont. She gave a bare hallo to George, whom she must have instantly seen as unpromising, probably also too young; and as she shimmied off in her tight doeskin pants her mother wished him goodbye in a flustered apologetic way while preparing to follow. She wondered if they would perhaps run into each other again, out walking?

Having no barbecue to go to, George and his father stayed late at the party, becoming happy and talkative – indeed a bit tiddly as Mrs Pusey had been accustomed to put it – and finally left amid a profusion of gratitude. Their hosts remained kind, although they would have preferred them to depart sooner. The pair went home to their usual supper, cooked – or rather prepared – by George. He could think of nothing but Martha's face as she had said goodbye.

In spite of Martha's goodbye, and the way George remembered it, it took some days of assiduous strolling about the neighbourhood for them to manage to meet again. When they did, it was the first of many such meetings.

George initiated her into his snug dark nooks among the conifer plantations at the frontiers of big gardens. Martha was fearful, imagining discovery: perhaps – horror of horrors! – by one of her own neighbours. Or suppose a dog were to nose them out, shoving a friendly panting face into theirs, while its owner called and whistled nearby?

But for her it was a fearful joy. She found George's local knowledge unexpectedly masterful, and he could always calm her fears, or at least reduce them to thrilling and tremulous excitement. And so they crouched together in whatever lairs he judged secure, whispering and kissing, and insatiably hugging each other.

They remained childishly innocent at first. George may have known every inch of the surrounding country but he knew almost nothing about sex. Martha had a natural horror of infidelity. But to be in love like this seemed different. When she was alone in the house, or walking down the street, her face sometimes had the look of a young girl's, who smiles secretly to herself in public as she thinks of her next meeting with her young man.

And George was a young man. She remembered that from time to time. She wondered if he remembered, at the same times, how old she herself must be. Yet it was not so much that age did not seem to count when they were together as that he seemed to her the elder, the wiser even; and she was like a small sister, timorous and ecstatically worshipful. Although in one way so intense for her, their meetings also seemed like a game, the sort of game that childhood had never given her. It was all wonderful, and yet at first she could feel that it was not 'serious'. It was not, at least technically, adultery.

Of course it soon became so; although George himself was undemanding. He only wanted to hug and kiss this wonderful being, and to talk to her. They both seemed to chatter without stopping, yet it would have been hard to say what they talked about. None the less, even while the simple charm of their encounters remained undiminished, Martha began to feel, as other women with youthful lovers had done before her, that she could only expect to keep him by means of sex. Of course nothing so brisk and worldly as that reflection went through her bumbling mind: she did not put the matter to herself at all. What she did begin to feel was that she could think of nothing else to give her George, and she passionately wanted to give him something.

Her old desire to oblige fitted naturally into this new dimension of love.

So it was she, the backward, awkward, and easily abashed, who initiated the seduction. It might have been quite the wrong thing for her to do, and have brought their relations to an abrupt end; but in fact it worked out very well.

George secretly dug out an old piece of painter's sheet from his father's stores, so grubby and splashed and splodged with colours that it made excellent camouflage. He rolled it up when they left their carefully chosen nook, the most secure and secret he had found, and pushed it under a mass of leaves and brambles, ready to unfold next time.

CHAPTER 2

The Hoard

Their actual love-making he left all to her, as if it were the washing-up. Martha's solicitous tenderness and clumsiness caused no tensions. It enchanted him to recognise that this must be the first time she had ever had to take any sort of initiative about such matters: and that she yearned to do it because she loved him. As she awkwardly fidgeted him into position on top of her, smoothing out the battered textile beneath them as best she could, he would become fascinated by some small detail of her only partly exposed person: the by now rather too obvious blue veins in the hollow of her elbows or the soft white flesh of an inner thigh. Their love-making could manage neither leisure nor inventiveness; but its childishly cheerful whispering and giggling buried them in a devotion and an intimacy unknown before to either of them. In each other's arms they were *ingénues* together.

Martha could think of nothing but what she could give him. In her mind she loved him all day and all night in a manner that amazed her, but brought her a joy she had never known. She was incredulous that he should love her, and humbly grateful for the certainty that he did.

She told him everything, at least everything she could think of, which to her did not seem much; nor did George have a great deal to tell her. But this never stopped them talking. Once he let go it was George who was the dominant chatterer. He might have liked to shed some of the perfect self-absorption of the young but he did not know how, not being aware of it. Martha loved this perfect selfness in him which had blossomed for her; and she always gazed fondly at him while he spoke. Life had made him wary, and conscious of what could or could not be said to other people, and to his parents. But Martha was not for him another person at all. She personified not only his timidities and his secretiveness, but the inner freedom these aspects of himself had once given him.

So their summer of enchantment, an unusually fine and dry one, had gone on; and apart from the possibility, never more than very slight, of being disturbed in one of their lairs, the risk of detection seemed non-existent. Mr Grey, though comfortably affluent now and close to retirement, clung to his daily commuting pattern; and George's father was too immersed in his own troubles to be more than absently grateful for his son's continued presence in the house. The couple in love never walked in public, even on the quiet roads of the estate; they met in or near one of George's little places, all of which had a thickly screened approach.

But the autumn rains, drenchingly cold and prolonged that year, soon made even their most sheltered woodland nest untenable. It was then that George brought himself to yield up the secret which he had been quite sure he would never reveal to anyone. Disclosure of it had seemed a total impossibility.

So did his relationship with this vaguely nice-looking woman. After each of their encounters she went back to looking like a lady at a church fête, who has never been even half undressed. Could she really be his secret mistress?

For her part Martha had daydreams about taking him home to the house, which she might easily have managed in daylight hours. Alexander was at his office, and her children, though still unmarried, only came home for occasional weekends. George could have called to leave a book, just in case any of the neighbours happened to be around. Not that any of them would have paid much attention. They all had better, or at least busier, things to do; and the Earlwood estate was definitely not the sort of place where old people peered from behind lace curtains. But although Martha yearned to be able to invite George to a meal and – all ecstatic and tremulous – feed him as if she were a youthful bride, in reality she shrank from the mix-up of emotions such a scene might induce in her, and all the guilt and fear that was so singularly absent in their happy liaison.

It would be really awful if her George should become a source of guilt and fear; and in their outdoor burrow life he represented neither. In some strange and wonderful way he was nothing to be ashamed of, nothing to feel agonized about. She could still look forward to their meetings as if they were a kind of hobby, something harmless and satisfying, like weekly classes in pottery or art appreciation, which had come completely to absorb her.

George, for his part, also preferred the secret and isolated pattern of their meetings, but for a rather different reason. Since domesticity was not only an impossible ideal but one he had no way of contemplating at all, he much preferred their meetings to be of their lives a thing apart, which he could think about, betweenwhiles, with all the detachment of tenderness and pleasure.

And so George had at last told her that he wanted to show her something: something of great fascination and importance.

She had no idea what it could be. She realised that it would be a part of their secret life, but what part she couldn't imagine, as the bracken would now be sodden and brown in their old love-haunts, and the dripping cedar coverts where she had lain and embraced him in the summer months would saturate any quantity of macintoshes.

Never mind, he would show her, and she took a placid satisfaction simply in the knowledge that he had something positive in mind, although as a general thing she doted with equal fondness on his reassuring lack of drive and purpose. He was not only her own darling but a kind of anti-son, in whom she welcomed and cherished all the weaknesses that she knew she must have deplored in a child of her own. So long as George seemed to need nothing but to love her, Martha was blissfully content.

She herself could think of no way in which they might make winter love other than in her own house; and she nerved herself to try to make some arrangement at home, the more readily because of a nagging fear that George himself would not be unduly put out if there were, at least for this purpose, no place to go. His appetite for her had never been exactly frenetic, which to poor Martha seemed all too natural; and three months or so had been enough to reduce it to a familiar and amiable domesticity.

But she loved George for everything, even for this slight diminishment in his ardour. There was besides in it something that reassured her; for if he loved her little – and he loved her more than that, as she happily felt she knew – he might also love her long. Of course she pined for them to be able to eat together, sit together, or be doing their separate things – she sewing perhaps, he reading a book – and yet all unconsciously she grasped, as many a mistress had done before her, that their days apart did much to ensure the warmth of their times together.

So when the winter came they walked; even venturing to walk along roads together hand in hand, if they were sufficiently far from home. Martha loved to cling to George's arm and to feel that he was her parent and protector. On these walks, which sometimes extended over the lunch hour, she would have liked to have sat with him in some unfamiliar pub. There were plenty of such little places not too far off, many of them almost empty at lunchtime, but Martha did not quite dare to risk appearing before a landlord who just might have remembered her husband or children; and George was as obedient to her in this as he was to every arrangement that concerned her security.

So Martha made sandwiches, and any little dainty which she thought might tempt him, interrogating him about this with an uncharacteristic degree of earnestness and authority.

Incidentally neither of them could drive, or at least neither had a licence. In George's case this was out of a general lack of enterprise which in former days his father, who didn't like his own Rover being driven by anyone but himself, had strongly encouraged. Martha had taken the test several times and always failed, to the not unkind derision of her family. Her husband had put up with the consequent inconvenience with a tolerance equal to that of George's father.

*

And then George had sprung his surprise. So there they were, on a damp drizzly November day, in a cellar lit by a Tilley lamp.

'It's quite simple,' George was saying, as he pulled something back on the mechanism he held in his hands. 'But absolutely deadly.'

Martha shuddered. Like everybody else she had seen plenty

of the things on TV, and in the photographs in the papers. They seemed a property of the media. She recognised the nasty-looking snout, with a sort of curve in the pipe thing behind it, and the box, also curved, that stuck out below, its dark metal surface fluted rather gracefully – like the columns of a Greek temple, she found herself thinking. One of their family holidays, and one of the few she remembered with some pleasure, had been to Sicily.

'All the African armies use them, and all the terrorist organisations. They used to come dirt cheap from Russia, you see. Most civilised countries – ha ha – our own included, have got their own version. But this is probably still the best, and it has this distinctive appearance.'

Martha saw that. In his enthusiasm George stroked the muzzle, and pulling out the box with a click, passed it to her. It was surprisingly heavy.

'Loaded with thirty rounds. Normally fired in bursts of four or five.'

Martha dimly recalled he had already told her that, but she forbore to remind him. She was still taking refuge in the Greek temples, and ouzo, the drink that went like milk when you put water in it. She hadn't liked it, but her husband had become quite fond of it she remembered, and so did their son Ben who was with them, although he hardly bothered to drink at home.

She longed to start chattering to George about these matters, as she always did about everything that came into her head; but it would not be appropriate now, she saw that; and she had a twinge of regret in seeing it. This was the first time she had had to adjust herself wholly to her lover's will; and for him this moment was obviously a serious matter.

So she must pull herself together. 'However did you find it all, my darling?' she found herself repeating.

He stopped looking lovingly at the weapon and looked at her at last. But his gaze flicked away. For the first time with her, as she saw with another pang, he seemed uneasy.

'Well Dulcie, you remember what I've told you about this house?'

Indeed he had done that; and of course she remembered.

It was an old rambling redbrick farmhouse, probably Georgian, now encircled at a distance by the big houses of the

Earlwood estate. The children or grandchildren of the original owner had long since moved away. Mr Pusey, who himself lived in a far more modest part of the area, had taken note of the place as it crumbled. When he judged that the right moment had come he had bought it from the trustees, paying quite a stiff price for the bit of land, and for a house which by then was almost a ruin. He could afford it; and he liked to play with the idea of rebuilding it, either for his and his wife's retirement, or as a speculative item. He had been too busy then to do it, but while his wife was alive he hoped one day to begin.

What he had done was carefully to board it up, fortify it against the possible attentions of vandals or travelling folk. Not that there were problems with persons of either sort around Earlwood in those days, except, of course, for his wife's own motley group of hangers-on. Local youth was swallowed up early by a suitable school, and was seldom visible in the area. The young males were busy on tennis-court or cricket pitch, or at dances with their girlfriends. And so Manor House Farm remained inviolate, boarded up as it was.

George, sole teenage vagrant of the neighbourhood, had early on found ways of entering or leaving the place without leaving any traces. He never told his father about these visits.

Local householders were rather proud of the survival of the relic. With visitors they referred casually to the old Manor House; it confirmed that the district had been genuinely rural in days gone by. It gave cachet to the big new Tudor and Georgian-style houses with their landscaped widespreading grounds nearby. Everyone knew that one day the old house would be done up and converted; and one of the amenities which Mr Pusey fully intended to exploit was the barn attached, a brick and timber affair of considerable size. Most of its tiles had fallen and lay about in drifts among weed-buried broken glass. George soon recognised their use as an early-warning system.

He visited the place seldom. It was not one of his lairs. But when he had begun to roam the area afresh after his father's bankruptcy he resumed his acquaintance with the old house and barn. They were just as he remembered, but even more overgrown with brambles and elderbushes, almost up to tree size in the barn. He made his discovery there in the early summer, not long before he met Martha.

He was in the dark barn, and feeling his way among the debris on the floor, when something gave way under him. He nearly fell through. Reconnoitring cautiously he found there was a cellar under the barn, access to which had been boarded over, presumably when his father's men had been mothballing the place and making it secure.

George did not leave the matter there. Though wholly unathletic by nature he brought a torch and a length of rope, and got himself down into the cellar. He constructed a new mode of access with the aid of an old mounting-block he found down there, made of oak and still sound. He brought an effective light.

And it was then he found the first package.

It was thickly encased in a plastic material, much newer than the rubbish in which it was embedded, though by now just as damp, dusty and mildewed. This wrapping material, all stuck to itself, came apart with a harsh sound as he tore at it, and there was the gun.

George had never seen an automatic rifle. But like everyone else he had been exposed to plenty of them in newspaper pictures and on TV. Freedom fighters from Africa and Sri Lanka, Palestine and Afghanistan, some wearing black masks and distinctive headgear, were all accustomed to brandish objects like this one.

He was fascinated. Many if not most young men of his age would have been, and George, born long after the days of conscription, had sometimes had fantasies in his childhood about joining the army. Of course he never did anything about it, just as he had done nothing about so many other things.

But this gun seemed like a dark finger beckoning from the depths of his own natural secretiveness. It was negative, like himself: but a negative thing charged by discovery into a positive metallic life. It was as perfect, and as much outside his own being, as the birds and trees, the dark places and snug corners with which he was more privately familiar.

After this first find he explored the ramifying old cellar very thoroughly. And from the surrounding lumber he soon unearthed what seemed to be the main cache: a dozen packages in all.

Some contained magazines, which like the guns themselves were thick with grease; in others there were neat boxes of bullets, packed nose to tail in a symmetrical pattern.

George rightly judged that the first he had found was a specimen weapon, perhaps for demonstration purposes, with its magazine ready fitted. He experimented in loading the magazine, pressing in each bullet with his thumb against the elastic resistance of a spring. He learned how to cock the gun's mechanism against a much stronger spring, and then he cautiously fitted the magazine.

Now he feared the thing might incontinently open fire, deafening him no doubt in the confines of the cellar and perhaps audible from far off. Gingerly he kept the weapon under restraint, pointing its muzzle at the floor. He couldn't resist putting a cautious finger inside the trigger guard. How did it work? There was a small lever on the side with two figures in the dark metal – an S and an F. After a suitable period of cogitation George moved the lever to S, and still holding the gun cautiously, muzzle to ground, he pressed the trigger. It was a sort of triumph when nothing happened. He felt he had mastered the demonic thing, and yet of course he wanted – some time – to let it off.

He carefully wrapped it up again, as it was. Further search revealed in one of the boxes a number of neat little manuals in picture language, illustrating how the gun must be employed and maintained, stripped, cleaned and cared for. There was also a series in English, and another one in the daggers and curves of Arabic script.

There were a couple of wooden boxes too, which had death's heads stencilled on them and exclamations printed in red. They had oiled paper seals under the lid, and carrying handles of rope with wooden toggles. George got one open and found, as he had by now already half expected, that there were blocks inside which must be some sort of explosive. Probably Semtex. Everybody nowadays knew about Semtex. George remembered from some newspaper or television thing he had seen or read that the stuff had been manufactured in Czechoslovakia; and sure enough there were stencil marks and instructions in a language he took to be Czech, as well as in English. The blocks were quite small and made up in different shapes and sizes. Here too there were printed manuals, and a separate metal box full of other gadgets, fuses no doubt. They looked highly complex, and George had no understanding of such things, and no interest in them either. But he was fascinated by the gun.

He was fascinated too by his last discovery – a box that contained six automatic pistols, with cartridges in separate packs. *Makarov 9mm* was stencilled across the box.

This extraordinary find had, naturally enough, possessed for a time the whole of the young man's consciousness, from which it was only driven out by the meeting with Martha, a few weeks later. During their enchanting summer he never once went back to the cellar. It seemed much better not to. But he thought about it from time to time, and when the winter came he realised its suitability as a snug place for them both. He was aware that he felt a slight reluctance to share the guns with Martha – they still seemed so much his own private and secret thing – but on the other hand he wanted very much to demonstrate them before her, and watch her face, and then take her in his arms.

But what about the hoard itself? Who had put these things down there, and where were those people now? How had they themselves discovered the place and, as it had later occurred to him, how had they known that whatever they put there would lie undisturbed? It was this realisation that suddenly sharpened his reflections. When he had found that dangerous and exotic treasure-trove it seemed at once to become so much his own. He could not feel that the rightful owners still existed, as if they had been a pirate crew, long since dead and gone from the Spanish main; buried treasure the sole anonymous relic of their infamous careers.

Infamous careers? Maybe those careers were still going on? Perhaps the terrorists – for who else could they be? – were even now dealing out death and destruction somewhere, with other weapons, other explosive devices?

The trouble was that George did not really see things like that. This new excitement seemed so much part of his own old private life, just as, a little later, Martha herself came to seem a part of it.

Once, when he and Martha were lying embraced in one of their fastnesses, and he was chattering to her at random as he usually did, he remembered those shadowy figures who had planted the hoard, and who must still be somewhere – but where?

What he said to her was not about them, however: he said how out of date they must both seem, except to themselves of course, and how out of touch with everything.

'But that's just it, Dulcie,' he went on, 'I don't think we exist at all except here. Other people seem so entirely different from us. And I don't think I existed at all until I met you, and we became like we are.'

Martha understood him perfectly. Her babblings in response reciprocated his, though they would have sounded, to anyone else, even more muddled. But to themselves what they said was crystal clear and admirably profound: practically the utterance of a pair of philosophers.

But the odd shadow remained. Although those 'other people' were so absurdly different they were undoubtedly there; and it was this thereness which had struck George as he thought of the ones who had used Manor Farm; who with a secrecy and stealth equal – no, surely superior? – to his own, had put their materials down there, to keep them safe until they were needed.

What was, what could be, the mysterious connection? And then he remembered the activities of his mother, who had been dead for nearly two years.

She had certainly known and nurtured some pretty queer fish. He remembered too, in the early days of the Irish troubles, how at television time she would express sympathy, usually of quite a temperate sort, with the hunger strikers, and with the goal of a united Ireland. It seemed incongruous to hear her talk like that; but of course she had been got at by her queer fish.

She had never positively approved of the violence; not at least that he could remember. He and his father had in any case turned off their attention when such things came up on the news. They switched off by tacit agreement, as they always had done where her affairs were concerned. She seemed not to mind: perhaps she had come to prefer things that way. She had developed her own secrecies, as George now saw, or thought he saw. Perhaps he had inherited that very trait from her?

Impossible that she could have known what was in the cellar, what had been put there under their noses, so to speak; and perhaps with her tacit consent and agreement? And yet, was it so impossible? George had to recognise that he had never known his mother. He had never tried to know her. He had preferred things that way. Perhaps she had too?

And George now preferred, very definitely preferred, not to think about his mother. He had Martha to think about, and that was quite enough. Of course he had realised that Martha might be, from his own point of view, a security risk. However much she loved him he could not be quite sure that her knowledge of the hoard might not so upset her – on his behalf of course, not her own – that she would let the secret out, in some way, to somebody.

His own unthinking decision had of course been to keep absolutely quiet about it. Not only could he not bear the thought of parting with it: he also saw that it was in fact the prudent thing to do. Were he to report the find to the police, wherever they were to be found these days, they were bound to ask him all sorts of questions, and require him to return for interview after interview, some of which might well be uncomfortably probing. His whole secret life would be unmasked. He, and his father too, for his father as owner would be drawn into the matter, might well remain under suspicion. He might be followed about, kept discreetly under surveillance. This could happen however polite the police were, and however much they might appear to accept the simple explanation which would be all that George could give.

He was bound to admit, as he reluctantly left the cellar after first making his discovery, that the unknown depositors of the hoard could scarcely have found themselves a better or a more secure hiding-place. Even the heart of a wood or the edge of a field, a quarry or a derelict cottage, would, he realised, have been far more vulnerable. Such places, however apparently solitary, were frequently disturbed, rebuilt, ploughed over, transformed into something else. Poachers, woodcutters, gamekeepers did their business in the most secluded places. In this way womens' corpses, vanished children, suicide victims, were always being discovered.

This reflection lead him back to the secret intelligence those men who made the cache must have had. George's mother must have known that her husband had made a longterm investment. He would have told her it was for their retirement, when he had the leisure to set about repairing Manor Farm. And his retirement would have seemed very far off then. Business was booming; the old house could wait.

Yes. Something like that would be the way it must have been. To one of her respectfully garrulous queer fish, her apparently helpless and aimless lame ducks, she must have unconsciously – or perhaps deliberately? – disclosed this information. It could have found a devious way back to the centre of the movement. Irish, Arab, Palestinian, whatever it was – there were so many different kinds. But, given his mother's TV sympathies, Irish seemed the most likely.

It never occurred to George, oddly enough, to be alarmed for himself in all this, or even for Martha. Somehow he just could not believe that the men might be coming back, that the hoard might any day be reactivated. It seemed so much his own place and property now. And he was sharing it with Martha. He was glad about that, even though his feelings, as a proud owner, were ever so slightly ambiguous.

Martha perhaps, as she crouched lovingly on the cluttered floor beside him, was conscious of that ambiguity.

None the less it was the first time they had shared in a project together, had, as it were, something akin to a business partnership: their new ownership of the cellar, and its contents. George was obscurely aware of the significance of this. It was a new kind of relationship with her. And what would he do now without her? Not just 'do', but live? She was in herself an occupation for him, and so could be his other great find, the cellar?

Until now he had no occupation; and in a sense for good reason. His father could not work, or at least did not work; and it had been for George a natural relief to join him. Pusey and Son, specialists in non-activity.

Now he had something to do. He was teaching; he was a publicity man; he was instructing Martha in the workings of the Kalashnikov, a gas-operated automatic rifle, of Russian manu-

34

facture. He was behaving like a trainee salesman, learning how to get an order.

And indeed the whole thing suddenly seemed highly comic to George. He began to laugh, as they did together all the time. And Martha began laughing too, but dutifully, as they both at once realised. In fact she was bothered, and though she loved to see George laughing, it did not this time sound quite the right sort of laugh.

George stopped laughing. Taking one of her hands he fondled it and laid it on the muzzle of the gun, but she could not help at once taking it away. None the less she continued to kneel beside him on the damp and dirt-encrusted flagstones, with her dutiful expression of wonder.

It *was* comical that she had sometimes worried to herself about her darling not having a job – a guilty worry too, because something in her preferred things that way – and here he was as caretaker and curator, at least in his own eyes, of this dreadful store of dangerous weapons.

The more attached they had become, the more conscious she had been that her George should in some fashion succeed in life: even though she wanted, at the same moment, that things should go quietly on as they were. She did not know that his own father also tacitly welcomed his son's idleness, because it appeared to complement and justify his own. But could she not be behind George in some positive way, helping him and furthering his career? Lately she had begun to think she could, and should.

In seeing this she saw also how clumsy she had been in the way she had fallen in love with him, with what a fatal absence of cool reflection! If falling in love could be thought of as a cardgame, surely she had played her cards all wrong? But of course it couldn't be thought of like that, at least not by her. Suppose, though, she had got Alexander to meet and to accept George? That should not have been too difficult? She could then have taken a legitimate interest in him, really helped him. And then, after that, at her convenience and opportunity, made love with him on the side?

Could she have wanted it to be like that? She thought of it with a shudder of disgust. Surely the honest thing was to love George in his own way, and hers, and keep it quiet? Only like that could she go on feeling normal, her proper self.

It must be more honourable for her too, funnily enough, to lead a double life. A double life could be for ever – that was another point. It was like a perpetual honeymoon. Whereas if she had been able to insinuate George step by step into her family life, to the point where he became her lover – ugh, how disagreeable it sounded like that! She would always have known at the back of her mind that the thing was just a phase. A step forward on his progress into life; a step backward on hers?

It had turned out that she had the nerve for a secret love. But she could not have brought him treacherously into her life, wangled him in among her family. With an absurd sense of virtue, induced perhaps by the cold stones she was kneeling on, she felt that such behaviour would not have been like her at all.

He was talking about those guns again, and how they functioned. She wished he wouldn't. It made her realise how much she had loved his rapturous and continual curiosity about herself, his interest in how *she* functioned! That was comical, or might seem so to others, but how much she loved him for it. He had questioned her about the birth of her children; and she could talk to him (as she never did to her husband) about her occasional feminine ailments and even about her tendency to piles. Much better, this last, she was able happily to assure him, since he had come into her life!

Martha could not help smiling to herself now as she thought of all that. The darling! He was her very special one – even if otherwise he could only be her anti-son, her anti-husband, even anti-hero. Suddenly she felt reckless and a bit bad. She began to want to make love to him, in this strange place among all the dust and chaos, the dirt, the damp floor. Careless of all that she held out her arms to him. But he was already engaged in carefully folding the gun up in its wrappings.

As for George, he had been unwise enough to look forward to this moment. Now he saw that the joy of sharing his discovery with Martha was not to be. Next moment he knew it all the more clearly. Before she could stop herself Martha had blurted out the words he might have known would come.

'Surely you ought to tell the police, darling?'

At once she knew what she had done, and looked at him piteously. That imploring look, begging him to forgive her, at once won over George. He seized and kissed her.

'I shall do sometime, Dulcie. But not yet.'

The silence that followed, and was so unlike them, seemed all the more constrained from the funereal gloom of their surroundings. Martha still did her best to gaze about her, in the livid light of the gas lamp, with a suitable air of awe and wonder. George turned off the lamp and switched on his torch, directing its beam towards the place where Martha would have to make a laborious exit.

To cheer them up he produced the little tag of poetry he had picked up from somewhere, and which he had once whispered to her, in deliberately thrilling tones, as they had left one of their love-nests. For Martha had looked fearfully back over her shoulder as they walked away, as if expecting some neighbour who had waited in ambush, to stalk up behind them now in grim outrage.

> As one that on a lonely road
> Does walk in fear and dread,
> And, having once looked round, goes on
> And turns no more his head …

At once she turned her big face to beam at him, as she had done, in fearful joy, on that first occasion; and in a stage whisper she completed the quote he had taught her.

> Because he *knows* a frightful fiend
> Doth close behind him tread.

As he was helping her up the makeshift steps below the trapdoor, some Gothic lettering sprang into view on the wall, lit up by the powerful beam of the torch.

FEAR GOD   HONOUR THE KING

'What's that?' exclaimed Martha, in real fear.

George was already familiar with this exhortation, although

37

he too had at first been startled by the gilt letters on the dark wall of the cellar, when he had made his discovery. It seemed likely, he had supposed, that the men who had stored the weapon cache must have stolen this hatchment, or whatever it was, out of a church.

It certainly frightened Martha. He could feel her trembling. This was not the fearful joy of their former encounters, their happy whispers as they left the nest. Martha felt unnerved in this dark place as she had never done in their tree-haunts outside.

It had occurred to George that the founders of the hoard must have put up that old church commandment as a private joke. It was as if the ancient dragon of Anglican authority was now condemned to keep unsleeping watch above what must surely be an Irish treasure.

CHAPTER 3

The Man in the Antelope

'Have the other half, then?'

George did not disagree, and his father picked up his glass and strolled over to the bar. A nightly visit to the Antelope had become one of his last pleasures in the limbo to which the collapse of his business had consigned him; and his son was always prepared to come along. There was no chance of seeing Martha in the evenings, and he liked having a quiet drink with his father.

The pair were in their chosen pub, a superior establishment at the end of the High Street, much frequented by local businessmen, who sometimes gave a dinner there for colleagues or children. The food was not good; but the place had an oldfashioned ambience that caused it to be favoured by residents. As a friend of the Greys had once said, there was nothing 'roadhousey' about it.

Although the bar was usually quiet it had surprised George at first that his father should favour a place where he might expect to encounter old acquaintances and former business connections. But the reason, he soon saw, was straightforward. His father welcomed the solicitude of those who had been more fortunate than himself. Their slightly uneasy deference, of the sort that might be given to minor royalty in exile, cheered and comforted him. They also stood him drinks.

His son's company was soothing as well. Like a number of fathers he had never seemed sure whether he would prefer his son to succeed or to fail in the battle of life. As we have seen, he liked George to remain dependent on him, even in his downfall; and the more so because his wife had always been, in her calm uncombative way, so extremely independent. He was sustained by his son's passivity and lack of will, and by the apparent absence in the young man's life of anything that seemed to offer

39

a challenge to their continuing relationship, which, however pointless, was all that the world seemed now to offer.

If George should get a job elsewhere, or show signs of wanting to get married? … The paralysed father shrank away from those possibilities, just as he did from any positive course of action to mend his own affairs.

And so they sat nightly, never more than for an hour or so, in the Antelope bar, which was not so much oldfashioned as merely shabby. It had certainly never even tried to look like a roadhouse, a concept itself quite obsolete in the locality.

A man from a firm of building suppliers suggested a game of darts. George declined, and while his father went to play he sat quietly with his half of lager, thinking about the cellar.

Had it been a mistake, showing it to Dulcie? The demonstration had not been a success. He loved to do things with her because she always loved them too, but this time she had not done so. That was clear. Perhaps it was bound to have been a disappointment, he now felt; and yet it still bothered him why it should have been so big a one. He should have realised that Martha would be frightened by the place, and of course by the guns, and by his determination to keep quiet about them.

A stranger had come in and stood now by the bar, looking bad-tempered until he had a glass of whisky in his hand. He was a tallish lean man in an old brown check suit, not the sort of suit to which the customers of the Antelope were accustomed. The local men dressed either for the office or, with aggressive suitability, for the weekend.

George watched him glance round the bar in a leisurely way, first at the darts players and then at George. He looked uninterested, but George's idle curiosity was already alert: it was unusual to see this kind of stranger here. As if becoming aware of George's interest the man picked up his glass and strolled slowly over; then seated himself at the adjacent table. There was a pause. Then he said: 'I believe I used to know your mother.'

George's curiosity instantly recoiled. He looked round for a way of escape but there was nowhere to escape to. From the way he spoke, it looked as if George himself had been his target. He might even have been waiting outside, and have seen them go into the bar. With an opening of that sort, and from the way he delivered it, it could hardly be that he was just bored, and in want of a chat.

'Or rather,' he was now going on, 'I used to know a young chap who knew your mother. That's how I should really have put it. Never met her personally, you understand. Wish I had.'

His lean upper half made a sort of bow towards George, as if in deference to his parent.

'She sounds a remarkable woman. Remarkable in all sorts of ways. Wouldn't you say so?'

George had no choice but to echo, in a modestly filial manner, the stranger's admiration and respect. None the less he resented it. The Antelope evening was quite spoilt, and he wished his father would finish his darts game, so that they could leave.

Although George's passiveness gave him the appearance and even the reality of good nature, he disliked social life. Since being in love with Martha he had avoided it even more. Solitude came naturally to him, and he would rather speculate about people, as he had done in the case of the unfamiliar figure in the bar, than meet and talk to them.

His mother had regarded the world as a hospital. People for her were there to be looked after. It was probably quite unconsciously that her son had reversed this instinct. He enabled his own imagination of other people by not actually finding out about them. He had been interested by the unfamiliarity of the stranger in the bar. Now that the wretched man was sitting beside him, and talking in this familiar way about his mother, George desired only to be rid of him.

George's love for Martha might have been unsuitable in a lot of ways, but it was surprisingly genuine. And becoming, in a sense, more genuine every day, though it never lost the fascination for him of his own peculiar brand of romance. In her ample comely middle-aged person Martha embodied all the mysterious allure of his secret lairs and hiding places, his sense of a passive and personal strangeness. No doubt it was pure chance that it should be so. Although one of them was young, the other not, both of them needed, in their own out-of-date way, their own Arabia.

And they had found it in each other. Ironically, their mutual feeling exaggerated rather than transformed their essentially

negative attitudes towards life. For George their love conse-
crated his lack of desire to do anything: for Martha it beatified
her general out-of-touchness with things.

Their affair would be over already probably, had this not
become the case. Its permanence was in the solitude to which
both clung by instinct, and such a mutual solitude is not likely to
be less than permanent. Even the closest familiarity with eye and
voice, clothes, body, speech, made each seem, and remain,
miraculously strange to the other.

For George, Martha's physical being was more wonderful
than anything else in the world. The more intimately he could
investigate her, the more divinely mysterious she became.

So it had been up to now. But something about this man
beside him, and what he was talking about, gave George the
horrors; as if he might be talking with the same indication of
hidden knowledge and insolent familiarity, not about his
mother but about Martha herself.

George found himself sweating, not only with resentment but
with a kind of fear too. It seemed to him the man was speaking
of this unknown young person's relation to his mother as if he
knew that George himself was in love with an older woman, and
was secretly amused by this knowledge.

As if almost uncannily to confirm George's fear the man said
meditatively: 'I fancy he was a bit in love with her, don't you
know? Natural enough.' George was silent.

'Natural enough,' the man repeated, looking at George with
friendly blue eyes, that seemed to twinkle with the hateful
amusement of how much they knew.

George swallowed. 'When was this then?' he said with an
effort.

'Oh some time ago. Some time ago. The young fellow must
have been about your age. In those days I mean.'

The man began slowly to fill his pipe. He seemed to have lost
interest in the subject. George hoped he might get up and go.

But he showed no sign of doing that.

'Young man all on his own, you know. Got into bad company.
Or maybe came from where the company was bad in the first
place.'

George naturally hated pipes, and the men who smoked

them. They symbolised ancient authority, and its attempt to intrude on the new generation.

Anyway he must keep calm. 'How did you know this young man?' he enquired, as if politely, and to keep the ball rolling.

'I was investigating him.'

So he must be some kind of policeman, thought George, almost in a panic. If he was investigating the unknown man he must have investigated George's mother. And his father no doubt. And why not George too?

'Heard your father had taken a bit of a knock,' went on the stranger, as if resuming a topic. 'Sorry about that. In his business of course it does happen. There was some sort of property he was going to restore, wasn't there? Never got round to it I expect? And what are you doing with yourself these days? Helping him get back on his feet?'

The man's familiarity was all the more odious for being so calm and polite. 'Doing with yourself' indeed! The phrase jarred on George beyond all endurance. He rose to his feet. 'I'm afraid I must be going now,' he said coldly, or as coldly as his natural amiability could manage.

'Your father hasn't finished his darts game yet,' the stranger pointed out, nodding his head towards the players.

It was true. George's father had always been good at the game, and he looked happily settled into a prolonged contest. There was a soothing sound as the missiles plunked into their cork target.

But the thought of having to sit down again beside this man was too much for George. 'I think I'll leave him to it,' he said, and then wondered what his parent would do if he found his son gone, and himself perhaps being questioned by this man?

George stood irresolute. The other got out his matches and began to go through the leisurely routine of smokemanship. He seemed to have lost interest in George.

George decided he must wait. As an excuse for doing so, and as a demonstration of good manners, he asked if the man would like another drink.

It was an offer expecting to be declined, but the stranger's response was disconcertingly prompt.

'Thanks. Whisky.'

43

Hang it, the man should really be offering him a drink, rather than the other way round. He seemed to know George's father was in low water.

How did he know about that? How did he know anything about George, or his mother and father? Presumably this 'young fellow' had told him.

George got the whisky at the bar and brought it back. He was anxious now to head off this man from his father. He wanted no more queries about this property, which had never been renovated and restored.

'Yes, I was investigating the young chap,' resumed the stranger, as if he knew exactly what was going through George's mind. 'Still am, actually.'

Again he appeared to lose interest in the topic, retaining it only for his pipe and the new whisky, for which he did not thank George.

George could not help himself, as no doubt the man intended. 'Why is that then?' he asked, with a slight effort.

Without replying the man asked a question himself. 'You'd say, wouldn't you, that Mrs Pusey could hardly do enough for these young folk?'

George agreed, without enthusiasm.

'The young fellow I was speaking of – Irish, you know, and Catholic – Roman Catholic that is – used to say she was like a St Monica. Watching over him. One of the Papist ladies I suppose. Brigid, Barbara, Mary. All that lot. Ever come across her? Did your mother ever mention her? No? Well, it's all in the religion no doubt, like the murders. Politics is all that's left of religion, and, when you come to think of it, religion's always been a form of politics. Does either of them appeal to you? Personally?'

'Not in the least.'

George spoke no more than the truth. Nor, so far as he knew, had they interested his mother.

'No? Well, you're a bit of an aesthete yourself, aren't you? I can see that. And your mother more the nurse type, wouldn't you say?'

George offered no opinion. He began to feel fear of this man.

'Among the kindnesses your mother did this young chap was keeping things for him. And for his friends. Store their belong-

44

ings for them. If they had any. Anything of that sort still left around, do you know?'

'Not that I know of. What sort of things?' It must be safer to ask the questions himself, if he could.

'One thing in particular. Could be quite small. Like in a small suitcase. The case might be heavy though.'

George felt a sudden relief flood through him. His fear of the man subsided. There was something laborious now about these queries; the mystery of the fellow's status diminished.

As if in recognition of this fact, and after George had assured him that his mother's young friends had left nothing on their premises, the stranger offered to buy him a drink, and George said he would have a whisky too. A single malt please. The most expensive. Actually he disliked the stuff, but to ask for it gave him some sort of revenge.

The man asked no more questions. They sat chatting, or at least he sat chatting to George, until the latter's father had finished his game. Then he wished George a good evening and went out. Mr Pusey did not see him, and George said nothing to his father about the encounter.

CHAPTER 4

Prentice Wood

Martha Grey sat up and looked uncertainly round for her bra and vest. Beside her George lay stretched out on the thin strip of mattress like a naked crusader on a stone tomb.

There was a blanket, though, from Martha's airing cupboard; and one of her old sheets under them, neatly darned in the middle. The duvet over them had been pushed aside. The cellar was dank rather than cold, and outside was a muggy November day, with a slight drizzle.

Before she started to dress Martha couldn't resist leaning over him to kiss his face and eyes. It was the first time they had made love in their new lair. It was exciting; and wonderful to have their own place, almost like a real bedroom. The cellar bothered her of course, and the proximity of those guns and things he had shown her, but she forgot all about that as they came to grips. When they lay down she had seen the enscrolled words, in staring gilt, confronting them in the gaslight, and she had asked George if he would mind taking down 'Fear God Honour the King', or turning it to face the wall.

A very happy couple of hours. Yet it continued to give Martha slight guilt feelings that in the midst of them she couldn't help remembering their outdoor summer places, the aromatic pine needles on her skin and in her hair, the giggles and whispered endearments and their half-dressed threshings about. About this new love-nest there was an almost matrimonial stateliness. Its stagnant slightly sinister calm, and gloom, gave her a twinge of nostalgia for idyllic summer days gone by.

These things confused with the present in her mind, and induced her to kiss George all the more passionately. She was conscious too of her new nakedness, which seemed somehow

47

drab and respectable after the nervous thrills of woodland *deshabillée*.

For she knew she must look decidedly middle-aged. That thought had given her the wish to resume her clothes. But before she could start to do so George ducked his head and fastened his lips to a breast as it drooped above him. Clasping hands behind her he held it to his face, gazing with rapturous intentness at the other prominent brownish nipple. He always loved the startled look such bits of her, as if never before exposed, presented to him. The next moment he abandoned his scrutiny with a soft groan and clasped her to him more tightly.

After this third encounter Martha felt they had really better be getting up, happy as she was to lie there with him indefinitely. Her watch was somewhere away in the shadows on the cluttered floor, but it must be not all that far off the time when her husband would be home from the office.

George had been immensely touched by the way Martha had cleaned up and arranged their new domestic burrow, and brought in her supplies. But he knew, and knew that she knew, that it was not really a home for them. It had been too much of his own place, and had definitely not become hers. The guns, after all, were there in the lamplit darkness, snugly packed all round. Yet their celebration had certainly been magical.

It had also, as they told each other, been a special wedding-feast. Martha had brought George's favourite, a cold mushroom omelette; and they had drunk, unusually for them, most of a bottle of white wine.

George had said nothing to her about the man who had spoken to him in the Antelope. The last thing he wanted to do, naturally enough, was to spoil their time in the cellar. But suppose that man found out about the cellar? He seemed already to know about George's father and his business affairs. He must have made enquiries in the neighbourhood.

These matters were very much in George's mind as he lay and watched Martha getting dressed. While she did so she was chattering to him happily, as if their love-making here had relieved her from her anxieties about the cellar, though she kept her voice low instinctively, as if in the musty hush of church.

He was comforted by her happiness, as well as reassured. But he could not entirely forget the lean reddish face of the man in the pub, nor the look in his eye

Back home again, Martha found she was still in plenty of time. She went into her kitchen, opened the larder door, and eyed the leftovers, sparse and tidily disposed. She peered into the big fridge. Alexander was particular about his food in his own way, disliking what he called anything fanciful. By this he meant, oddly enough, what his wife had been brought up to think of as good plain English cooking: roast lamb and mint sauce, say, followed by the Queen's Pudding.

When they were first married Martha had taken a lot of trouble over such dishes, and she was confident that her efforts had not been unsuccessful. But to her chagrin not only Alexander but her children too, as they grew up, let it be known with emphasis that they preferred junk food.

She had sometimes, and rather forlornly, wondered why. She felt deprived of her status as home-maker, about which she had in any case never felt confident; and as time went by she seemed less and less needed. No 'dishing up', that hearteningly strenuous traditional activity. Alexander and the children could easily get what they wanted for themselves, and usually did, although Martha had continued to try to serve her meals in a regular way. It was odd how they went on living without such convictions, but in the former style of the big house. How did others live – their neighbours? She had really no idea. It seemed as if they were all inhabiting the still intact ruins of a former culture. Provisionally living: while waiting for it to come to its destined end?

Not that Martha or her husband considered this possibility themselves. But they behaved in a way that might have suggested the idea to a thoughtful outsider.

What it suggested to Martha was that now she and Alexander were alone together for most of the time it would have been nice to eat out more. To join the expanding restaurant culture. With this in mind she had lured him to a new little place off the High Street, which was run on very contemporary lines by an enterprising couple. They had called it the Bayleaf.

Confronted there with a warm salad of goat cheese and pine kernels Martha's spouse had soon fallen silent, withdrawn himself. They were the only diners, since it was still early, and Alexander was accustomed to having his supper at half-past seven. Martha would have liked to chat with him about what seemed to her a fascinating menu; but as things were she was driven to doing so with the friendly young waitress, who struck Martha as being decidedly a social cut above her partner, the chef. Curious about this, and despairing of Alexander's co-operation (they had not gone to the place again, or to anywhere else for that matter) Martha had done her best at the time to be warm and appreciative; and the waitress proprietor, looking very fetching in a miniskirt and an apron of leaf-green baize, had welcomed her interest. She had stood by the table for a gossip, while the plump young chef grinned shyly over a louvred swingdoor of stripped pine, displaying his spotless kitchen.

Working to keep up the animation, Martha appealed once or twice to Alexander, who declined to be appealed to, and ignored the Bayleaf girl without being positively rude to her. His rudeness, fortunately silent, he reserved for the food. He neither ate it nor remarked on it; which was discouraging for Martha as well as for their hosts.

Remembering this occasion (it was some little while before she met George) Martha felt a slight twinge at the thought that he might not have shared her husband's indifference towards the charming Bayleaf girl. Perhaps it was just as well she could not take him there. But how much she wished they could spend the night together, and that she could cook him a proper dinner!

She poked some elderly Double Gloucester cheese. It would only be fit for a Welsh rarebit, which Alexander sometimes liked. What she prepared for him and ate herself she hardly noticed, which is why she would have enjoyed the little restaurant, and its amusing things to eat. A meal at the kitchen table with Alexander was not exactly fun; and possibly he thought so too, for he usually got up to watch TV in the big study, which he preferred to do on his own.

That was not a bad thing, as Martha hated it. She sometimes wondered why, almost guiltily; and she noticed she was becoming increasingly alienated from the radio as well. Nothing but soundbites, as they seemed to call them, and what she still

50

thought of to herself as vulgar remarks on the tedious game and chat shows. No straight talks any more.

She abandoned the cheese, deciding that to give him his usual treat would be simpler: anchovies and plain scrambled egg. She would fry some sliced bread. As a concession to dietary wisdom she always did this in the best olive oil. She knew that George and his father lived on much the same things, probably minus the extra-virgin oil. She loved to chatter about food with George, as about everything else. Surely, she sometimes thought, love – real love – was nothing but the longing to chatter with the loved one, and finding it so easy to do so. But then, as Martha vaguely knew, nature and the years had accustomed her to being an untalkative person. She accepted that silence all the more eagerly now that she could talk to George.

She wondered about a bath. She used to have one when she got home from seeing George, though she preferred not to, because she loved to feel him lingering about her. A glass of sherry instead? Alexander, who never seemed to smell George on her, would certainly smell the sherry, and she knew that would discompose his mood if he happened to be in a good one. He had always stuck to the rituals of return, and he liked her to come and kiss him in the hall. She liked that too; and still did.

A few years before, when going through a bad lonely patch, with her children hardly ever seeming to come home, Martha had suddenly discovered the solitary joys of midday drinking. Vodka of course – vodka and lime – said to leave one 'clean'. She looked forward to it all morning, and often all the previous evening too. Settling down to it at last, with the World at One on the radio and the Archers to follow. Those were the days when she had enjoyed both programmes, and the drinks seemed to make them positively sparkle. By three o'clock she had felt extremely comfortable; and after a doze and a cup of tea she was quite ready to face the evening, with nothing untoward seeming to have occurred.

But after a few weeks of that happy regime, with an irregular but steady increase in the vodka intake, she had become all too aware that even with such home comforts a law of diminishing returns soon set in. She had given it up, not as abruptly as she had begun it, but by fairly painless degrees.

51

And then at last, and it could be said at long last, she had fallen in love.

There was Alexander's key. The sweetest sound a wife hears – where had she read that? Some ancient woman's magazine probably. Not that she disagreed. It did give a lift of the heart – always had done. Suppose it were George's key? Her mind, as they used to say, boggled: and for a moment she stood quite still, parting her lips. No, it couldn't be: she couldn't imagine it. George was George and her husband was her husband. Best so? Well, anyway, that was the way it had to be.

She should have remembered to put the mortice lock on – Alexander was always reminding her about that. Besides, in these days of women's lib, as well as of endless burglaries, there were plenty of other things for stay-at-home wives to do instead of listening for husbands' keys in locks.

As she crossed the big hall she remembered there were also plenty of bananas. Mashed up, with cream, it was the only pudding he liked.

At one in the morning she lay listening to Alexander not quite snoring. A comfortable and on the whole a soporific noise, but Martha felt wide awake none the less. Lying on her back, and looking up into the darkness she suddenly had a vision of that painted board, with its scrolls and curlicues – seventeenth century? eighteenth? – FEAR GOD HONOUR THE KING. How startled she had first been when George's torch had revealed it. More than startled – frightened.

But shouldn't the words have been a kind of comfort and reassurance? A little, Martha found herself thinking incongruously, as the vodka had once been? If her father had seen those words on a board in church he would have said nothing, but squared his shoulders in silent approval. She hardly ever thought of her father, but she found herself doing so now.

And what would he think of George? It was unthinkable to think about what he would think of her relations with George; and then the thought of all those 'thinks' made Martha smile.

She had never known her father, though she had loved him. A dark, upright, mysterious man. Or perhaps not so upright – how did she know? Perhaps if he knew what she was up to now he would give her one of the occasional smiles that she remembered – how happy they had made her – and say as he said at rare intervals 'Good for you, my lass!' There was no telling.

Now her mind was really rambling, and faster than ever. Those sudden words imagined out of the darkness had woken her up still further. What about Alexander's odd behaviour as they were going to bed?

Over the years she had treasured as much as relied on the fact that he had become so wholly uncommunicative. Her husband's lack of speech had suited her own silence. She had come to depend on it, as on the house, the money, her children, mildly scornful of her as they had always been. True, since her life-giving discovery of love-chatter with George, it had crossed her mind to wonder whether there was some other place where Alexander *did* talk. Perhaps with his ex-wife, and her husband? She had always known about that. Or perhaps with some quite other man or woman, of whom she knew nothing at all?

In any case it had been most unusual for Alexander to get all of a sudden quite excited; and at what was for him the normally absent moment when he sat on the side of the bed, putting on his pyjamas.

This abrupt animation at bedtime had made Martha feel embarrassed. It was her guilty conscience she supposed; although the idea of that conscience was really just a theoretical and even a familiar one: some obstruction she had to walk warily around, as it were, in her daily doings. Now she was on guard, not because there was the faintest chance her husband was going to accuse her of having a secret love affair, but just that he seemed to have something in his mind, which automatically made her feel careful.

And what he had in his mind turned out, as she correctly guessed, to have nothing to do with her. At least only indirectly. And yet, when he started to talk to her about it, he might almost have been telling her about some love affair of his own.

In an odd way perhaps he had been? For he had started to talk about Bobby, the elder of his two younger brothers. In Bobby, to his wife's mild but continued surprise, Alexander had always shown an extraordinary degree of almost furtive interest. He could seem almost like a girl, affecting indifference towards the man she was really hooked on, or at least intrigued by. Bobby, and all his doings, seemed to fascinate his elder brother.

In her own quiet way Martha couldn't stand Bobby. Bobby bothered her even by his name, which seemed incongruously innocent and wholesome. That disinclination to communicate, which somehow reassured her in her husband, repelled her in his brother – she could hardly have said why. She had come almost to dread their infrequent meetings; and although Bobby had never been to stay she had made up possible excuses why they could not have him, were the question ever to come up. Fortunately it never had: and yet, as a bachelor, Bobby might be said to have some right to the occasional hospitality of his brother and sister-in-law. Since leaving the army, in circumstances that remained obscure, he had mostly lived abroad; and that was a relief. Martha never wished to hear about him, but she was well aware that her husband was still fascinated by his sibling's activities, whatever they were. At one time it was even rumoured that he might be in the business of smuggling drugs.

Martha always felt terminally soothed by her husband's preparations for bed: they signalled the end of the day of her own wifely duties. But this evening, as she sat at her dressing-table and he was putting on his pyjamas, Alexander had suddenly asked without any preamble if she would mind Bobby coming to stay for a few days. She felt appalled; but as she continued putting her hair and face to bed it was no trouble to continue to seem placid and amenable. Nor was she deceived by Alexander's air of weary tolerance where his brother was concerned.

'What did he do, darling? Ring you at the office?'

Martha was prepared to hint that a civil note addressed to his sister-in-law would have been the polite thing for Bobby to have written.

'Just what he did, and of course at the most inconvenient moment. My secretary interrupted me at a meeting.'

'You poor dear. But really, I don't mind a bit.'

'Well if you don't mind, I do.'

He was obviously happy to make himself the martyr, giving in to his wife's ignoble permissiveness.

She knew in fact that he was grateful; and the next moment he showed it by condescending to explain why Bobby wanted to come.

'Tells me he's going to be doing a job of some sort down here, and could use us as a base of operations. Base of operations! I ask you! That man never lets anyone forget he was in the army!'

'I really don't mind a bit, Ally. I'll do out the big spare room. It'll do us good to have somebody here for a bit.'

Martha broke off, aware that she had not phrased that very happily. Perhaps because it was the opposite, of course, of what she felt. Having the wretched Bobby here could do her, and George, no good at all.

To conceal her feelings she leaned across the bed and patted his pyjama-clad knee. He was really grateful to her, she knew, for not making any sort of fuss. Though when did she ever make a fuss, come to that, in their domestic relations?

Because he was smiling with pleasure at the thought of Bobby coming, even while he pretended to be put out, she came round the bed and sat down beside him, giving him a kiss. As she did so she had the uneasy feeling that his face might have worn just the same amiable expression if he had somehow found out about her and George. Would he, she wondered, even let her know that he had?

When they were in bed he abruptly, and most unusually, rolled over to her side and started to caress her. After he had gone to sleep Martha lay awake, looking up into what seemed a hopeful darkness. She was glad he wanted her from time to time, or at least thought that she might be wanting him – it hardly mattered which – and touched that she might herself have encouraged him, however accidentally. She had been made love to four times today. Probably not a record, though it certainly was one for her.

Alexander was sixty-six, or was it sixty-seven? And she was fifty-four. George was the youthful one, and he had done most of the love-making. Would he mind about what had happened just now? She really had no idea. Although they chattered about everything they never bothered to talk about the fact that she was a married woman with a husband, although they never seemed to avoid it either.

Long before she had a lover – an astounding thing in itself – amazement would from time to time over come Martha at the

55

idea of how she seemed to be living: living she meant, as a married woman. At moments she could hardly believe it. She must be unadaptable, for it was after all the ordinary state in which most people's lives were lived? It was just the fact of it that overcame her from time to time, and not any of the things – nice things they were, surely? – with which the married state had surrounded her.

She supposed, none the less, that it must be because the life she had lived had never been quite believed in by somebody inside herself that she went on the spree of those lunch-time drinks. She could not really think of it as solitary drinking, any more than she could think of George as her 'lover'.

Did all women have this recurrent sense of not *being* what they were actually *doing*? Did men have it too?

She would never find out. Yes she might! – she would ask George! And she was sure of one thing. With George she was her true self. He had found it for her, quite accidentally no doubt. She had often chattered to him about all this, and he seemed to understand perfectly what she was getting at. He said he felt just the same with her.

He was so young of course. But she never felt that when they were together. Then she knew she had become what she should be: and she knew, too, that he felt the same.

Smiling up into the bedroom darkness Martha felt pleased with herself as she had never done before. It was shameless of course, but there it was. Evidently she could easily be two people, and with some success, but she knew which person she really was. She was her George's girl, his little sister. The sickly-romantic idea made her almost start giggling. But look at the way she had knelt obediently beside him, while he had instructed her about those guns? And the way they had made their underground nest, where she had undressed properly today for the first time.

Instead of sleepy she began to feel hilarious. No doubt little girls did not, or should not, take off their clothes and lie down with their big brothers, but never mind about that. The whole day had made her feel quite uncharacteristically splendid.

The word reminded her all of a sudden of that nice Mrs Stringham, another Earlwood resident, whose husband had been accused of soliciting in a public lavatory. There had been a court case. As a result of all the scandal and fuss Mrs Stringham's reputation in the district had risen by leaps and bounds. Everyone said she was splendid; that she was behaving splendidly.

No doubt she was. But Martha remembered none the less having the unworthy thought that 'splendid' behaviour must be the easiest kind to demonstrate in such circumstances. So much easier and simpler than to be furiously angry, or dramatically prostrated.

What equivalent kind of splendour would Alexander, and the neighbours, find it best and easiest to produce if she, Martha, and her George, were to be revealed one day as lovers ...?

Martha nearly started giggling again; but at that moment, and with its usual unexpectedness, sleep must have come to her.

*

Bobby Grey stood meditatively at the window of the best spare room in Prentice Wood. It was a big room, with wall-to-wall Wilton carpeting, immaculately hoovered; but in the dark morning it felt as unused as it was. Outside the December rain fell warmly and quietly on the big gloomy lawns and garden. Some way off, through the beech trees, the lights of another house were visible in the fog.

He had just shaved, and carefully cleaned his oldfashioned razor. Now he dried it on the innocent lining of the William Morris curtain beside him. Soft, thick, and clean – might be made for the purpose. The towel was damp: and he wouldn't have used it anyway: it gave him pleasure to misuse his hosts' property. His hostess no doubt took the curtains down for cleaning at least once a year.

It cheered him a little to think how much he despised his brother and sister-in-law. He was well aware of Alexander's undercover hero-worship of him – was that the chief reason for his own contempt? – and he had a simpler and more massive scorn for Martha. He smiled: his smile was charming but slightly twisted.

It had just struck him that out of sheer nervous politeness, and desire to do the right thing (like washing the curtains at least

57

once a year), his sister-in-law might not absolutely refuse him, were he to make a heavy pass at her, as people used to say.

She would be terribly bothered no doubt, and not a bit flattered either. He did not flatter himself about that. She would agonise over what the right thing to do would be. Earlwood was not exactly a wife-swapping area, he realised that; and in any case he had no wife to swap with Alexander. No, poor dear Martha would do what she thought, or feared, the proper up-to-date thing to do would be. The custom of the country. But no again, that was hardly fair. She would give in, if she did, out of the compulsion to oblige, to be of service. As if he had asked her to mend a hole in his jacket.

Not handsome of course, but not a bad looker either, if her face wasn't so big. And still a good figure, if on the full side. Awkward. Always reminded him for some reason of that Greek sculpture job – Venus arising from a shit, or whatever it was called. That was what it looked like anyway.

Why didn't he try it some time? He was good, he knew. Mustn't boast: but he had a kind of quiet hypnotic insistence.

She might be afraid of her husband of course. He sensed that Martha knew of his close relation with Alexander, or rather of Alexander with him, and that she dreaded it in some way. And yet she might easily feel – not think, he could not imagine Martha thinking – that if she were to oblige him in secret she would detach him by that much from her husband. She would share a secret which her brother-in-law could hardly let out – so she would feel – and one that she could even hold over his head?

How wrong she would be: and he smiled to himself again. Alexander felt about him, Bobby, as he felt about so many other men – his ex-wife's husband for instance. Martha, he was sure, knew nothing of that.

Of course Martha amused him no less than she exasperated him. No man worth his salt would pretend to want sex if he didn't, but women like his sister-in-law might think they had to supply themselves for all purposes. No real desires of her own at all, probably. And what did his brother feel when making love to her? Imagination might do much, but his brother's imagination could hardly turn her into a man?

He fell to wondering about his other sister-in-law: young

58

Peter's wife. That had been a surprise, if you like. Peter, of all people, getting entangled with that dim female who worked for a publisher. He remembered meeting her once, at the seaside. She'd fallen for him a bit of course. He could probably have had her then, if he'd wanted; and a time and a place, and all that. Carnal relations with both his sisters-in-law? Nice thought.

Anyway this other dim female – what was her name? – seemed afterwards to have taken Peter away from his Russian wife. He, Bobby, had a great respect for that former wife – wasn't she called Vera? – although he had only met her a couple of times. Once worked for the KGB, probably still did. And God, that lot were more unpredictable than ever, now they'd been privatised.

But Vera had been reliable – absolutely hundred percent – one could be sure of that. Without Vera Peter seemed to have given up on all his former enterprises.

God knows what he and his new wife lived on. He'd heard they'd had a baby too. Ghastly … As if the world wasn't in enough trouble.

What did he live on himself, come to that?

And yet this caper he was on at the moment could bring in quite a bit, if he played it right. The trail might have gone cold by now. Yet somehow he didn't think so. Where that young fellow George Pusey was concerned, he'd been following up a hunch. The young man had something to hide; he was now quite sure of it. Pity the boys hadn't leant a bit harder on that Irish bastard, when they got hold of him. Too many kid gloves on that side of the game – altogether too many.

And now he couldn't afford not to watch out himself. They must have his number. But the oppo didn't know what game he was playing, or trying to play. They though he was straight. There'd be some laughs on their side if they knew what he was really after. Not that it mattered a tinker's cuss, to his real employers, if the Irish had the right stuff, or if they hadn't. As long as his cut was handed down from higher up he didn't care if the KGB were screwy about this or not. They didn't care themselves probably. As long as there was money in it, it must be OK.

Money. That was all there was to the business, these days. Putting away his razor he remembered the time he thought he'd made a killing on those drugs. Must be getting on for six, seven years ago.

He'd liberated them from a female colleague – what was her name? – over six foot tall, but quite a nice piece. And when he got to Madrid he'd found they were a dud lot. God, he'd had egg all over his face that time. Not the six-footer's fault, he had to admit that. Someone had taken her for a ride further up the line ...

While her brother-in-law ruminated malevolently in her best bedroom, Martha was bracing herself downstairs for the arrival of her cleaning lady. Mrs Jones was highly vocal, though she lacked two front teeth and never seemed to have done anything about it. She gossiped all the time though she did work as well: Martha had to admit that.

This morning it was a friend who had lost her cat and was that upset she was undergoing counselling. A purgatorial duty, Mrs Jones implied, but one bravely borne. All done in her own house; the social workers came by appointment. 'And when you think what they earn ... But there, where your health's concerned money's no object, is it? And they wanted her to get a new cat – perhaps a Persian – but my friend said no – she'd rather have to undergo the counselling ... She's that determined, Mrs Grey, I can't tell you. She wanted what they call to come to terms with her loss.'

Martha exclaimed and wondered; and had the idea, while Mrs Jones was talking, that she might set the cleaning lady on her brother-in-law – would the cat bereavement amuse him by chance? If so, it would make up to her in some degree for his continued presence in the house. Mrs Jones must have someone to talk at; and Martha had normally to undergo the duties of handmaiden, bringing coffee at eleven and sometimes a glass of sherry before Mrs Jones left in her car.

In the days of her less demanding predecessor Martha had worked mornings part-time at Oxfam and another charity shop. But now she had to go there in the afternoons, which made things difficult in the matter of George. This problem was still unsolved.

Martha would have gladly dispensed with Mrs Jones's services. But she was well aware that householders like themselves

60

had an obligation, and that if she were to attempt easing Mrs Jones out the cleaning lady might go to Alexander with a grievance. Able to dispense untroubled generosity as he was, Alexander would certainly decree that Mrs Jones might stay. To have no cleaning woman at all, and with Mrs Jones volubly advertising the fact, would entail a grave loss of status in the community.

Bobby's presence was an alternative torment for Martha. But at least it was soon plain, in spite of the big news about the friend's cat, that the presence of this apparently unemployed male in the house excited the cleaning lady to the point of frenzy. This nerved Martha for her attempt to brush off Mrs Jones against Bobby.

Mrs Jones made it clear that she would like nothing better – Martha was painfully conscious what a poor audience she made herself – but the hateful Bobby did not, of course, co-operate. He sat on at the breakfast table, and afterwards in the drawing-room, and gazed at Mrs Jones without speaking. This clearly unnerved her, although she continued to chatter sycophantically – she had always bossed Martha – and to hover hopefully around him.

Bobby had the same unnerving habit of gazing in a meditative silence at Martha herself. It seemed a friendly silence, she had to admit, nor were his eyes at all hostile. Indeed they had a kind, pensive look; but something about his silence, and the way he regarded her, caused Martha to break at once into a nervous gabble, scarcely knowing what she said. No wonder he must think her mad.

Once he flummoxed her by suddenly demanding why she called her husband 'Ally'. There was an intrusiveness, even a brutality, about the abrupt question, which really upset her. Odious man, even if he was Alexander's brother! He seemed to be breaking, deliberately, into that unspoken closeness – a purely domestic, not a family one – which she and her husband might be presumed to have. Indeed did have, surely? Brooding about the moment afterwards, Martha found tears coming into her eyes as she thought about her married life.

For it *was* a married life! And now this brother of his seemed to be not only questioning the fact, but in some way suggesting by his rudeness that her marriage itself was some kind of pretence. The sign of which was that she had to perpetuate a pet name for her husband, which his relatives no longer recognised, and disliked.

Martha was well aware that she was making too much of all this. It was her guilty conscience raising its ugly head, she supposed, however little she really felt she had one. Yet this intruder did make her feel sort of guilty, for the first time. Even made her feel that he must suspect something. Even made her feel that only his own indifference, or amusement, might prevent him from giving her away.

Perhaps what really upset her, or upset her the most, was the sweet secrecy there should be in pet names. For George she was sometimes his Dulcie, which she loved to be. So why shouldn't Bobby's brother Alexander still be her Ally?

This was the fourth morning of Bobby's stay, and the strain was telling on Martha. He had the habit of leaving the house at about half-past ten, sometimes remarking that he was going for a stroll. This was a relief, but before she had even begun to relax he was usually back again. Only to disappear once more, at some inconvenient moment, and for an equally unpredictable period. Even without the lack of George to distress her, Bobby would have been a most unwelcome guest.

Her husband continued his daily commuting, down to the station in the car every morning, or bicycling if the weather was fine. But his brother's presence excited him. He arrived back each evening in a state of anticipation which was almost vivacious. While the pair of them sat with their whiskys and sodas before dinner, Martha in the kitchen could hear Alexander making his own efforts to find out just what his brother was doing in the neighbourhood.

When Bobby arrived, Martha had made a feeble effort to improve supper-time standards. But neither brother seemed to care or notice. On the second day her fish pie, which she knew she did well – it was more like a fish soufflé – caused her husband to bestow one of those looks of muted disapproval which always discomposed her.

Quietly smiling, and charming his elder brother, Bobby remained wholly uncommunicative. Martha's face, on the other hand, could be a great deal more expressive than she was aware, and this might have been on account of George.

She had not been able to bear not seeing him any longer, and on the Wednesday she wrote him a letter.

Love-letters between them had been few and meagre. Martha's own security-consciousness had always been obsessive, and George honoured it with equal or even greater precautions. Ensuring Martha's safety and reputation was the only way he could take care of her as a husband; his zeal in protecting her was uncharacteristically meticulous. On his own side he had his father to watch out for. Unemployment had made Pusey senior absent-minded, and George could not bear to think of a letter from Martha being opened by him accidentally.

So now Martha found endearments and regrets and simple longings flowing from her pen. She had no idea she could be so eloquent on paper, and she revelled in page after sprawling page. But she wrote the address very large and clear, and she stuck up the envelope with numerous bands of sellotape.

She proposed a meeting for Thursday: the day her lover would get the letter, as she hoped. Then she bent her mind to concocting reasons to give the unbearable Bobby why she would be out at lunch. Out in the late morning, and the early afternoon. She found it absurdly difficult to think of anything she might be doing, harmlessly and legitimately. Bobby's presence in the house had benumbed her mind to that extent. She would have to fall back on her work at Oxfam.

But her luck was in. On that Thursday morning, which was warm, damp and foggy, her guest pre-empted her own excuses for absence by saying he had business in Chalfont St Giles, and asking what would be the best way to get from there to London, where he had things to do later in the day. Martha joyfully informed him that a Greenline bus ran to London through Chalfont, and she rang herself to ask about the timetable. Would he be back that evening, she enquired, hoping he wouldn't. Oh yes, he would.

Martha was too elated to mind. Her eyes were sparkling. Her involuntary looks of joy were not lost on Bobby. He had tested her deliberately. Now he had decided to wait nearby until she left the house, and to then follow her.

CHAPTER 5

Zeiss

On Thursday evening George and his father paid their usual visit to the Antelope.

George would rather have stayed at home. Although he had been longing to see her, and had been elated beyond measure to get her letter that morning, the ensuing meeting in the wood had been marred for him, if only momentarily, by a curious event. Although disconcerting it had seemed unimportant at the time, but afterwards it had begun to worry him. He was glad he had not mentioned it to Martha. Her joy in their afternoon, and his too, had been so great that he could not have borne to upset her, or to have disturbed their time together.

Besides, he might have been quite wrong. What he thought he had seen might not have existed, or at least could have taken place in a different world, a world unaware of theirs.

He did not in the least feel like a visit to the Antelope. He wanted to stay in the house and brood over what had happened, and comfort himself by reading over again and again the words in the letter that had arrived that morning.

She had said to meet her in the derelict park, one of their most secluded places, and one which she knew now almost as well as he did. Along the old paths and avenues, which however overgrown still just suggested a ghostly tunnel through and among the dense growth of rhododendrons, they groped their way, clasped together; and in what survived of the clearing that had once capped a landscaped prospect, they had paused under a great tumbledown cedar tree, one of George's old landmarks, or sacred stations.

It was almost as safe as their cellar lair. And Martha, stepping back still further into the shade of the great cedar, had pulled up the front of her skirt for him, like a wanton milkmaid offering her lover a lapful of flowers. There was something so touching and incongruous about her gesture, accompanied as it was by a bashful and beamingly timid smile of enquiry, that George drew her to him at once. At this reunion after their days apart he had thought only of being with her in their old familiar haunts, and filling what time they had with a torrent of talk. But now, as he clasped her bare flesh under the skirt she held up for him, he could only murmur that she was his darling. Nothing less banal could have conveyed the tenderness he felt for her comically awkward pose, as she stood straddled for him against the trunk, one solid white thigh marbled with a rosy pattern of capillaries.

When almost inside her he had caught the sight of a sudden glint among the trees of the adjoining slope of woodland. At least a quarter of a mile away. But someone must be there, with something that shone briefly as it moved.

George buried his face in Martha's neck and carried on; but even as he shut his eyes he was aware of the agitated ghost of his visual impression. Was anyone else in the wood, and if so, had they been seen?

In the wet leafless wood they had never made winter love like this before. The bulk of the cedar gave an impression of safety from any prying eyes; but this could be misleading: its very size made not only a landmark but a gap among the perspective of lesser trees. The park was officially private and totally unfrequented; but there just might be an amateur poacher about, or more likely a birdwatcher, who would have fieldglasses. The thought still bothered George as he sat that evening by his father in the bar.

As he worried, sipping the bitter for which he had never acquired much of a taste, his father was called off to play darts, as on that other and still recent evening. And then took place a further and nightmarish repetition. As if on cue the same stranger walked into the bar.

George had somehow been confident – he couldn't have said why – that he would not be seeing that man again. The thought of him had not crossed his mind when he entered the Antelope. But here he undoubtedly was.

He seemed at first not to notice George. And yet as soon as he had gone over to the bar, and had a drink in his hand, he came and sat down beside the young man as if he were already an old acquaintance.

George had been irritated by the interest the tiresome fellow had taken in his mother's affairs; he seemed a bore to be avoided, though nothing much worse than that. Now George was trapped again by his father's absence, and he resigned himself to fending off the brute for a further period of annoyance.

The worst thing about the worst bores, as George was beginning to find out, is that they are not content to ramble on, but insist on your attention, even on your own considered opinions.

This was what now took place. As on the first occasion the man would ask him questions, but these were now of the most tedious kind, relating to the locality, and its amenities.

'I've been taking a quick shufty round the place, since we last met, you know. Charming, isn't it, wouldn't you say, really charming? And so rural. Who could guess you were a mere twenty-five miles from London? Not much more, is it?'

George said he supposed it wasn't. And he had no idea what a shufty was. Probably some ghastly colonial expression, of the sort this fellow would use.

'Today I ventured a bit further afield,' the other went on. 'Found myself in a sort of park. Must have been a fine place once, but now all let go anyhow. Sad, isn't it, the way these old places can't be kept up any more?'

A vague uneasiness took hold of George. As if to head the man off he embarked on a laborious exposition of the Roman Camp site, the most notable of the local places of interest. Said to be from Caesar's second expedition to Britain. Or his first perhaps – George could not remember. Anyway it was a protected area of outstanding natural beauty, or historic something or other ....

George tailed off, lamely observing that in what was becoming a built-up area there were not many such places left.

'Ah, but that's what's so delightful about the ones that still are,' said the other with animation, beginning to light his pipe. 'Delightful. Exciting too.' Pipe in mouth he gave George an arch look.

George made a deprecating noise. He had begun to feel a little sick, and something more bitter than the beer rose at the back of his throat. He saw Martha holding her skirt up, her lips to his,

67

and then something bright among the trees, winking over her shoulder.

The other returned to business with his pipe. Gazing towards the bar George strove to wipe away the look of consternation that he knew must have showed on his face.

'Just the sort of place I would have chosen to take my girl, when I was a bit younger,' mused the stranger indulgently. His eyes softened into a look of retrospection.

All George had to do was to stay blank. Or so he told himself. His urge was to get up and run away. But he must adopt another animal subterfuge: to crouch down and wait. He did not trust himself to pick up his glass of beer.

'And apart from love's young dream', the man went on, with his friendly laugh, 'there are birds in those woods I wouldn't believe I was seeing, this distance from London. A sparrowhawk for instance. Flew right past me, chasing a goldcrest. How about that?'

'Ornithology is it you go in for then? Birdwatching?'

'Just so. My old man was in the forces. He got the chop, as they used to say, in the very last week of the last war. Tough luck, what? – really tough. His jeep ran over a mine when he was out on a recce. D'you know, I've still got his glasses. German pair he liberated somewhere or other. Zeiss. Quite the best. He used to say the German army always did have the best. And, this'll surprise you, they're quite undamaged. Lenses clear as clear. Super intensification. Brings anything you're watching right into your lap.'

He drank off his whisky.

George, tension mounting in him with every word the man uttered, beheld inside his own head a soundless explosion. A small vehicle was tossed high in the air, its occupants disintegrating in the cloud of smoke and dust, even as a pair of binoculars landed safely in a distant hedge. Later on they would have been retrieved, no doubt, by a faithful and grieving sergeant ....

Too late he saw that the other was studying his face, as if admiringly.

'You get the hang of things quickly, I will say. Quick as a flash.

68

Pity you young chaps never had the chance to join the army. You'd have enjoyed it, I shouldn't wonder. I know I did.'

George felt he could stand no more of this. It was plain that this man had seen him in the park: just as plain that he had seen the woman he was with. But he could not know who she was.

He stood up. 'I'm afraid I haven't got the time to buy you a drink tonight,' he said, as if facetiously. 'I must be going.'

He waved towards the exit and then in the general direction of the darts board, as if in reluctant need to fulfil some engagement which involved leaving his father behind in the pub.

'Oh come,' said the stranger, as if with a sudden authority. 'You can spare just a moment I'm sure. Sit down. I've something important to say to you.'

*

George turned himself over, yet again. He judged it to be about four o'clock. Perhaps only three. Whichever it was he knew he hadn't slept at all; and he was reluctant to turn the light on and look at his watch. He preferred the darkness.

He knew that if Dulcie had been there they would have relaxed together and slept. They would have made love of course. And then she would have been there all night beside him: ample and smooth, warm and comforting. He could feel her exactly as if she were there. But what was the good of that, when she wasn't? They had never been all night in a bed together. Probably never would be. Not now.

And the awful thing was that he couldn't avoid starting to think of her in a new way. It was almost as if this man had himself been intimate with her; as if the pair of them had come in some way to share her.

He turned on his back. That was the most uncomfortable, the least womblike, position: the most suitable for his present state of mind. And he realised that he must in fact have slept, for however short a time, for he was remembering what seemed like a waking dream, or a nightmare.

It had begun rather well, if conventionally. He had been walking across a wide moorland towards a fire glowing in the distance. As he got closer he saw it was a wall of flame beyond

69

which lay Martha like Brünnhilde, on a pyre, in a blue nylon nightgown. Without any hesitation he strode through the blaze, which proved harmless, even heatless. He had never seen her in a nightdress, and her big bare feet were unimpressive, which made them all the more dear to him. So far so good. He stooped ecstatically to rouse her with a kiss, wondering at the same time, and in the manner of dreams, what they actually did about feet in the opera – were they shrouded in some suitable drapery?

As he had the thought, and as his lips met hers, he saw out of the corner of his eye two men standing just beyond the flames, laughing at him.

Yes, he must have slept, for he had certainly dreamt something like that.

Those men knew about him and Martha. And it amused them.

On and on in the darkness he heard the voice of the man in the bar, repeating what he had first said after George had reluctantly sat down again beside him.

'So, my lad, you've been cuckolding my big brother? Well, well: I suppose I ought to congratulate you.'

*

Martha was lying in bed beside Alexander, thinking of her day with George. Only three or four hours really, but it felt like a day.

Seeing him again had set her up so much that she felt she had almost danced through the evening. And now, lying beside her husband, she experienced an imbecile serenity. It was a great benevolence towards the human race, which at that moment even included her brother-in-law. She was so happy she didn't care how imbecile her feelings were. She went over in her mind every moment she had spent with George.

Of course she had been looking forward to it, but the pleasure of actually seeing him again had surpassed all her hopes and fears. And making love in the open, in the sunshine and among their trees and hidden pathways, not in that murky, ill-omened cellar! Even their parting had been happy, as they held hands and knew they would meet again soon, although they could not arrange quite when.

Home again, with no Bobby there, and no Mrs Jones of course, she had gone first up to her bedroom and put her pants back on. She had taken them off, on spec as it were, before she had gone out to meet George. As she smoothed down her skirt she must have smiled an involuntary smile, intercepted by the looking-glass. She had gone on grinning amiably into it, and even started laughing.

There were more usual days when that glass reflected a strained apologetic smile of anxiety, which seemed to beg for the toleration and forbearance of humanity. Why shouldn't she look at herself, smiling in this cheerful helpless way?

Perhaps her mood had been infectious. When Bobby returned, some time after Alexander but still punctual for dinner at eight, he had himself seemed positively cordial, almost skittish. And she had striven of course, though for once with no conscious effort, to play up to him. She had never seen him in such a good mood.

Alexander too seemed to sniff the warm gales of euphoria; and he went away, humming to himself, to open a bottle of claret.

In her happiness Martha had allowed herself to do a bit of real cooking, and the men didn't seem to mind. Watching her husband, as he drank his wine and ate her lamb casserole with some show of enjoyment, Martha felt like a biblical wife, dispensing the comforts of the evening ritual among an extended family. She even felt a kind of Christian contentment. Like most people in their neighbourhood she went to church; and she had found herself coming increasingly to depend on it. It gave her a nice blank sort of solace, a comfort that was quite without meaning, and for that reason all the more dependable and habit-forming. It went with the blankness she gave to her husband and took from him, which seemed to suit them both.

This evening, she felt, religion had not only blossomed but produced real fruits: the fruits of her joyous day with George; and now it was these pleasures and satisfactions she was helping to spread for the ones at home.

*

71

George had simply stared at the man, incapable for the moment of uttering a word. The other had seemed to find that natural.

His conduct to George so far had always been polite, even mildly deferential, as when he had talked about the young Irishman who had worshipped Mrs Pusey and called her his Santa Monica. Now he suddenly turned rude, as well as jocular, as if they were members of the same family, accustomed to the give and take of old jokes: the kind that went near the knuckle.

With appalling suddenness he had become a kind of relation, close kin to Martha, perhaps closer to her than that.

'She's in luck, catching a good-looking young stud like you.'

To do him justice George had never given a thought to his looks. Did Martha think of him as a handsome boy? That would be intolerable – he knew she didn't. She loved him, and never thought what he looked like.

Or did she? Had she fallen for him because he was a good-looking stud? The notion was not only unbearable but ridiculous. And yet Martha's brother-in-law, her husband's brother, was taking it for granted. Almost as if it were a family joke. Martha's well-known weakness for good-looking young men, which was regarded with indulgent amusement in her family.

The idea that this man, this odious man sitting beside him in the pub, should be a relative of hers! Even though it was only by marriage.

'Are you going to tell her?' he found himself saying. The nightmare of her relationship with the man had made him find his voice. Perhaps she knew already that this man knew? Perhaps it had already become a family joke?

George realised with sudden clarity that Martha was still for him not so much a person as an extension of the private life he had always lived. A marvellous extension of course. He loved her, knew she loved him: and yet in this relation she could only be the embodiment of his private solitariness. Their love was their secrecy. How could it exist in a social context? Or inside a family? Her family.

What could she feel about it – Martha herself? She must feel the same as he did? And yet, why should she? He couldn't really know. All he knew was that she was happy with him. And because she was so, that happiness seemed for him to be natural to her, in a way that it was not for himself. Probably he was not made to be happy, just as he wasn't made to be a footballer, or to listen to great music, or to know how to savour a choice wine.

Somehow he must save Martha, save her for himself, get her away from these people. And yet how absurd! All George's negativism rebelled at the very idea. He might not be made for happiness – exciting holidays, shouts of children, communal laughter – but he was made to be with Martha, as the two of them had always been. Separate from the world.

Martha's brother-in-law puffed quietly at his pipe, his smiling eyes wrinkled against the smoke. He seemed to be considering the words George had got out. When he spoke he did not answer them directly.

'Kissing and telling,' he at last said meditatively. 'Never fancied it myself. No, I'm not going to tell her. Or anyone else for that matter. But fair's fair. I think in return you should tell me a lot of things. If you can, and I think you can.'

He paused, and relit his pipe.

'Suppose we start with what your mother's friends could have tucked away somewhere. There's just one little item they seem to have got hold of in which I should be interested. You know the area, and I have the feeling you may know where it's likely to be.'

*

After dinner Martha had put the two brothers safely into the drawing-room and returned to the kitchen, humming that same tune from 'The Mikado' which her husband's croak had made vaguely recognisable when he went to open the claret. Both brothers seemed in a good mood now, and she was happy to leave them to have a chat together.

Bobby lighted a cigar, having asked permission with an irony that was not lost on his brother. Alexander liked the sound of his wife's cheerfulness – he could hear her rendering fairly adequately the tune he had been trying to recall – and he hoped much from Bobby's present expansiveness. He longed to learn something of what he was up to in the area.

73

Bobby was well aware of that. It amused him to wonder how Alexander would receive what he was about to be told.

'I've been pottering around that bit of run-down parkland over towards the main road. Privately owned, I suppose, but nobody challenged me. Rum sort of place, what? Must have been a fine estate once?'

Alexander was not in the least interested in such activities. If his brother chose to waste his time – or was it still the army's or the MI5's time? – wandering in the locality, that was nothing to him. He wanted to hear about something more businesslike, or even about some amorous adventure that Bobby might be pursuing in the neighbourhood. His brother's sex-life was still something of a mystery to him. Could it, for instance, be anything like his own?

He was a little irritated, too, at Bobby's hint at being more familiar with the world of parks and estates, however run down, than his bourgeois elder brother would be likely to be.

'Martha had the idea of getting a dog,' he said carelessly, as if possession of a dog, even if hypothetical, showed an easy familiarity with country lifestyles. 'She likes to walk in that park sometimes.'

'Yes, I ran across her there today,' said Bobby. 'But I don't think it was a dog she was with.'

At that moment Martha opened the door, still wearing the apron she never remembered to take off in the kitchen. She paused and beamed approvingly at her two men. She told them she was off to bed. It had been a busy day.

As the door closed Bobby knocked the ash off his cigar and remarked that for Martha it probably had been a busy day.

Something was in the air, and Alexander sensed in himself a feeling of growing excitement. His brother had something to tell him; something he actually wanted to tell him, or so it looked. And coming from the reticent Bobby that was itself a cause for excitement.

'Your wife's having an affair, you know.'

Bobby calmly stubbed out his cigar as he said this.

The excitement that had been continuing to mount in his brother changed direction, and broke into a run, like a delirious crowd at a football match. He got up and took two tripping steps across the carpet.

'*What's* that you're telling me, Bobby?'

'What I say, old boy. Saw her in that park this afternoon. With a young man. A good looker, too.'

Bobby Grey was not given to enjoyments. But it gave him pleasure now – perhaps the only pleasure of which his sunken nature was capable – to watch the dawning of animation in his elder brother. Betraying young George Pusey was nothing: it had been an almost automatic reflex. The pleasure would be in seeing how Alexander took the news.

Alexander took it very well. He merely became more and more interested. That disappointed his brother a little. Bobby looked grave and sad now, conscious of duty done, reluctant to intervene between the news he had given and the upset it must be causing.

But reluctant as he was, or seemed to be, he brought himself to venture a further suggestion.

'Of course Martha didn't see me. I vanished discreetly away. And if I were you I shouldn't say anything to her, old chap.'

Alexander was well aware that he must dissemble the thrill the news had given him. Bad for his blood pressure too, probably.

He was excited, none the less. It took him back to the time when he and Martha were first married. The time when he had resumed relations with his former wife.

Naturally he had said nothing of that to Martha. But he was soon aware that she knew, and he was pleased to find that out. How she knew was not easy to say, but her awareness made her seem more than ever a comforting and domestic person, a good wife. He felt that he was full entitled to that, after Fiona.

As he sat with Bobby, digesting this fascinating news, and trying to dissimulate the fact that he found it so fascinating, he did find time to wonder just how he knew, in those far-off days, that his so obliging and ingenuous new wife was perfectly well aware of things. She knew that her predecessor was still performing a wifely office, for her old husband as well as for her new one.

That was true, but what she hadn't known was the real reason.

It was his – Alexander's – own deep and helpless attachment to young Nigel, the fair-haired stockbroker with whom Fiona had fallen in love. She had got him, insisted on marrying him. He had been flattered no doubt, for Fiona was a good-looking girl.

And then she had found – what? – that after a month or two of marriage Nigel didn't like sex with her any more.

But Fiona's *amour propre* required a husband, and two were better than one. So she hung on to Alexander. And that had kept them all together, like a family. Indeed they had been an invisible family: invisible, that is, to everyone except Martha, who was mysteriously heartened by her unknown co-adjutors, as she set about raising a family of her own.

Fiona, Alexander knew, had never wanted one. No doubt she had taken her own precautions. But she needed a family around her. Her ex-husband and her new one suited that need very well; and when they had become boyfriends it suited her even better. She indulged them just like a couple of boys. She was as well aware of the relations between her couple as Martha had become aware of her continuing relations with Alexander. Fiona liked having two husbands, one older than herself, and the new one, Nigel, a good bit younger.

So all had been well, reflected Alexander. As it still was. His work with the company had given him every opportunity to be away from home. Martha, bless her, had always been eager not to interfere with his job, and with its demands on him. There had been plenty of phantom courses and conferences, accepted by her without demur. Busy weekends, at Fiona's and Nigel's house, had been one of his accepted pleasures: they still were. And sometimes it was a real conference, in which case they often made a threesome at some hotel close by.

And so now – Good Lord! – a parallel situation had arisen, putting him, Alexander, in the very position his wife had been in before! She had not minded, he knew, so why should he? But Martha – of all people! The thought did give him a sudden and quite unwonted stab of jealousy. Perhaps he was more possessive of her placid being than he had realised? But he put that thought quickly away, to concentrate on this young man Bobby had seen with her. A good looker, so he had said. Who on earth could it be?

The thought dragged him back to Bobby, who was regarding him, pipe in hand, with a look of pacific apology.

'Martha's got her friends, you know. Probably met one of them while out for a walk. Walked on to the park together. And I believe there's a young fellow who mows our lawns from time to time. Earns a bit of pin-money that way.'

Bobby considered his brother's suggestion, as if judiciously.

'Well, they weren't actually walking. They weren't even talking.'

'Not talking?'

'No.'

'Then what were they doing?'

'They were copulating. Under a big tree.'

Alexander started to stride about the carpet. He had the eager excitement of a man who has just heard wonderful news. Bobby continued to smile at him, unanxiously.

'Your wife's a good picker. This young fellow is OK.'

Alexander suddenly realised that he was most annoyed by his brother's tone. What the hell did it matter – should it matter, rather – what this young man looked like? He must remind Bobby, and forcefully too, of his own status as an outraged husband. In this locality – and at their time of life!

'I don't care a damn about the young man! Have I ever met him?'

'Well, I wouldn't know, would I? He looked to be a nice young fellow who wasn't doing anything much.'

'Except rogering my wife!'

'Just that.'

The brothers were silent. Bobby had felt pleased at first with his little experiment, but the pleasure had not lasted. Boredom had set in. He wasn't really awfully interested in his brother's love life, although the move he had made at least confirmed what he had always felt sure of anyway. Alexander liked the men, the men who liked his girls. What a bore sex had become nowadays. Always on view. Like sticking a BMW in the garage and leaving the door open.

With a neutral sourness he thought of the girls in his own life. That six-foot creature Pinky, for instance, from whom he had pinched the suitcase that should have been stuffed with heroin.

He'd lugged it about the continent. And in the end found it was worthless.

Life for him had been a bit too much like that, all the way.

The reflection did not perturb him particularly. In any case, the caper he was on to now could be worth much more than that suitcase full of chalk should rightly have been. Very, very much more.

He decided to go to bed. His brother looked hurt, as if the significance of the news he had just heard required them both at the very least to stay up, mulling it over into the small hours.

After Bobby had gone Alexander continued to pace about the room. He fiddled with the bits of unburnt log on the wide stone hearth. Because of the central heating the fire was not needed, and it always smoked. But Martha thought it nice to light a fire.

He felt a sudden wish to see her, though not to talk to her. She was asleep. He gazed at her a long time with an expression of amazement; and indeed he did feel incredulous. Something of the glamour of this newly revealed and astonishing liaison seemed to hang around the familiar form under the bedclothes.

What sort of young man had she got? As he stood gazing at his wife he was filled with a sober and steady joy at the thought that he must now inevitably find out.

CHAPTER 6

South Ken

When Mrs Peter Grey received an invitation to spend Christmas with her husband's brother and his wife she was delighted. The invitation came early, and would give her plenty of time to get herself ready for the occasion.

Peter had been asked too, of course, but would he come?

A model husband in many ways, he was also a man of irregular habit, who came and went as his business or pleasure dictated. His wife Virginia, or Ginnie as she was usually known, did not mind this at all. Peter was an excellent father, and he often took charge of their daughter, who doted on him. Then Ginnie could more easily get on with her own work at home.

She was a publisher's reader. Before the birth of her daughter she used to go to the office three or four days in the week, but now she did most of her work in her small flat. In her own quiet way she enjoyed it: particularly the editing, and the reading of proofs.

Ginnie was not to know that Martha had been told by her husband to invite them for Christmas. She thought well of Martha, and wished they could meet more often. She always remembered Martha's kindness to her, before and at her wedding, and the way her large features had beamed a smile of goodwill. That smile had a look of collusion in it too, as if she and Ginnie understood each other separately, in the midst of the family into which they had both married.

When she thought of her own marriage, and of that wedding, Ginnie herself could never get over a feeling of amazement, indeed incredulity. It was by far the most improbable thing that had ever happened to her. By far the most.

She had not so much loved her bridegroom (whatever that meant: she was by no means sure she would ever find out) as found herself given away by herself to an alien mode of being. She might as well have been sold as a slave to the barbarous Turk, like the heroines of old opera and rhyme, or even in some of the trashy sex romances she was sent to read and report on. Often, she had to admit, she rather enjoyed them.

Well, that was putting it too strongly. No doubt all women experienced something of the sort when their lives changed – if they did. Ginnie had got in the habit of assuming that hers never would very much, and she supposed she had come to prefer things that way. Calling her soul her own, could one say, although she only thought of it like that after what had happened to her.

And what had happened to her? For one thing she had been pregnant, and her daughter was born four months after the wedding.

She had been living quietly in her little flat and getting on with her modest job. Seeing her mother and one or two friends, not bothering anybody. Her boyfriend at the time, if he could be so described, was a young Oxford philosopher she had met when invited down to lunch with an elderly don. Her firm had sent her to discuss the layout of a volume of memoirs.

Ginnie then had been getting on for thirty-six. The boyfriend, as he had more or less become, was some years younger.

Less rather than more perhaps. From a mixture of diffidence, even distaste, and a lack of opportunity, she had never been made love to, at least not by a man, Her philosophical boyfriend had hardly so much as kissed her, and seemed to prefer things that way. But when he invited her down to Oxford, some months after their first meeting, he had suggested, in his precise philosophical manner, that they should go to bed.

Well, you never know your luck. Tim, she felt sure, had anxiously planned the encounter, and it had been gruesomely unsuccessful. Ginnie's fault no doubt, as she was quite prepared to admit; though if she had been clueless, so had he. But things have a habit of happening all together, if they happen at all. The following morning she had met the Captain.

The circumstances had certainly been extraordinary. She could never afterwards imagine quite what had happened, although she possessed a fanciful mind, and like many solitary people she had always enjoyed making up little stories about herself and an interesting-looking man, or woman, seen on a bus, or on the opposite side of the street. It had been a painless and pleasant way of imagining herself taking part in a love scene. And then it had happened in real life.

Poor Tim! She had not seen him since. She had written to explain things, and his reply had been decidedly brief, although she had heard from Dr Bowser, the elderly and benevolent don who had brought them together, that he was soon having a long-term relation with a very pretty young undergraduate. Dr Bowser seemed glad of that, for Tim was his protégé. Ginnie was glad too; for it was due to Tim, after all, and to his well-meant attempt to put some sex (which he had supposed she must be in want of) into their friendship, that she had met Captain Peter Grey.

And that had begun as a case of mistaken identity. By coincidence she had once met his brother, down at the seaside, and this man she now met was very like him, although – as she thought then and was quite sure now – he was very much more attractive.

It was because of this close resemblance that she had actually spoken to him, at the end of Tim Kent's morning lecture. Peter, it seemed, had been in the habit of dropping in, because he was interested in the things that Tim Kent was talking about. With his usual charm and good manners exuberantly in evidence, he had seemed greatly amused to meet her.

From then until the day they got married she hardly knew what had happened.

Peter and his Russian wife had the job of looking after a country house near Oxford. At first, when he took Ginnie out there on the day of the lecture, she thought he was the owner; and he hadn't disabused her. And she certainly hadn't realised how much he had abruptly needed her.

That was a strange business! She had never fully understood it, not that she had really tried. A crisis had occurred. His wife left him: his employer, whom it seemed they had been attempting to blackmail, threatened him. So Ginnie had all inadvertently been his salvation.

Not as a wife of course, at least not then. It was as a screen, a blind, a protective device, that she appeared to have been heaven-sent. She was a clueless and innocent bystander whose mere presence had stood between Peter and something very serious indeed. They might even have made away with him, if she hadn't been there.

So at least he had told her; and she believed him. Nor in this case was she wholly wrong to do so, although she later found that in almost all circumstances the truth appealed to Peter much less than what his own lively mind could make up. (He had once told her his was a 'toy mind'; it, and the truth, were a box of bricks which he enjoyed playing about with, like a child on the floor.)

She had been left a clueless and innocent bystander, whom it had entertained him to pick up at the end of that Oxford lecture, as if she were herself a toy. But without knowing it she had interceded for him, he said, as if she had also been the Virgin Mary; and as things turned out she had still been a virgin on that extraordinary night when his employer had unexpectedly returned, two men with him, and her presence had evidently saved a situation which had been quite uncomprehended, at least by her.

By then she supposed she had been helplessly in love, or whatever one called the state she certainly had been in. She had been determined to stay with Peter in some role or other – as houseguest, housemaid, mistress, she didn't care what – and at the end of that singular evening they had washed up the dinner things and walked upstairs to bed together as if it had been the most natural thing in the world.

Next day he had asked her to marry him. She was genuinely surprised, far too surprised to say yes. She was too happy even; and she thought he couldn't be serious. It looked as if he loved her, though quite why she couldn't see. And, to be honest, she still couldn't see. True, his wife had left him; and he appeared, surprisingly, to be the sort of man who needed one. But why her? He had everything going for him after all. Fantastic good looks, charm, kindness, self-assurance. Women should, and no doubt did, fall for him in droves.

Oddly enough, Ginnie had never felt in the least despondent about this. Although she still could not see why he should have fallen for her, except out of the improbable motive of gratitude, she recognised that most women meant nothing to Peter, however many might love him and pursue him. He did not like being pursued.

As for herself, she was old enough to feel fairly philosophical. Romance for her had always been brief, satisfying, and pointless: the object of it seen from the top of the bus, or encountered on holiday. She had never expected to have to do anything about it.

But of course on this occasion she had done something. After leaving that enchanted house and returning, comfortingly and thankfully as she thought, to her flat, she had suddenly found herself bursting into floods of tears, rushing off to Paddington, getting on a train, going straight back to him.

When they said goodbye, after that memorable night, she really thought she mightn't see him again. But he had rung up and asked her to marry him. More than that, he had rung several times. That day and the next and the one after. He had always been on business somewhere. She had got quite accustomed to chatting with him on the phone.

But she still could not believe that the whole thing wasn't over. And in a way she wanted it to be: it had been so perfect. So days, weeks, more than a month went by, and they hadn't met again.

He was still away on business.

Then she found she was pregnant.

It had never occurred to her that such a thing could, or might, happen. Perhaps she had taken it for granted that once a virgin, always a virgin. Something like that.

She had been incredulous, and then frightened: more than that, appalled. She still remembered that feeling with horrid distinctness. How could it have happened that her body had suddenly trapped her like this, when she wanted to sit dreamily in her flat, and think of Peter? As a wonderful thing that was over. She had been quite happy talking to him on the phone, and getting on with her daily work. She had been quite sure then that he would get over it, whatever it was; and in the meantime it was nice, very nice, to hear his voice; sometimes several times a day.

But then it was just as if she had contracted, at the same

83

moment as the love affair, a fatal disease. Something quite separate from the state of being in love.

She did not tell Peter Grey, when he next rang. She could not have brought herself to do so, any more than she could have told him she really had some awful disease. But three or four weeks later, when he rang, as usual, at eight or so in the morning; and when he told her he longed to see her, and joked about wanting to do the washing-up with her again, she suddenly broke down and told him what had happened.

Of course even then she might have been wrong; she had not taken the test. Just the possibility had totally unnerved her.

She would never forget her astonishment at his reaction. He seemed genuinely delighted. Thrilled to pieces. He was up in Peterborough at the time, for some reason. As she shed tears on the phone she thought how comically suitable for him the name of the place sounded. Peter at Peterborough.

He said with decision that he would be coming down to her at once. And he had done so. Within two hours, as it seemed, he was with her at the flat, and they were in bed together. Then he had taken her out for lunch, and they had drunk a bottle of claret. She could remember the year, and the way in which he had held up the bottle, smiling at the label. They would have another bottle, in private, on their wedding-day, he said. Never mind the champagne.

But, of course, he was married already.

Except it turned out that he wasn't. His Russian wife, Vera, had married him according to the Orthodox rite. But there had been no civil ceremony: they had never been officially married.

Naturally enough Ginnie asked more about Vera.

Vera, yes – well, she and Peter had been happily married for years. During that time he had never looked at another woman (Ginnie could believe it, oddly enough) and at this point in his narration Peter's eyes slowly filled with tears. There had been a frightful misunderstanding with Vera, as he told Ginnie later.

Yes, they had been married, but only in the sight of God. Vera believed in God.

'Do you?' he had asked Ginnie, raising his head from her stomach, where it had been comfortably pillowed. (After return-

84

ing from the restaurant they had gone back to bed again.) Ginnie had said she thought she did not, on the whole.

None the less it had seemed otherworldly, almost mystical, to lie there on her own bed, with his head on the place where their child was apparently growing, and to know that the three of them would be joined together.

Quite horribly sentimental it seemed, now that she was both married and middle-aged. She remembered how she had thought of the Virgin. How old had Mary been? – quite young presumably. She, Ginnie, had never got pregnant again: not that she had taken any steps about it. And looking back that seemed to have been the best for all three of them.

They had decided to call the baby Elizabeth. It was christened in church, the church in Kensington where they had got married. Ginnie's mother had been there of course, as she had been at the wedding, where she had looked happily dazed – absolutely staggered in fact – at Ginnie's achievement. Resigned to her daughter never having a husband, she had regarded Peter with awe. And she was enchanted by her grandchild.

The child Elizabeth hardly heard the name. At her first attempts at speech, when her father was holding her, she seemed to try to say his name, producing a noise like 'Pinky'. Or perhaps it only sounded like Pinky because of the girl Alice whom Ginnie had known. The genuine if improbable surname of this girl, anglicised from the Ukrainian Pinkorenko, had been Pinky.

In any case, from then on the little girl became Pinky; and Pinky she obstinately remained.

Ginnie had kept on with her job. This was partly because they always seemed to need the money, such as it was; but more because it still seemed to her to be her real life. Her husband and child were phenomena she could never quite get used to, wonderful as they no doubt were. Deep down she always felt they might disappear one day, and leave her stranded, back in her former existence.

After more than five years they were still in her old small flat. The only change was that the bed was bigger. Peter said the little place suited him, and he loved it because it was hers. He was away a good deal, and Pinky was often with her grandmother.

Fortunately the friend who lived with Ginnie's mother also adored the child.

Ginnie soon found that her husband was the reverse of masterful, whatever had been her impression when she met him, and when she had fallen in love in that disconcertingly new way. He preferred leaving things to her. This might have been a recipe for non-success in marriage, as her own temperament had always inclined her to passivity rather than action. In practice, like many apparent misfittings, it worked out very well. They talked all the time – he loved to talk to her. She remained vague all the time about whatever plans and projects he might have in hand; and that was the way she preferred it.

They had a joint account, which usually seemed to have a sufficiency of money in it, if not a great deal. Before they were married he had sold the BMW he had used for his business trips. Now he told her, and thankfully, that he did not need it any more. He would go by train, if he went at all. That suited Ginnie, who did not drive and had no wish to learn. She took Pinky on the train from Victoria, when they went down to her bungalow at Greatstone-on-Sea.

It had been bequeathed to her by Alice, the odd girl whose name survived, as if by coincidence, in Ginnie's daughter. The bungalow was a sort of reward for Alice having taken Ginnie for a ride in her shady dealings. Alice had then gone off on a trip to Australia, more than five years ago now; and Ginnie had not seen her since.

But she often thought of Alice, whom she supposed she had loved in a way, and who had certainly made a decided impact on her life.

It was through Alice, after all, that she had met first her brother-in-law, Major Bobby Grey, and then her husband; although Alice's relations with Bobby had also been shady to say the least, and she had never known Peter at all.

But she had given Ginnie her ticky-tacky cottage beside the sea and the sand dunes, on Romney Marsh.

Ginnie's sojourn with Alice at 'Silver Spray' had been brief but eventful, even dramatic. She had nearly been raped by one of Alice's smuggling friends, a young Irishman whom in retrospect seemed not so very frightening, or even unamiable. If that was surprising it was no odder than some of the other things that had happened to her with Alice. Ginnie remembered how they had lain in bed together talking, and watching the lighthouse beam slide across the ceiling. She often thought of that time, and she loved Greatstone, and its grey featureless sea. She had taken Peter down there, and was very happy to see him fall in love with the place as she had done.

After Pinky was born they had spent more time down there by the sea than in London. Peter played golf; and though Ginnie never attempted the game herself she loved to walk round with him, hearing the larks in the wide sky that stretched from Dungeness to Folkestone, almost always a fine light blue. Peter would carry the baby in a sling, handing her carefully to Ginnie before he played each shot.

At home he performed the offices of child care with elegant devotion, and when the little girl was two he would scamper her across the sands, and gravely initiate her into a world where black sea-pods could be popped, and small pink shells discovered.

It amused Ginnie that her husband, normally an immaculate dresser, made no concessions to seaside attire, resembling an Edwardian father as he pottered with his daughter beside the wide edge of sandy foam, his trousers rolled up a few inches, and his shoes and socks removed.

With her mother Pinky began to take an interest in the flowers to be found on the fairways of the links in June and July, and particularly in their names – trefoil, houndstongue, ladies bedstraw. Her greatest pleasure was a trip in the small carriages of the Romney Hythe and Dymchurch Light Railway, which ran briskly across the reed-bordered fields of the Marsh, trailing a miniature corridor of steam, and whistling at the rare road crossings.

Peter Grey's approval of this innocent world, and the enthusiasm with which he took part in it, never ceased to astonish his wife, and gratify her too. Her predecessor, Vera, could have told her that Peter Grey not only loved everything he undertook, but put a fine imaginative relish into it which used to captivate the Russian woman, sombre in her own nature as she was. Vera had always doted on her husband's high spirits, though Ginnie found them a little tiring sometimes.

But in their own domestic world she was grateful for them, as she was for him.

She hardly ever recalled now the comedy – indeed the absurdity so far as she was concerned – in which their relationship had begun. She had encountered him under such very different circumstances: in that exotic mansion which appeared to suit the style of his being so perfectly, and to harmonise with it. Now he loved to sit shirt-sleeved in the tiny living-room at 'Silver Spray', reading with bland concentration some script which his wife was working on for her firm. She quickly came to value his judgement and advice.

And yet there remained for her a kind of unreality about him. It was the very thing that had been so marvellously seductive when they had first met. She recognised now, although it had ceased either to worry or to fascinate her, that his beautiful oddity as a person must often have licensed fantasy in others, as it had done in herself. So it must originally have been with his Russian wife, Vera; and perhaps Vera had always been able to think of her Peter in the light of her own foreigner's fantasy: a fantasy of English innocence, and flower gardens, and firelight winking on panelled walls.

It sometimes occurred to Ginnie to wonder if Peter's evident delight in herself, and in his daughter, resembled his feeling for other properties that had become part of himself. His waistcoat, the worn flannel shirts he washed by hand, his two pairs of ancient and glassy brogue shoes. He revelled in his various toys. Perhaps that was natural in a man? And yet she had to admit that there was nothing exactly 'natural' about her Peter, as he had become. He remained mysterious to her. But she didn't mind that. On the contrary.

His business doings were obscure to her rather than mysterious. He seemed to have remarkably few friends. He once told her that his old activities on the fringe of the secret services, and in the netherworld adjoining, had not exactly promoted a sociable way of life. And out of preference he'd always been a one-person man. The company of Vera had been enough for him.

Ginnie loved to hear him talk of Vera, both from a natural curiosity about her predecessor, and the wish to find out what she could about her husband.

And come to that, she had not so many friends herself, although the few she had were all charmed head over heels by Peter; and great curiosity about her new husband was shown at the office, where she numbered most of her acquaintance. She had taken him once or twice to an office party; and in that setting found herself looking at him with something like pride of possession. She felt incredulous that she had him; and she couldn't help but feel gratified at the looks of incredulity visible on some of her colleagues' faces.

She looked forward now to going down to Martha for Christmas. Martha was kind and cosy, and got on well with Pinky the few times they had met, although Ginnie surmised, incorrectly, that her sister-in-law might be no more fond of children by nature than she herself was. Martha's family was grown up of course, and she was a lot older too; but somewhere inside her there seemed to be a privacy that could be recognised by another woman, to whom it also came by nature. Her sister-in-law, Ginnie felt, showed symptoms of a well-concealed surprise at finding herself in the situation in which life seemed to have put her.

At five years old Pinky was a shy little creature who usually remained speechless in the presence of strangers. Ginnie suspected that her daughter was reassured by the secrecy in Martha she thought she had noticed herself. Martha's 'insider' situation, with her big house and solid family, conveyed a sense of the problematic; as if Martha knew too well that her only hope of making sense of the world was to do what it seemed to expect of her.

What did Martha feel about that big opulent house, in its graciously landscaped surroundings? Did she feel it was 'her' house? Where she herself was concerned, Ginnie knew she sometimes had a twinge that the little place in Kensington where she had lived many years was now 'their' flat: not hers anymore. An unexpected effect of marriage, she found, was both to sharpen and to dissatisfy what had previously been her own unthinking sense of possession.

89

She had never seen herself particularly as an outsider; but now she was a married woman with a child she sometimes felt she knew what that notion signified.

And she continued to experience, from time to time, a mild sense of desolation, as at something lost. It had never occurred to her when she was pregnant, or when she was first married; but sometimes she was reminded that she and her new life were now locked in together, to serve an indefinite sentence. Being alive had acquired too positive a meaning, too much of a point. She had done without such a point in life before. And it was when that brief horror, or nausea, overcame her that she realised she could do without it again.

The vague dreams and comforts and vacancies of her old life had ended. And they should have ended, vulgarly speaking, beyond daydream's wildest expectation. She couldn't deny it, nor did she – not even to herself. But something in that self, when she woke in the night with Peter beside her, remained obstinately unimpressed. She hoped to placate it, whatever it was, when Peter was away, and Pinky was with her grandmother; but even when she was alone again in the little flat her former being would not come back to order. It would not revisit her just because she was by herself, or rather without her husband and child.

She had lost whatever was once inside her, or in her head: there was no denying that. What survived was something of her old solitariness and scepticism, which declined to be impressed by her good fortune. They silently scoffed at the guilt feelings which sometimes told her she must be an ungrateful and unloving wretch.

But why should she be? Just because she baulked, in her inner thoughts, at the idea of love and marriage didn't mean that Peter and their child were not now part of her. The part that failed to come to terms with herself, as she used to be.

She developed a morbid interest in her mother's reactions. In her devotion to her grandchild the old lady seemed to have found a new mode of being. And this looked to Ginnie like the opposite of what she herself had experienced.

From her mother-in-law in Florida, whom she had never met, she had regular cards, and even 'newsletters'. Peter was a little satirical about his mother, who had long ago as a widow left her sons in England, to remarry in her native land. She was older than Ginnie's mother; but she and her husband were still very much alive; and at the proper seasons lavish gifts of dolls, games and candy arrived for Pinky.

The little girl was polite about these – she had always been a polite child – but it was clear that they meant nothing to that inward life which, as her mother was secretly disconcerted to discover, had something in common with the sort that used to be her own.

But Pinky had other characteristics which surprised her mother much more. Although normally shrinking from contact with anyone but her parents, she had taken a tremendous shine to the social worker who came on reconnaissance from the child guidance clinic in New Romney. Ginnie had the feeling that in this quiet seaside spot the welfare personnel might be under-employed, and have every incentive to be inquisitive. She and her daughter, when on their own at 'Silver Spray', could be seen to offer themselves as a suitable target.

At any rate Mrs Peabody took a professional but slightly disturbing interest in the wellbeing of the pair. Ginnie felt she was suspected of being a single mother, an undercover one. But Pinky became suddenly animated when Mrs Peabody came to call about their rights and benefits. When the car drew up she would dance down the short sandy pathway to the sand-covered concrete road; and when it left she hung about it, suspending herself on its open door. She seemed to be trying to hold the woman back, in order to revel in yet more of her society. It was not, Ginnie had to admit, as if Mrs Peabody made much of her, or attempted any move to extract the child's confidence. The woman's kindly but always formal manner was irreproachable; and it seemed this very impersonality which made Pinky regard her as a bewitching reservoir of romantic and life-enhancing matter. She would stand by the gate in a trance after the woman had gone, murmuring ecstatically to herself.

Never normally a tiresome child she sometimes none the less importuned her mother to visit the office of the authorities represented by the lady she called 'Muz Paybody', so that she might get the chance of glimpsing her idol. Ginnie humoured her if they could combine the longish walk and busride involved with a shopping expedition; but she had no talent for mateyness with the staff at Welfare, or with the young mums who haunted the building. She hung back shyly as Pinky made these forays, all but pretending that the child had nothing to do with her; and indeed it was on these occasions that her sense of her own unreality as a parent, often latent, was at its most obvious. Though the staff there called her Mrs Grey it sounded to her like a courtesy title. She felt they thought her standoffish and dishonest, trying to keep up appearances in the bad old way instead of mucking in with the teenage unmarrieds who flaunted their status and its assets, and lounged about the Welfare Centre like queens, displaying their noisy children with an indolent patronage.

From other children, even comparatively well-behaved ones, Pinky had always shrunk away. Ginnie was secretly rather glad that she did not want little friends about the place. She felt chagrined but also amused by the child's determination to substitute Peabody fantasies for the company of her own age-group. She suspected that Pinky would have liked to ask the woman to tea, and bear her off into the garden to play at shop assistants or Red Indians. And she was startled one day when after a more than usually prolonged fit of abstraction Pinky came out with an unusual claim.

'Muz Paybody is going to put a notice in the back of her car, saying "Fuck the Kids".'

'Oh Pinky, I don't think she is.'

'Yes, she is. She is going to ask me to put it there for her.'

Ginnie remembered that Pinky had been impressed once in the bus by a notice in the rear window of the car ahead, proclaiming a love for the Rain Forest, or had it been for Toads?

'Muz Paybody hates the children.'

'Well, aren't you one of them?'

Pinky turned away, looking deeply offended. But after a moment she turned back and said forgivingly: 'You and Peter will write it for me, please, won't you?' She pondered a moment. 'Peter shall print it for me.'

At a disadvantage, as she not infrequently felt with her daughter, Ginnie thought it best to try a new line.

'I don't think it's dignified to use that word with grown-ups.' Ginnie felt proud of turning the tables, but Pinky remained unmoved.

'I know,' she said scathingly. 'It's a *children's* word. That's why Muz Paybody wants it in the back of her car. So that all the little buggers will understand it.'

'Well you mustn't use those words with Peter and me, Pinky.'

'Peter says them. He says them to me when we're pretending to be children. They are bad words, and that's why we use them when we're pretending. It's a horrid game Peter likes to play.'

Pinky did not look as if she thought it was a horrid game at all.

In fact Peter, for all his charm, had been a failure with Mrs Peabody. This amused him, and Ginnie, although she had been careful to conceal their amusement from Pinky. Deep down, the woman had probably had a suspicion that Peter was a love-them-and-leave-them type. The Child Support Agency would one day be knocking on his door in some far-off town.

At the sight of Peter Mrs Peabody pursed her lips when she came to call. Confronting the woman, Ginnie found herself drawing her arm through her husband's, with what, for her, was a smug and unfamiliar gesture. She suspected Mrs Peabody of wondering whether Peter might be capable of abusing his daughter in his spare time.

Thinking rather distractedly about her daughter as she went to pick her up from playschool, which Pinky detested, Ginnie tried to concentrate her mind on the problem of Christmas. She would really enjoy seeing Martha, and over a longer period, but she was dubious about Pinky's reception at Prentice Wood, and she doubted that Peter would want to come at all. He was adept at not doing what he should do without giving offence, even to her. Without him, Pinky and her sometimes disconcerting utterances could cause a difficulty, although Ginnie herself might be the only one to be bothered by it. She was often aware that she didn't feel at home with her daughter. Would she ever do so?

It was a feeling, she knew, that would have seemed incomprehensible to Peter, presumably because he revelled in his paternity, and could manage it so effortlessly. It was no good for her to try to be like that, and to feel like that. Or, rather, to take the whole thing so wonderfully for granted.

93

In some obscure way it was for this sort of reason that she was looking forward to seeing Martha. Not necessarily to talk to; there would probably be no chance of that; but to share and to be comforted by the secret understanding that they were two of a kind, who had the same sort of difficulties with the world.

None the less she wondered again why they had been asked. Ginnie had nothing against the rich; and in any case she felt that Martha and her husband were, so to speak, only rich by accident. And yet she had felt, on her few previous visits, how different they all were, Martha's grown-up children especially. She feared that these sophisticated and superior beings might be there, looking down on her. It was different for Peter of course, but then everything was different for Peter. She would miss him, and his support, if he didn't accompany them. Without him, she knew, or even with him, she could never come up to the standard of his elder brother's family, and their particular style of conformities.

CHAPTER 7

But Once a Year

The church of St Nicholas, Victorian Byzantine in style, was girding up its loins for the next Christmas service. The long neat cemetery at the back was well filled for such a comparatively young foundation. Where it ended, among fir trees leaning over an ornamental wall of yellow bricks, a more than life-sized angel beckoned. This statue presided over the grave of the young wife of the nobleman who had once owned the surrounding acres.

In the shadow of its six-foot marble wings stood George, keeping an eye on the arrival of the worshippers.

Martha's attendance at matins was regular. Sometimes, not often, she went to the early service. During the past summer of their meetings George had been regularly on duty behind his angel for both Sunday occasions. He saw Martha arrive and go into church, and he waited till the service was over, when she often spent a minute or two in conversation with churchgoers, whom it was likely she knew in no other context.

To look at her, when she was being what George thought of as 'normal', and among her own sort of people, was an immense pleasure to him. But he had never spoken of this to her: it was the only thing he had never told her about. Secrecy was so natural to him that even from Martha he still had this secret.

The glimpse of Martha that he got on these occasions accentuated for him, in a manner almost intoxicating, the split between Martha as she was for others and as she was for him. The two would never be brought together: he would hardly have wished they could be.

Suppose that magic could have turned him into her husband, into the unknown figure of Mr Grey, while of course leaving him also as his own familiar self? In such a disguise he would have no idea how to behave, or what to do; and Martha could only be a person so different from his own Martha, that he couldn't have known how to talk to her, let alone how to love her.

But it was that other Martha whom he had loved to watch, on these summer Sunday occasions, from behind the angel in the churchyard. She was different, quite different: and yet she was the same. Crouched behind his angel George gazed adoringly upon the paradox, like a simple shepherd worshipping at the nativity.

Sometimes he thought of the guns down in the cellar. Although Martha and the guns had not mixed they belonged in the same way to a different world; just as she did when she came to him, and when she was at home, or in the church. If George's hoard were to be revealed, or reclaimed by its original owners, it would cease to mean anything for him. He was prepared to recognise that. Then suppose the two Marthas were to become one for him: the 'ordinary' one, the one he saw going into church? How would he feel about her then?

He wondered about that; but it had not in the least diminished his wish to see Martha going into church, or his pleasure in doing so.

Normally he kept well behind his angel. The last thing he wanted to do was to discompose Martha at what must be a peaceful moment of her week. He had even liked the idea that she was free at that moment not only of her domestic bonds and arrangements but even of her attachment to himself. In her freedom was his own peace. He could contemplate her as she was; and there was great charm for him in the fact that she who loved him was away at this moment, and yet would certainly come back.

But this was Christmas morning. Their first one. And Martha was not alone. She was accompanied by a man, who must be her husband, and by a woman. For the first time, and to his own surprise, George felt a stab of jealousy, not only of the man, Martha's husband no doubt, but of the woman too. Who might she be? Martha had never said anything about a friend of the sort who might come with her to church on Christmas morning. His delight in Martha's solitude and separateness was dispossessed by more upsetting emotions.

Impelled by this new jealousy, and by curiosity as well,

George stepped smartly out from behind his angel. Martha and her companions had disappeared into the church: and today he would follow them, come what may. With outstretched arm and lifted forefinger the angel seemed to be warning him not to be rash.

He gained the church door and paused. He had never been inside before, and every pew seemed crowded; but he slipped into an end one at the back, with a look of apology at an old lady on her knees there, who paid him no attention. He could just see his loved one at the front, the mousy-looking woman on one side of her, and the man who must be Martha's husband on the other. The congregation rose, and George, unfamiliar with the drill, was briefly left behind. Once he was on his feet his height made him conspicuous, as well as letting him see over the heads and backs in front. He saw Martha open her hymn book, and glance round, in a decorous way, to estimate the size of the congregation, and to see, perhaps, if there were any acquaintances nearby who should be smiled at.

She saw George. Her mouth opened. The beam of joy shone on her face, and he could feel she was longing to wave to him. Then the organ stirred itself vigorously; her head turned to the front again, and he could see her mouth joyfully opening and closing as the choir got into their stride with the Herald Angels.

George was so enthralled that he could think of nothing else throughout the rest of the rather dull service. How predictable it was in all its efforts to be jolly. There was something forlorn about it, as if emphasising all the exclusions in which people round here lived. No wonder his mother hadn't liked it – she never went to church. The thought of his mother reminded him disagreeably of the Manor Farm cellar, and the man who now threatened it – threatened him and Martha too. Martha's brother-in-law, the man he had met that fatal day, not long ago, at the Antelope.

The beam Martha had thrown back at him across the pews and the aisle was of course not so indiscreet as George had thought, indeed in a way had hoped. It was perfectly normal nowadays for such radiant expressions of goodwill to be bestowed all round, on strangers as on acquaintances, as a preliminary to the kiss of peace exchanged more self-consciously at a later stage of the service. George might have felt a little dashed if he had known that. The youthfully middle-aged rector was evangelical by temperament, although some of his congregation would have preferred the high church practices they associated with villages in the real country.

Before his wife died and his business collapsed Mr Pusey had a vague idea that his son, who had after all been to university, would help to raise his local status, which was already quite high, since his wife was so powerful a figure in the field of good works. But George remained as passive about social awareness as about so many other things. Since he had loved Martha he had sometimes wanted, none the less, to get to know the places she frequented in her own life. For this reason he had made attempts, once or twice and on weekdays, to get inside the church. Unavailingly. The rector may have encouraged tokens of love in the Sunday service but he was a prudent man. Since he could not spend much time there himself he had the big building kept locked up.

When the invitation to a Boxing Day drinks party had arrived from the Greys the week before, Mr Pusey had been as surprised as he was gratified. He knew of the Greys, of course, but had they ever met? Perhaps his wife had done so in the old days? With a rare degree of animation he interrogated George. Had they ever met the Greys? George was negative, but he knew that they had: at that other local party where he had seen Martha for the second time. He would always remember that.

He said he thought he might have mowed their lawn; he had mowed a good many. That so clearly constituted no possible reason for the invitation that his father gave the matter up, but remained looking bright-eyed and hopeful, turning over and over in his big hands the card with 'At Home' in the middle. Alexander and Martha Grey requested the pleasure of their company. Possibly this Grey was a kind man who had heard of his difficulties, and knew of something that might be a help?

And yet poor Mr Pusey's unemployed and becalmed self rather dreaded such a possible explanation. He preferred to hope that the Greys had heard what nice people he and his son George were. Natural assets at any social gathering.

As for George, he could think of nothing but that he would be seeing Martha at her house. She would be, as the card so literally put it, 'At Home' for him. But what about this man who claimed to be her brother-in-law, the man at the Antelope? Surely he must have gone away, vanished back into the nightmare limbo he had come from? Illogically, in his love and in his youth, George was sure that he and his father would not have been asked if that man was going to be there. He was sure too, although he scarcely dared to think about it, that Martha herself had asked them. No one else could have had the idea.

He was going to see her in her own place, where she lived before she met him!

There had been moments very early on, as he had to admit to himself – and the thought of them now rather embarrassed him – when he had imagined himself actually living with Martha, in her own house or in a similar one: one equally choice, and opulent, and well-furnished. Although he had never seen these furnishings, his fantasies, ever insistent on detail, were quite able to supply them. There he would live: cherished, prosperous, wearing a tweed suit. Beloved, an object of total devotion.

He was ashamed of these fantasies now. His love for Martha had, he liked to think, matured. He knew it was for ever, but it was more capable now of confronting the realities of their situation. What George meant by that, although he might not have admitted it to himself, was that the permanence of their feelings for each other depended on their situation remaining in its present form.

Martha knew this too of course, but did not trouble herself to be particularly conscious of it. Christmas was the thing at the moment and, in spite of all the anxieties it had brought, she was by no means not enjoying her Christmas. Its high point was that blissful moment when she had suddenly seen George standing at the back of the church. She had become aware of him rather than seen him, as if he had been some sort of divine manifestation; and she had smiled at him joyfully, knowing that Ginnie and her husband beside her would realise, if they saw her smile, that this was just the way one should behave in church, especially on Christmas morning.

That was only one reason why it had been an unusual Christmas. It was her first with George, as she liked to think of it,

99

walking happily out of church. Then there was Alexander's insistence that Ginnie and Peter should be asked to make up a house party, which had surprised her a good deal, but delighted her too. She had bought presents for them, paying rather more in the local craft shops than she would have done in Oxford Street, but she had never liked going to London at Christmastime. She had cooked, for once, all the proper things; but as Alexander had nothing but contempt for turkey she had decided, rather daringly, to have quails for Christmas dinner, stuffing them with herbs and a paté. It meant a lot of last minute work in the kitchen, but Ginnie helped her nobly, and it was all being a great success. She had really got on with Ginnie; and they had spent most of their time chatting in the kitchen, only joining the two men at the last moment.

The two men? Yes: for Peter had not come, or rather was not coming till Boxing Day. But Bobby was still with them. Bobby's continued presence was the real cross Martha had to bear; but she bore it the more willingly because he had sometimes been absent, and because Alexander had seemed so pleased to have his brother still around. Most of all, because Bobby himself had become really nice to her, not only affable but positively helpful and kind; and anyone – even Bobby – who was nice to Martha won her over without further difficulty.

Then there was the extraordinary fact of Alexander suggesting the Boxing Day cocktail party. And not only that, but inviting the Puseys, father and son, remarking that he had heard they were down on their luck, and that it would be a kind act at Christmas. To her own surprise Martha had been not at all disconcerted by this. She could only think, with a great leap of joy, that she would see her George at Prentice Wood. And when he had appeared in church, and she had beamed at him, it had struck her that there would be no greater problem when it came to smiling and talking with him at the party. Because of the time of the year George seemed able to enter her life like a Christmas angel, without anyone remarking on the fact, or being surprised.

Martha had the sense to see, too, that although George might – indeed most certainly would – appear nervous and embarrassed, this would be only natural and becoming in a young man invited to the house for the first time. Alexander had said something vague about Pusey senior being a useful man to consult on the subject of house alterations. If any of their guests showed curiosity, which was not likely, George could be accounted for quite simply as the son of their builder.

She was glad, none the less, that neither Penny nor Ben were coming home this Christmas. The presence of her children – of her daughter especially – would have unnerved her. Penny, it was true, had for years been of an age when she was absorbed in her own affairs of the heart, and took no interest in anything at home. Indeed her children seemed to have stopped thinking of Prentice Wood as their home: something that gave Martha a pang when she thought about it, which she had not done much of late.

What would they feel about it if they knew their mother had a young lover? Martha was slightly horrified to realise, as she considered it, that the idea filled her with a sort of furtive joy. What she had got up to might still surprise the young? Not that anything did surprise them much apparently, nowadays.

Ginnie would be a great help at the party. So attached had Martha become to her sister-in-law, during this Christmas period, that it had even occurred to her once or twice to tell her the secret, since George would be coming to the party; or at least to drop a hint about it.

Yet she knew quite well she wouldn't. Never accustomed to the pleasure of confidences, she was now committed wholly to the secretiveness which had been growing in her since marriage. And now George was inside her secrecy: he *was* it. And that was the way it would always be. She would never tell anyone.

Ginnie was preoccupied herself, as it happened. But she said nothing to Martha, for she was enjoying too much, if a little guiltily, being with her at Prentice Wood on her own. Never disobliging, as he was never unaffectionate, Peter had told her when they had been invited that he really couldn't make Christmas Day, but hoped to get down on Boxing Day. He had a conference in Birmingham. Ginnie didn't bother not to believe him. As an automatic liar Peter often told odd lies. He probably did have a conference of some sort, though not necessarily in Birmingham. If another woman was involved she would never know anything about it. And really she hardly cared.

But then had come a snag. The three of them had always been together at Christmas before. Peter loved it; he made a small tree and did most of the preparations. And when Pinky heard he would not be coming with her mother and herself to Prentice Wood she refused to come at all. In her silent way she could be very obstinate.

'Muz Paybody hates Christmas,' she told her parents.

'How do you know she does?'

'I just do know.'

Peter was amused. Then he suddenly suggested that Pinky could come with him, if she wanted. They could stay in the hotel together. She had never stayed in a hotel, had she?

Pinky was in ecstasies. Ginnie was doubtful. Knowing Pinky, she had been resignedly looking forward to telling her sister-in-law that they couldn't make it after all, or at least not until Boxing Day. That would have been very awkward.

What was in Peter's mind? Presumably he was not going to meet a woman, if he was prepared to take Pinky with him? Ginnie had to admit that Peter could look after the child better than she could herself – far better. A glance at Pinky was enough to tell how determined she was to go.

Ginnie gave in. It was weak, she knew; but she could not face the prospect of a reluctant Pinky at Prentice Wood. Though the child was never morose, her lack of enthusiasm could be unnerving. Never able to think of her as other than an adult Ginnie had quailed at the thought of her daughter being treated and humoured as a child, during what she feared would be the forced-draught festivities of the grown-ups at the big house. On her own she thought she would enjoy it there. As a private holiday. So an elated Pinky went off with Peter to some notional Birmingham; and her mother got on the Uxbridge line at Earls Court, for what she hoped would be an interlude in the midst of her own private anxieties.

For there was another reason why a day or two on her own, which she was bound to be in this other and alien family environment, would be welcome. There was something about which she would have to talk with Peter, as soon as he was available and had time to listen. Improbable as it might seem, it looked as if she might again be pregnant.

102

A most worrying thought. Indeed she hardly knew at the moment what to think about it, nor did she wish even to try.

Peter, whatever his other deficiencies as a husband, was instantly and reliably sympathetic. And, in his own inconsequential way, decisive. She would feel very much better, totally better, when she had told him all about it. Matrimonial communing, affectionately cryptic, stopping and starting between embraces, and ending in bed, had proved the most absolute and, by her at least, most unforeseeable asset of the married state.

On the other hand she wanted a chance to think over the matter first of all by herself. Calmly and dispassionately: which should be possible in an unfamiliar place, where she was on her own. She might of course feel more harassed than ever, the more she thought about it; and in that case the arrival of Peter on Boxing Day should be timed just about right. Then it would be a relief to pour things out to a husband, even though she had never really managed to see Peter as qualifying permanently for that role; just as it was surprisingly hard to think of Pinky, who would be accompanying him, as her own daughter.

Had she always instinctively sought to gravitate back to her own being, her own lair, after her experience of marriage and childbirth? It looked as if life might not be going to let her do that any more. Life was like a hunter, pursuing her. Or perhaps waiting patiently until she was finally held in his trap, without hope of further escape?

These had been melodramatic thoughts to accompany the rattle of the tube train as it ran out into the country. At that moment too she had even more urgently looked forward to Martha, though not necessarily to talk to. Martha might give her the feeling of a refuge. Ginnie intuited, though such intuitions, she knew, were usually off the mark, that Martha too might have a private lair of her own, a safe house of some kind, whose invisible presence would be a comfort. It was to Martha she wanted to come for Christmas, even if Martha was already appropriately submerged in her own mode of living.

It certainly looked like that when Ginnie arrived. But for the moment this cheered her up as much or more than any reachings out into an imagined 'sorority' could have done. And even her two brothers-in-law were hearteningly friendly and forthcoming, Bobby in particular.

'Do you remember our meeting on the links?' he asked her.

Of course she did. 'And you told me all about the wild flowers.'

It had been down at Littlestone, less than a mile along the coast from Greatstone-on-Sea. When he spoke she remembered it all, and she warmed to him at once. Here, in the Christmas cheer of his brother's house, she was certainly not going to enquire about other things, which she remembered just as vividly. There had been his betrayal of Alice, going off with her precious suitcase. Peter had often remarked that his brother Bobby had a heart of gold, really; and she had never bothered to dispute it. The main thing was that he was being nice to her now.

The atmosphere had certainly achieved a sort of festivity, and Ginnie had to admit to herself that it was a relief not to have Pinky with her. Down here, and at least for a day or two, she could be something like her old self. She had always liked a drink or two, though she must be a bit careful about that, in the role she hoped to allot herself as Martha's handmaid and assistant. There might be other more pressing and private reasons why she should be careful now; but she refused for the moment to think about them.

So she did full justice to the burgundy at supper on Christmas Eve, and even earned a word of commendation from Alexander.

'Not many women would see the point of this one,' he observed as he refilled her almost empty glass, turning the bottle over in his hands and gazing knowledgeably at the label.

Clearly not a woman to be counted among those who would see the point, Martha minded not at all as she beamed round on them. Soon she would be serving a lemon soufflé, one of the dishes she was proudest of. Great was her joy when Bobby, after tasting it, declared he would give all the mince pies in the world for a plateful.

'Ah, but you'll be getting everything like that tomorrow,' Martha told him, flushed and joyous with what seemed like newfound family pride.

Ginnie noticed it with interest. Comfortably full of burgundy as she was, she felt warm towards Martha and, as she hoped, closer to her. But she couldn't help noticing, too, that in some indefinable way Martha herself appeared further off. Not as if she were entirely preoccupied with her happy Christmas family role, but as if some other matter, more secret and inside herself, were causing this outward glow. Her high spirits excited Ginnie at first; but, as the burgundy wore off, left her feeling a little desolate, and remembering her own urgent preoccupations.

She had been put in one of the grand guest-rooms – grand at least they seemed by her own modest standards, with a pink and blue bathroom attached. Martha hoped so much she would be comfortable, with the twin beds, and the one she had put in for the little girl. Not so much to interest her hostess as to console herself, Ginnie had explained that Peter and Pinky were at that moment having a high old time in a hotel. It cheered her a little to imply that her husband was such a good father. But she felt a bit low as she got into the comfortable bed. Being on her own at Prentice Wood was turning out to be not so restful as she had hoped.

*

Deciding against a taxi, Peter Grey picked up the lean leather suitcase with his father's initials on it, now barely decipherable, and began to walk up the long slope from the station. He was alone.

He needed to think, before he arrived at his brother's house. He had not been able to do any thinking on the train.

He had just encountered his wife. His first wife that was: but for her, and indeed for him, his only wife.

She had made that absolutely clear. And he had agreed of course. Or rather there was no need to agree. He knew it as well as she did.

What had happened was this. Peter Grey had indeed gone to Birmingham, just as he had said he was going to do, to meet some people. They were business people, but they had also been spy people. He had known such people when he was himself in the Service, some years ago now. Like most others in the Service he had never quite left it: for a number of reasons one could hardly afford to do that. His old colleagues had put things in his way, helped in various projects of his own. And, of course, with the big project he was now engaged on.

There could be a great deal of money in it. A very great deal of money. So far so good. But he had no idea that his wife was involved. His ex-wife that is.

Indeed she was more than involved. She was running it. She had arrived from Russia the day before.

Vera and he had been married for many years; after he had left the Service, and she had left the KGB. It was a cliché, a matter of common knowledge, that the KGB had become a privatised mafia, operating for its own and its members' profit. What was less widely known to the public was that every other intelligence service had, in a usually quieter and more discreet way, done much the same thing.

Neither Mr nor the original Mrs Peter Grey had discontinued their previous activities; and they had also operated together, on the whole with good success.

There had been the country house they had run together, as a 'couple', for its very rich absentee owner, a Swiss Lebanese businessman. They had both loved Bleedon Court, and they had been able to live there almost as if it were their own place. A good life. With Vera the ever-loving woman, who doted on him and adored him. What a treasure she must have been to the KGB! And what a treasure she had been to him! They had been almost ridiculously happy together.

Older than he by seven or eight years, she must have been nearer fifty than forty when they married. He was her child, her English child, and he got all the tenderness which had been absent from her life in an arduous, exacting, at moments even gruesome profession. His own childhood had been short on tenderness.

Sometimes he had said to her in a jokey way (she liked what she thought of as English jokes) that everyone in their line of business was either a child or a mother. He knew which he was, and which she was too.

Peter Grey reached the top of the slope and paused, shifting the suitcase from his right hand to his left. He sighed. It was a good deal more than a mile to his brother Alexander's house, but as he walked he was going to have to think what to do. And for almost the first time in his life he had no idea what to do. None whatsoever.

But matters must somehow be explained to Ginnie. That seemed evident. Would she be able to tolerate such a situation, dear kind and good as she was? Or was she dear kind and good? Peter had really no idea. Assuming that she were, what sort of form would dearness kindness and goodness take at this present juncture?

Peter had never thought about such things in relation to his present wife. Perhaps because he never had any trouble in being dear kind and good himself. Or the opposite, if it came to that.

One of his troubles, as he sometimes saw, although always with a degree of complacency, was that he had the kind of nature that was perhaps becoming not so uncommon, as was said, at this present moment of time. One which was capable of responding in almost any way to any given situation.

Take himself for instance. You really could not say just how good or bad he was. Nor could he: not that he would have tried very hard, or very often.

In any case – and he sometimes did think this – the way we live now has no 'guidelines'; the world we live in at the present time is edgeless. Nobody knows their place: nobody, indeed, has a place. The world had got rid of decorum and propriety, and the other things that kept you straight. Never mind about morals. They had only ever existed in terms of things that were, and were not, done. And everything could be done now.

Peter Grey loved decorum, of a certain kind. He personified it in his dress and appearance, his manners and his mode of life. He loved it all the more because it was vanishing, or had vanished.

He loved it in Ginnie. He loved what Ginnie had made of him, quite without meaning to, no doubt. But he had no idea what she really thought of him. Or what she would do when he told her.

Well, she would have to do the best she could. Just like everybody else. And so would he. That was what it came down to, as it had done with that final business at Bleedon Court. He had been really lucky, looking back, to have got out of all that alive. Then there was that girl, Caroline, whom he and Vera had kept there for a bit, while blackmailing her father, Lord Hatchcombe.

But it was not she who had been his downfall. It was Ginnie herself. He had picked her up, quite blamelessly as it happened, but Vera had found out.

And she had left him at once, without further ado: only pausing, as it were, to save her Peter from the consequences of their joint operation. She had gone back to Russia, and he had heard no word since. He hadn't expected to. He knew his Vera, and he knew when her mind was made up.

And now, abruptly, she was back. And he was hers again. There was nothing he could do about it. Vera had reclaimed him.

He remembered the moment when Ginnie had told him that she was pregnant. Her tears; the general upset. To calm her down he had shown great joy at the unexpected news. And perhaps he had really felt it? Pretence with him, as he well knew, could be like that. Almost indistinguishable from the genuine article. He and Vera had never made it to having a child, naturally enough. She was too old. Ginnie herself had been a bit long in the tooth, come to that. So it had been a surprise. And she had been prepared to marry him then. He had genuinely wanted that too, for some reason. Presumably the loss of Vera.

Why had Vera come back? Had she engineered the job so as to get him for herself again? It looked like that certainly. Had she missed him so much in Russia? God, what a moment it had been when he'd seen her, yesterday, in that hotel lounge, looking at him in the old way!

Women were odd, certainly. Why had Vera decided so uncompromisingly to leave him, and then come back to make him hers again? Was it for the same sort of reason that had made Ginnie at first refuse to marry him? Had Ginnie eventually married him only because she was pregnant? What mysterious gratitude to her he had found himself feeling, in any case. Until that moment he hadn't realised what gratitude was.

Peter Grey frowned to himself as he walked along, and shifted the suitcase again to his other hand. You never knew with these things. He had never regretted his second marriage. Not one bit, not for one moment. And he didn't think Ginnie had done so either. She had never been exactly communicative. That was one of her most restful characteristics. But he always remembered how she told him once, after their first meeting, that she had gone back to her flat, looking forward to the comforts of her old existence, and how she found they weren't there any more. She had been so miserable that she had had to come straight back to him. She had helped to save his life by doing so, but never mind that. The point was that she had been compelled to return. He had been greatly touched when she told him that.

He groaned a little as he walked. The memory was painful now. Vera had got him again – there was no doubt about it – and with his own full and fervent consent. He would go not only quietly, but eagerly. But what was he going to say to Ginnie?

He was getting on for the place now. He turned from something called Bristow's End into Gannet's Path. Rum names they had around here. He remembered noticing them, the only other time he had visited. Nearly there now, and still no idea how to explain himself. The seemingly unused road, full of potholes, passed quite close to a surprisingly derelict building, an old brick-built farmhouse. Nice-looking old place. Odd that in this area it had not already been pulled down, or tarted up.

At last he turned into Gallions Way. He could make out the dark bulk of his brother's house now, behind its thick screen of cypress, or whatever they were. He could smell the woodsmoke. At Christmas they had fires in every bedroom, his sister-in-law had once told him, as if he had a right to know.

Crunching his way up the curling drive he passed without seeing it Martha's giant old crab-tree. What *was* he to say? A big white front-door confronted him, under a porch with a lantern, brightly switched on. At least the door was not one of those fluted jobs in 'natural' oak, he found himself thinking. With bottle-green bullseyes ....

Dark shapes of cars, all over the spacious gravel sweep. Plenty of room for them. The December air was almost tepid, as if riches – well, moderate riches – could control the weather, like all the other things round here.

There was a steady hubbub from inside the house. Of course! – they were having a party. Ginnie had warned him about it. He should have been here before it started, but there were reasons why that would not have been possible.

He knew his wife well enough by now, for God's sake. And what was the point of being married if you had to account for everything? He had never needed to account to Vera. Until that final reckoning of course, when he had had nothing to say.

He put his case down and rang the bell. After a minute or two the door was opened by Martha. She was herself looking more than a trifle distraught, he noticed, but she welcomed and embraced him in her conscientiously enthusiastic way. She looked around and beside him, with a little intake of breath, as if about to produce a question; but she was distracted by steering him towards the disciplined uproar of the party. It was not deafening, but loud enough to excuse postponement of the polite queries directed at a new arrival in the house.

Then the drawing-room door opened and Ginnie hastened out on a rising volume of sound. She exclaimed when she saw him, and lifted her arms to put around his neck. Perhaps she had listened for the bell? He saw her smiling at him, and then her arms dropped and her smile came away. 'Where's Pinky?' demanded his wife, with uncharacteristic vehemence.

*

The party had actually been going rather well, although certain aspects of it had surprised Ginnie. She and Peter on their own had very little social life; but her office had given her experience in gatherings of this sort; where, however, she had played only a passive role. Here, as one of the family, she had felt she must try to help, and to pull her weight. She had enjoyed doing that. But it had become clear that the titular host, and senior member of the Grey family, was making little attempt to pull his. He did nothing at all to help with introducing guests, distributing drinks, and keeping the sharp eye open which should help to make things go. Martha rushed about trying to do all that.

Ginnie sought to aid her as junior receptionist, fully aware that neither of them must look convincing in the part. Although Martha was so taken up with trying to be a hostess Ginnie found herself giving her sister-in-law an occasional reassuring pat, and a secret smile as if they were fellow-conspirators.

110

Martha had seemed excited at the prospect of the party, to which Ginnie had been looking forward with mild apprehension. But Ginnie had enjoyed the afternoon they spent together in the kitchen, cutting squares of toast and putting smoked salmon and two kinds of paté on them. Those preparations had been restful and agreeable, even though they had given her no chance for a chat. She found herself longing for the arrival of Peter and Pinky; and she looked forward to the end of the party and to bedtime, when she could talk to Peter and tell him all about her fears, or hopes. Whatever he really felt about it he would be sure to be comforting and supportive. She still didn't know what she felt herself, except worry, alarm, and fatigue.

Bobby Grey pottered about the party as if it was his own, grinning benignly on all and sundry. Then he sat himself down in one of the drawing-room armchairs and played the part of a distinguished semi-invalid, to whom persons are brought up to be introduced. Martha fetched him canapés, or a new drink, and introduced him in an eager distracted way to neighbourhood friends, who would stand awkwardly chatting by the arm of his chair, glancing furtively about in search of a relief to take over. Bobby all too clearly enjoyed such difficulties.

The guests knew their role and kept obligingly on at it, familiar as they were with the local modes of enjoying party discomforts which would give them, at the worst, something to talk about later.

The scene that drew Ginnie's eye, as she stood becalmed for a moment in an eddy of noise, was over near the fireplace. Alexander stood there in close conversation with a goodlooking young man, who seemed in almost as much of a state of nervous excitement as did Martha herself. It looked as if Martha, often going back to this couple with a plate, in spite of her many other preoccupations, was delighted that they seemed to be getting on so well together.

When Martha did get over to them the three together had the air of a family – father, mother, son – engaging in some private and domestic raillery before plunging back into the more impersonal fray. While Martha was away on her unresting social attendance, the male pair went on standing by the fire as if

111

nothing would separate them. Once Ginnie saw her brother-in-law, in what was surely a most uncharacteristic gesture, seize the young man by the upper arms and burst into a roar of laughter, which the other seemed to try willingly, though vainly, to imitate.

Parties like this look as if they will never end, until they suddenly begin to do so. There was no sign of that when Ginnie, in search of a moment's respite, went out to the kitchen with the excuse of looking for more canapés. To her surprise Martha was there. She was attempting to do something with a loaf, her big face set in a blind way. Ginnie hastened to leave her to it, as if she had accidentally disturbed someone being sick, and feeling agitated herself returned to the drawing-room. It was at that moment the bell rang, and Martha rushed past in the same blind way to open the front door. It was Peter arriving, and in a few seconds Ginnie was too upset herself to bother any more about Martha.

The voices of the party went on, high and unperturbed, but couples began to take their leave at last. Martha had been taking care to visit Bobby's chair at intervals, to offer another guest or to make sure he had enough to drink; and on one such occasion he put his freckled hand on her arm, and looking up with that newly winning smile he seemed to keep for her, he had remarked: 'Alexander is really enjoying your boyfriend.'

*

When the last guests had gone Ginnie and Martha took refuge in the kitchen with the plates and glasses. While washing up together they talked about the party as best they could, passing things carefully to each other to be put away. Ginnie had already explained that her daughter was staying on for a day or two, with family friends. Pinky had enjoyed her Christmas with them so much, apparently.

Peter, Alexander, and even Bobby, had made ritual offers of help which had been gaily refused. They had been advised by Martha to have a snug chat in the drawing-room. It must be years since all three brothers had been under one roof.

Later that night Peter and Ginnie sat together on one of the beds in their room. It was after one o'clock, but neither of them thought of sleep. They had the air of a couple waiting to part at a railway-station, for Peter was holding her hand. Ginnie let it rest in his as if she had nothing better to do with it. She did not want to pull it rudely away.

How well she knew that Peter never told the truth if he could help it. Lies were a part of his lifestyle; and they were the probable reason for that self-contentment which shone forth visibly from him, like a ray. One cause at least of his good spirits.

This mendacity was all of a part with kindness. Right at the beginning, when Ginnie had so absurdly and happily fallen for him, he had told her some whoppers. But when she found him out it only made her feel closer to him. It even gave her a secret satisfaction. She was the one who could love and believe in him, just because she so comfortingly knew that he always told her lies. Jolly lies, if there were such things.

But now she knew he was telling her the truth: and the unfamiliarity of it appalled her.

What a long time it was since she had seen him come in at the front door alone. She had shouted at him about Pinky, literally shouted. A rare thing for her. The rest of the evening had been got through somehow, without verbal damage, in the same way that she and Martha had broken none of the glasses at the sink. They all had some supper. The party was voted to have been a success.

Somehow then she had concealed her fright and her apprehensions – 'ongoing' ones, as people said nowadays – under a show of equable acceptance. Pinky had been so eager to stay on with the close friends Peter had been visiting – there was another little girl there – that he had not had the heart to refuse her. In the privacy of the loo, seeing her taut face in the mirror, Ginnie had not been able to help smiling a ghastly smile at herself as she thought of this. The idea of Pinky wanting to stay on somewhere because there was another child there! The very idea of Peter's 'close friends'! But this had been his cover story, both for herself and for the family party at Prentice Wood; and she had had no choice but to accept it.

Ginnie knew he was lying of course, but this was a different sort of lie: it could only be a dreadful one. And for the first time since she had known him the knowledge of his lie was causing her extreme distress of mind. Such a lie, such a mode of lying, could only be a looming promise of the truth.

And there was her own 'news'. And the way she had looked forward to sharing it with Peter, and being reassured by him, one way or another. Perhaps she would never tell him at all now; indeed something in her already felt sure of it.

There were other things she could be sure of. For instance, that their daughter would be quite safe, whoever it was Peter had been with; and also that Pinky would rather have been with him than with her, though the child had been too polite to emphasise this. The harmony of the three seemed to take for granted that Ginnie didn't have to play at being a mother, because Peter, without trying at all, could be the best father in the world.

Promptly, and most uncharacteristically, when they sat down in the bedroom, she had ordered Peter to tell her what was really happening. And, just as uncharacteristically, he had at once proceeded to do so.

He was going to leave her. He was going back to Vera.

For his part Peter found this unusual exercise of truth-telling far more easy than he had expected. As soon as he had Ginnie's hand in his the truth, the whole truth, came flowing out of him: inexorable, unstoppable, candid, clear as water.

He could see that Ginnie knew it was the truth; and that she was appalled in consequence.

He himself could still hardly believe it. What had happened?

There she had been, Vera, in the lounge of the hotel by Birmingham airport. For he really had been to Birmingham, just as he had told Ginnie. Normally, as he knew quite well, if he had been going to Birmingham he would have said he had to go somewhere like Glasgow; and she would have understood, and been quite happy. Perhaps the very fact that he had unthinkingly told her the truth, before he even knew what was to happen, had been a kind of warning. An omen?

However that was, there she had been. Vera: sitting in the hotel lounge.

It should have been a routine meeting about the job he was on.

Meeting the boss, the big cheese, whoever it was who was in charge. Naturally he knew very little of the plan. No point at this stage in trying to find out. He would know all he needed to know in time, and he would get paid: he knew that. This first time would not even be a briefing, probably. Just wanted to look him over. Pinky, as it happened, would be good cover. A father and child would hardly be going to a clandestine spy meeting together; and her mother had, after all, made him excellent cover for several years now.

And so he had entered the hotel lounge with Pinky beside him, a little girl too rapt in the wonder of the place to do anything but tread silently with round eyes, holding his hand. A charming couple. At least he knew he always looked charming; and Pinky, though not a beautiful child, always behaved well. She seemed too inwardly preoccupied to show off. So there they had been; and the burly woman in a black dress who sat smoking in an armchair had glanced at them, and stiffened like a big cat.

All this he poured out to Ginnie, who could see it all very clearly. Just as she could see that she would not now be telling her husband about the fact that she appeared to be pregnant. It was an unlikely thing to have happened, but there it was, or seemed to be. And she would have to sort that one out for herself.

She had never taken her husband's goings-on at all seriously; and she had certainly never suspected her own unconscious role in his secret affairs. They seemed like the games of make-believe which he had played with the aid of Vera; which he had been playing, no doubt, when she had first met him, and been with him at that big house. All that had seemed not to matter. But apparently it did matter, or could do. And now it would be breaking her heart; or something like that.

How strange they were, the three Grey brothers! How genuinely, incomparably sinister they were, or turned out to be; for after this evening Ginnie was apt to see them all as a single unit. Peter was no longer hers: separate and lovable. He and his brothers now seemed to represent to her something nightmarish in the whole of the society in which they were living. Peter's charm, Alexander's money, Bobby's pleasantness, all a kind of collective irresponsibility: going nowhere, fitting in nowhere.

She saw that Peter wasn't thinking about her at all, although

115

he still held hold of her hand. He must be thinking of the wonder of meeting Vera. Perhaps he was dreaming of their wedding in some Russian church, with the gold crowns held up high over their heads, and a choir, deeply intoning ... Somewhere or other, in the course of her reading, Ginnie had heard all about those exotic procedures.

She was right. Peter had been thinking, or dreaming, of something like that. But, more specifically, he had been thinking of the way in which Vera had told him yesterday about the time she had heard the news – the news of his marriage to Ginnie. That had surprised as much as it had displeased her. She had thought of course that he had been having an affair. That had been the reason – though only one of the reasons – why she had decided to leave him, and go back to Russia. And afterwards she had found out she had been wrong: there had been no such betrayal. Her Peter had been innocent.

No wonder she had been all the more displeased at the news that he was married. And to the very woman with whom he had *not*, in fact, been having an affair!

How had she found out about his marriage? That was quite simple. Vera had smiled indulgently as she told Peter that it had always been the duty of some pensioned-off underling in the Moscow KGB to read *The Times* every morning.

So she had determined to get him back. He was still hers. Never mind about the trouble brought to them, however little she had intended it, by the woman who thought she had become his wife.

Peter, as both his wives had come to know well, was an incurable romantic. (So was, or had been, Ginnie herself.) Vera was nothing of the sort.

Peter was understanding enough to recognise that Ginnie the daydreamer had gone into eclipse, following marriage and motherhood. He knew that he himself had long ceased to be her daydream, but that could hardly be expected to bother him. They had been happy, he knew, in other ways.

Now that Vera had so astonishingly returned, he couldn't help doing a bit of fantasising on her behalf. He must have been dead and buried to her, with no hope of resurrection. But then the miracle had happened!

116

God, or some benevolent ex-KGB high-up (much the same thing in such a daydream) had recalled her to England. The same miracle had forgiven Peter, and brought her to him, or him to her, in the lounge of the Airport Hotel. Mysteriously redeemed. Led by the hand of a little girl.

And it was true that Pinky had been standing beside them in her speechless way, gazing as rapturously at Vera as Vera and her father were gazing at one another.

Nothing of all of Peter's dream had been lost on Vera. Let him imagine a miracle, which she could see he was busy doing. The great thing was that she had him back again.

In his gratitude Peter could only see that he was loved and accepted once more. What was Ginnie, beside Vera? What was he himself, come to that?

And yet he had been genuinely delighted that day, more than five years ago now, when Ginnie had broken down in tears as she told him he was going to be a father. (Her agitation had made it sound very Victorian.) He would never quite abandon her, any more than he could abandon their daughter. And it had really been quite easy, as he had gazed in rapture on Vera regained, to see the four of them as figures on some holy icon. In a mystery of eternal fellowship.

Pinky had gone to investigate the magazines set out on a corner table. Her father had been talking to her in the train about birds' nests, and how his old friend Peter Pan used to sail in one on the Serpentine. But there proved to be no birds' nests in *Country Life*. Pinky put it down and stealthfully manoeuvred the *Tatler* towards her. Soon she was at a Hunt Ball, enjoying a joke with a hefty girl and a foolish-faced young gentleman.

But Vera's real presence had drawn her back like a magnet. Abandoning the *Tatler* she cruised round the lounge and settled beside this sublimer Muz Paybody, an idol a thousand times more worthy of admiration than the once idolised Welfare lady. She stood by the arm of Vera's chair, a respectful foot or two away, and adored her silently.

The new goddess hardly vouchsafed her devotee so much as a glance. But Pinky only worshipped adults who paid her no attention.

117

CHAPTER 8

When Troubles Come

Vera had indeed been wholly absorbed in the rediscovery of her former husband. In Peter's eyes his daughter had become an angelic being, whose mission was to restore him to his former wife. Soon aware of that, Vera indulged him in the way that she had always done. She caused a bed to be installed in a corner of their double room; and after her supper Pinky had been put into it in great state by her father and the new divinity. She had always liked going to bed; and with this face above her, beside her father's, the miracles of the day reached a climax and she sank into blissful unconsciousness.

Close by, as she slept, her father and her new stepmother were soon consummating their own reunion.

Peter did not tell Ginnie quite all of this, as she sat passively with her hand in his. The truth did, none the less, continue to pour out of him. He was compelled to specify the true details of their daughter's infatuation, for how otherwise to account for her absence? And how adroit dear Vera had been! It had been part of her training, of course, to seize every opportunity, to exploit every weakness that an opponent might involuntarily offer. Just as in chess. Pinky had been a small pawn upon the board.

No doubt her existence had come as a total surprise to Vera. And yet his Russian wife had at once known what to do with her. Peter saw that, and could only see it with admiration. It was true that the child, though she was never anything but civil, had on this occasion shown a remarkable obstinacy. She had refused to be parted from the object of her new infatuation, over which Vera herself had come to preside with smiling benevolence.

Let Pinky's treat by all means be prolonged. She, Vera, would take good care of her, and deliver her back home in a day or two, when the new goddess would next be seeing her father.

Of course Peter could have put his foot down, and taken a highly disappointed Pinky away with him to Prentice Wood, to Ginnie, and to his brother's family party. But he was again with Vera. He had no need to trust *her*; but he knew that she was, all so gently, ensuring her own trust in *him*. And the child's own resolution never faltered. Unconscious of it as she was, she would herself be the pledge of a new fidelity.

When Ginnie heard all this, rendered in that inimitably emollient style of which no one but her husband could be such a master, she was suddenly reminded of a newspaper story she had once found herself reading. She remembered that it had upset her beyond the point at which she might have forced herself to stop. She had had to go on reading to the end.

But the story it told had no end. It was about a woman who had been followed by a man in the street, plagued with anonymous phone calls, sent incessant notes and letters. When the police had been appealed to, it was regretted that nothing could be done until an offence had been committed. None was committed; but the presence and the persecution had gone on.

This unknown woman, who had been Peter's wife, was now doing the same thing to Ginnie.

That was her first coherent thought, after her burst of indignation with Peter, and alarm for Pinky. She knew at once then that Pinky would be quite all right. If she had not known it she would presumably have gone off the deep end, like any other mother. But she knew that whatever his oddities Peter was too fond a father to let anything happen to his daughter; and she was only too prepared to believe that Pinky was having a wonderful time with her new stepmother. That, no doubt, was what Vera would have to be called.

Would there be a future in which Peter, and Pinky too, were both there and not there, haunting her together with this other woman in a kind of unholy trinity? She herself would be neither alone nor with her own two, but in some limbo reserved for the maritally dispossessed?

In old days, when she had asked Peter about Vera, there had been a fellow-feeling with her predecessor; nor had she ever felt excluded from the other attachments that Peter must in his time have had. His invisible harem, in which she had been raised to an unexpected prominence, were not jealous of her, so she had felt, but benign and well-disposed. That was all part of Peter's original magic.

She could readily have shared him with others like those, provided she knew nothing of them, but not with this Real Presence, this spectral monster from Russia, who had made such an unseasonable Christmas appearance. It was a threat not so much to her marriage, which she felt she never needed to take all that seriously, but to her own self, as marriage had brought it to be.

*

Elsewhere, in the spacious upstairs of Prentice Wood, muffled by thick curtains and carpets, Martha was similarly afflicted with a husband who would talk, and go on talking.

Alexander had never let her alone since the party, except for that all too brief intermission when she and Ginnie were washing up the party glasses in the kitchen, and he was with his brothers in the drawing room. He had been on to her as soon as the last guest had gone, his voice vibrant with a geniality quite new to her; and, as it seemed, intoxicatingly unfamiliar to himself.

'I say, what a party, old girl, what a party! We haven't given one like that in years! All *madly* enjoying themselves, like that *nice* young man who came with his father. What's his name? George, wasn't it? But you remembered him of course?'

Martha murmured something.

'You were wonderful, I must say. Getting it all ready, and then making it go like a bomb!'

Over Christmas Martha had not only enjoyed herself but had felt, and for the first time in years, the centre of her home, to whom others applied and deferred; the one whom they teased and congratulated.

She had felt like 'Mother' in some ancient joke in *Punch. Punch* had vanished now of course, but it used to lie about the house when she was a child. Her mother never opened it; but she

121

remembered her father turning its pages when he was on leave, his face remaining grave but with a somehow satisfied look, as he were observing a ritual. When she had first arrived at Earlwood all the houses around would have had their copies delivered. Not at all the thing now; and yet those old *Punch* stereotypes – parlourmaids, kindly policemen, comic foreigners – had surely soaked themselves into the comforts and reassurances as well as into the repressions of local society, that invisible tribe in which she had never felt herself to be included.

Together with that recall of *Punch*, there came a surprising realisation. Her guests tonight had seemed to accept her totally, as her house's potent presence. How could that have happened? Invisibly, yet palpably, she seemed to have been made much of: by family, husband, guests, everyone.

Everyone except George.

For the first time she saw him as he was. A separate young man. A little awkward but presentable, tall, good-looking, standing in his stiff suit on the hearthrug, talking to her husband. And her husband was treating her now almost in the same fashion as he had treated George.

Martha loved George? Then why had George, in the midst of all this, become so shadowy a figure?

She had stood at the sink, rinsing while Ginnie dried, and chatting mechanically about the guests. Who was this, who was that? It had kept them going, but Ginnie clearly didn't take much in; and – come to think of it – Ginnie too seemed to have something on her mind. Probably she was worrying about her little girl, who hadn't turned up with Peter. Martha herself had been glad to see Peter. She liked him, but his resemblance to his brother Bobby had unnerved her as she let him in at the front door, and now she heard that sentence yet again in her head.

'Alexander is really enjoying your boyfriend.'

What did that mean? What was that wretched Bobby really like? Full of venom, and mystery. Or was he just being jocular, harmless, facetious?

How could she find out? Surely that 'boyfriend' was no more than a tease? Wasn't that it? No more than that?

And yet it might mean more – very much more. She remembered the washing-up with Ginnie, and how her hands had been

122

shaking as she rinsed the glasses in the hot soapy water. She knew the truth herself, even if Bobby didn't. She knew how much George meant to her.

She knew – did Bobby somehow know too? And tossed about between all such possibilities was the dread fact that her own image of George, hugged to herself once as she had hugged him in the flesh, would keep turning now into that simple public image of a 'nice young man'. The young man who had been at the party.

Why should the evening have lost her George? But in some dire way she felt it had.

She had known Ginnie was too close beside her to see the tears in her eyes, and she kept her eyes looking down at the sink while she had found herself apologising, yet again, for the fact that the washing-up machine was out of order. There was always something going wrong with it; and of course there had been no hope of getting the man to come over Christmas ....

*

And what about George himself? His sensations, had they known it, were much the same as hers. For him too that was the worst of it. Normally, and naturally, he spent a lot of time being with Martha in his mind: seeing her big face, and other bits of her; seeing her smile; doting on her in fact. And quite suddenly this habit of love had been shot through with alien vibrations, like trouble on the TV screen.

He clung now desperately to that last moment she had really looked at him; in her church, as he thought of it. The Greys' invitation had helped to bestow on George his own style of secret *hubris*. She was, must be, welcoming him into a family circle. He was to be made free of it; while keeping, of course, his own special and secret relation with her. He had been consumed both with excitement and with curiosity when he and his father were walking towards the Greys' house.

He had been sure that Martha would in some way signal to him, across a crowded room. She would be his, and she would somehow let him know it, even at moments when she was also being a zealous and preoccupied hostess.

That had not happened. Or at least it seemed to George not to have happened. Instead, and no sooner had they arrived, than he had the sensation of being harassed, almost assaulted, by Martha's husband. An assault of the most benevolent kind, it was true; but he had been compelled to spend every second fighting it off. Or so it had seemed to him at the time, although afterwards he realised that he had simply let the man have his way with him. Like an ingenuous girl under an attack she has neither the wish nor the experience to discourage.

Worse than that. The smiles of pleasure and encouragement which Martha had undoubtedly sent from time to time in their direction must have been as much for her husband as for himself? Or so it now seemed to him.

Martha's husband had taken them over. That was clear to George as he sat miserably afterwards at home. Instead of watching the television and rambling restlessly about, as he usually did in the late evening, his father had gone to bed, relaxed and made happy by the party. It had made him talkative for a while, too; but as neither Pusey knew much about the other guests there was not a great deal to say. The party itself had been the thing for Mr Pusey: and the success which his son had been having with their host.

That success might well seem as dazzling as it was inexplicable. His son George was going to receive every kindness and encouragement from his new friends, the Greys. Alexander had been full of promises, which were, after all, no sort of trouble for him to make. George in the future should come to lean on the husband's advice and experience, just as he would come to value and to enjoy the wife's warm heart, and her womanly understanding?

Such desirable things were implicit in what Alexander Grey had said. And still more promissory had been the way he laid hands on George's shoulders and looked into his eyes, chuckling and exclaiming in his pleasure, as if he himself had decided to take over responsibility for paying to George what had once been Martha's loving attentions.

Not, again, that George had objected: it wouldn't have occurred to him to do so. Alexander Grey, as it happened, had one characteristic in common with both his younger brothers: an

124

authoritative and oldfashioned tone of voice. He was the sort of person who begins a sentence with 'I say', or 'Look Here' – locutions which might seem aggressive, or even possessive, to a sensitive addressee. And yet it might well have been such a habit of speech which had unconsciously attracted Martha, in the days when she was a girl, and the eldest Grey was courting her. Her own father, after all, had been a military man.

That tone in the Grey voice had made George obedient today as it had once made Martha; she had once found it appealing too. It had no appeal for George, but he did not resist it, and not until some time after the party did it occur to him that Martha's image in his mind had been in some subtle way altered by the way her husband had behaved. It made him most unhappy to realise this.

If her husband had behaved with distant civility or, better still, with marked reserve, he would surely now be feeling differently. He could not suppose her husband to suspect them; but his sense of what was appropriate, what would have gratified his knowledge of Martha's love, and his own, would have welcomed a little stiffness in Alexander Grey, even a touch of possessiveness about his wife. Perhaps it was childish on his part, but George would have been more comfortable if Martha's husband had behaved as least a bit more like a potentially jealous husband.

As it was, the only thing he had seemed to feel possessive about was his new toy – George himself?

Martha suffered too, had George but known it, from her husband's attentions when the party was over. They were not uxorious attentions, although he did give her a kiss as she sat at the dressing-table, but the same kind of wooing by words that he had visited upon George at the party. Going to bed, he talked at poor Martha untiringly. As he went on and on she had even found herself reminded – and to catch herself making such comparison was really awful for her – of the chatter which bubbled all the time between her and George, at their meetings.

Both lovers were tormented by the sense that something vulgar and public had stolen in upon their secret intimacy during the evening: and, in its own demoralising way, was miming that intimacy.

But there was all the helplessness of being in love about the way in which Martha and George talked; and there was nothing in the least helpless about this sudden conversational display by Alexander; even though its new and startling insistence had its own air of exhilaration.

'I say, look here Martha, he's a really *dear* young man you know – that son of the builder fellow.'

So it had begun. Martha was repelled by the adjective, because it was so much what she felt herself.

'Did you find him nice, Ally?' she murmured, trying to brush her hair. 'I'm so glad. I hardly spoke to him. I seemed to be always trying to cope with someone else. Dick Stringham is rather a trial, isn't he?'

Alexander ignored her. 'We'll have him round here, Martha. The sooner the better, what?'

'I'll ask them again some time by all means.' By referring to him and his father collectively she had some idea of distracting attention away from George himself. But of course it had not helped.

Martha was both appalled and mystified by the line her husband seemed to be taking. Could it in some way relate to that jocular comment his brother Bobby had made to her, and which had so suddenly discomposed her at the party.

'Alexander is really enjoying your boyfriend.'

She couldn't forget it. What *had* he meant by it? Was it – could it be – in some strange way reassuring? Bobby must have been thinking of Alexander's own behaviour at the party, which had certainly been boyfriend-like, even flirtatious, and connecting it facetiously with herself. The boyfriend's comic girlfriend, so to speak? No more than that, surely?

Trying to brush her hair, and to prepare herself for bed under this unexpected shower of husbandly chat, Martha sought for any crumb of comfort and reassurance she could give herself. Perhaps there were no connections, except in her supposedly 'guilty' mind? Perhaps Alexander really had taken a sudden liking to George, as she supposed he must have done to Fiona's Nigel? But if so, what sort of effect on them all was it going to have?

She could hardly ask Alexander. He stopped behind her as

she sat before the mirror, and gazed impressively at her bemused reflection.

'Look Martha, we should try, you know, to help these young
people. It struck me tonight just how caring and decent most of
them are. That's one way this present generation is better than
ours.'

At that Martha had got up and plumped down heavily on to
her own side of the big mattress. The customary bedtime civili-
ties were beyond her tonight. Just before the blessed release of
sleep she could hear him still going on in those new earnest tones
with some stuff about the 'human condition'.

*

What was George himself, some days later in the Antelope,
feeling about the human condition?

Not much. With a sense of even more disagreeable things to
come he raised his half-pint glass of bitter to his lips and stared
hopelessly at Bobby Grey, who was sitting on the bench opposite.

George had scarcely seen Bobby at the party. Overwhelmed
as he had been by the unexpected attentions of the host, he had
no time to look around him and take in the identity of other
guests. He had barely even identified Ginnie, the mousy lady as
he thought of her, whom he had seen the previous morning with
Martha in church.

His state of mind that night had been as bemused as Martha's
as she sat at her dressing-table. He hardly knew how he had
reached home with his father after the party, nor how he got
through the next few days.

Then a letter had arrived for him. The note inside was signed
'Major Grey'. With a military terseness in keeping with that
signature he was directed to present himself in the Antelope at
twelve the following morning.

George had been awake most of the night, which was not
unusual for him nowadays. For the first time Martha's big features were not to be summoned up, in his mind's eye. All he
could see was the face of her husband, aglint, as it seemed, with
some inexplicable animation. In a dreadful way, too, they actu-

ally resembled his wife's, as if his features were representing, or standing in, for hers. George had heard that married couples came to look like one another. He saw now what that might mean.

To be fair to George, he was striving to be rational. How could he expect Martha to be all the time what she obviously wasn't? How could she help but wear the party face he had seen yesterday evening, even if it had been like a variation of her husband's, whose excited features had confronted George so unrelentingly throughout the party? As a result of that evening all three of them – he and Martha and her husband – had simultaneously, as it seemed, entered the public sphere. The pair had become a trio: he and Martha had lost that private world of two, in which they had lived with and for each other.

Four days after Christmas had come the snow. George had not seen Martha since the party. He wandered about in the wintry landscape, hoping she too might be out for a walk, as had happened when they first met. The dark bowers of larch and cedar, into which they had once snuggled, would be filling up with snow.

His father still talked about the party, but with an air of resignation, as of something vanished and unrepeatable. To the grandee Greys, their social task done, he and his son were no more to be thought of. The snow was so thick that he did not even suggest a visit to the Antelope. In the evenings they stayed at home, and the house felt cold.

The day after the party George had written to Martha; and instead of entrusting it to the post, which might still be disorganised by the Christmas holiday, he took it round to Prentice Wood late at night. With many precautions against making a noise he dropped it through the Greys' front door. In it he asked Martha to meet him the following afternoon – the day she should be getting the letter – in the churchyard. The church was not far from the Greys', and Martha might be going there for some reason, even through the snow. It could look like an accidental meeting, and there was cover behind the fir-trees, or even beside his angel.

He marked the letter 'By Hand'. It could possibly be some guest's thankyou letter for the party, should the envelope be seen by Martha's husband or by her in-laws, all of whom seemed to be staying in the house. Although he sealed it with tape he did not dare address the envelope in block capitals, which might make it look odd. He trusted that no one but Martha would recognise the writing. Her husband would surely be back now in his usual routine at the office?

The neighbourhood of the church was undoubtedly a practical spot for a rendezvous; but George's real reason for suggesting it was the fact that Martha had smiled at him there at the Christmas service, before the party. It was the last place in which he had seen his own private Martha, even though she had been in the church with her husband and a friend. The image of her, as she was then, had been slipping continuously away from him, dissolved and overlaid by the way she had seemed to behave at her house. Seeing her must surely bring it back to him?

He spent the afternoon in the churchyard, but no Martha. Had she chosen to ignore his letter? Her husband had forbidden her to come? (George was prepared for the moment to entertain the wildest and most oldfashioned ideas about the authority of husbands.) Had she herself preferred not to come? Had she been too frightened?

The last was the only tolerable possibility to entertain as he patrolled the solitary churchyard, with his feet getting wetter and wetter, for the snow had begun to melt. Enough remained to make his white angel positively dingy, and her Victorian features more vapid than ever. Her sweeping wings remained her best feature, and he paused frequently beside them, as if they could still promise him shelter. He even mounted the plinth once and touched her cold rough lips with his own, imagining they might be Martha's. The sculptor had caused them to pout slightly, giving them an overlip, or moustache, of still unsullied snow.

Certainly Martha would have come, had she received his letter. She was longing to hear from him, still more to see him. But though Ginnie and Peter were gone, the wretched Bobby remained, and so did her husband, who had not been back to his office since Christmas. He seemed delighted that his brother was still with them.

All that notwithstanding, Martha would have found some

way to come if she had heard from George about the proposed rendezvous. But she had not heard from him.

Bobby had intercepted the letter.

Now he sat opposite the young man in the bar of the Antelope, in what might have passed for a comradely silence. He had guessed that George would write to Martha, and he had got up before six and gone quietly downstairs in his dressing-gown to verify the guess. Sure enough, in the gloom of the unnecessarily spacious hall he could just make out a letter lying on the mat. With this possibility in mind he had switched off the burglar alarm after they had all gone to bed. He could pad over to the front door and gather up the letter without fear of disturbance.

'You write a charming love letter – I'll say that,' he commented pleasantly, drawing on his pipe.

He was disappointed if he hoped to provoke a strong reaction in George, who only stared back at him morosely. Somehow George had already expected nothing else. The note from this man, ordering a meeting at the Antelope, had seemed a death sentence on himself and Martha.

So this man had read what he had written? Had he sealed up the letter again and passed it on? But no – if Martha had received the letter surely she would have come? – that was the point.

She had heard nothing – could only have heard nothing!

So enthralled was George by this sudden realisation that he first glanced furtively at the other man before setting his own face into a look of what he hoped was numb and stoical indifference. If this shit expected him to break down he had made a mistake. He would find he was wrong.

'Shit' was not normally a word in George's vocabulary: and yet how well it seemed to suit Major Grey! The odd thing was, however, that George had never really thought this, and still did not quite think it. Although unaware of the fact, he still obstinately retained, from his childhood reading and film-going, a simple belief in the integrity of certain classes of English society. The police, the clergy, Doctors, Army and Navy men. They feared God; they honoured the King. Whatever shits they might be in private life they kept their public standards.

However much he hated Major Grey, and by now he hated

him very heartily, George could still not help himself taking for granted that such a man would not go back on his word.

He had made a bargain with George over Martha: he would not betray it. Even though, like the secret agent he was supposed to be, he had now taken to intercepting George's correspondence.

George's innocence had helped to make Martha love him.

And now his spirits suddenly rose. He remembered the horrible words this man had used to him. A stud was it? – a toyboy? – something like that. When he heard those words he had felt not only shocked and revolted but as if his person had been accurately defined. So that was what he was, for others?

But no, he wasn't! Triumphantly he knew it. This man, who thought he knew everything, knew nothing. Martha did not lust after George, nor he after her. What being in love had given them was their own world together. And it was not lost, that world. This man, and the others, would never find it. As for the other place, his old private lair, that could go: and good riddance.

George stretched himself luxuriously, smiling into Bobby Grey's face. He jerked back the last dregs of his disagreeable beer – it tasted mysteriously better now – and began to tell the other all about the hoard, and how he had found it. A kind of authority even seemed to possess him, as if he were the bright young staff officer briefing some worthy but rather slow senior about the latest plan of attack.

*

Pinky's new passion for hotel life was being sated. The three of them – herself, her father, and the Russian lady whose coming had replaced the old magic of Muz Paybody – were now installed at the Kensington Palace, within a short distance of her own home.

She knew the Park already of course, but now she was seeing it in a new and exciting way. She sat with her father in the window of their room, which was actually two rooms, and that was a further source of excitement. It was a thing called a suite, a word she had never heard before, and which she mouthed over frequently and luxuriously, in her silent way.

131

They were installed in the window of the sitting-room, which had arm-chairs upholstered in velvet, and her father was pointing out landmarks she knew well: the Round Pond and the Albert Memorial. He was telling her again about this man called Peter Pan, a distant relative of his, who lived by himself in the park and who hated children. The best moment of his day came in the evening, when all the children and their nurses or parents had to leave, and he could stroll by himself among the flowers. A sort of cousin he was – they had the same name – but Peter admitted he had never met his namesake.

Something exciting was always happening. Big burly men – in suits – visited their suite from time to time. Pinky silently mouthed the difference between suite and suit, which pleased her.

Seeing his daughter's lips moving, Peter wondered what words she had got hold of now. Loved words, that little thing, though she was so quiet about it. He'd got her a Christmas present when they were at the other hotel – a bottle of *Crème de Menthe*. Rum choice for a five-year-old, but it went down like a bomb. He'd seen her looking at it in a window, and saying the name to herself in the way she did. Wouldn't open it of course, not for a few years yet. And where would they all be then?

He'd left Pinky with Vera, hugging her green bottle to herself, as pleased as Punch. Like a doll, except of course that she hated dolls.

Vera was sitting in the bedroom, combing and arranging her dark wiry hair. She'd had a lot to say to the men who came to see them, talking Russian of course, and that had fascinated Pinky too. Vera was out of practice in her English, or did the presence of Pinky inhibit in some way her once total fluency in that language? Sometimes she made deep chuckling Russian noises to the child, which entranced Pinky as much as the fact that this wonderful new woman normally paid her no attention at all.

*

Her mother was also standing at a window, as she used to do sometimes in her flat, in the old days. It had usually been a pleasure then, but now it seemed to show that she did not know what to do with herself. Words of no use to her situation ran through her head.

With a mixture of relief and foreboding she recognised that what she still thought of sometimes as normality – her old pre-married self – might just possibly be coming back to her. In some form or other. First she must see if she needed an abortion; and then have one if she did. She quailed at the thought of what she would have to find out, and the arrangements she must make; but at least it was something that needed action; and she had no doubts at all about what she must do.

She still hadn't said a word to Peter, nor was she intending to. What he had told her that night at Prentice Wood was quite enough to have between them.

The fact she might be pregnant as well seemed almost an irrelevancy; and she positively writhed at the thought that she could use it to 'win her husband back'. Or whatever. She actually found her face grinning a bit as she wondered how Peter would take the news. Just for once he might be entirely flummoxed.

But no, he wouldn't be. Her Christmas encounter with all three Grey brothers had coalesced them in her shocked mind as creatures not only grotesque but alien. With so many distancing and exhausting peculiarities that it seemed incredible she should ever have known them; have married one of them, borne his child. On her visit that morning with her father Pinky herself had partly reassured her: taking the whole situation so entirely for granted that Ginnie found herself doing the same. But she was not going to meet the other woman. About that she felt very certain indeed.

At any rate it was time now to have the operation she had not had in the first place. Would she have had it then, if Peter had not seemed so anxious to marry her, and have the baby? Yes, she would. No one-parent family stuff, even if Peter did continue to look after her. And she could by no means rely on that.

Looking back, it struck her that she might have herself become entirely different – surely most women did, and without too much effort? – at the time she first had the child. However much wrapped up in their jobs and careers women seemed to turn all those energies into maternity, when it happened. She might have done so too? But somehow she hadn't. When Pinky was a baby Peter seemed to have done almost everything himself. It must have come naturally to him. She felt sad for a moment to think how he might have welcomed her news now.

But she must deal with things by herself this time. And how absurdly inopportune were the ways in which things happened! Yet she could feel, and with a certain pleasure, something obstinately selfish growing and swelling in her, like pregnancy itself. As if she could herself grow plump on this desertion. Something – she supposed it was her own inadequacy – might always be there to welcome her back.

But she would not see Vera. And it was no use telling the police about her. Pinky loved the hotel they were at: they must be quite rich? She hoped only that the woman would not ring her up, or come round to the flat.

On that occasion, nearly six years ago, had she been crying at this same window out of love, or for her lost freedom? She had found she could not bear not to go back to him, not to be with him. Yet it was not the kind of love she had known, or wanted.

Perhaps the whole thing had come to her from reading too many books? And that reminded her she still had a report to write. She had been too happily busy with Martha to get down to it at Prentice Wood, over Christmas. The report was on the third novel of a trilogy about pensioners, done by some old person who was quite cultured and yet hardly literate. None the less he had known how to describe things. The first two parts – *Still in Our Ashes* and *Wonted Fires* – had been surprisingly successful; and Ginnie's boss had been pleased with the way she had edited them into a fit state for publication.

What a subject, pensioners, but the public seemed to like it. Perhaps it was only old people today who read ordinary novels? Her boss should be interested in that view of the matter ....

And yet she knew, with despair, that she didn't in the least care at the moment whether the report got done or not. Would her old life ever welcome her back, since the new one seemed to be over? Would it, like a grudging landlady, ever let her take up residence again on the old terms? Even if it did, could she ever feel an interest in being her old self again?

And suddenly she did begin to cry, though in a feeble half-hearted way. Not like those almost heroic tears she had shed – it must be getting on for six years ago – when she found, safe home in her snug flat, that she simply had to go back to Peter. No one, and no place, to run to now ….

And yet, could it not be that there was? A sudden idea struck her; and made her feel almost purposeful again. That was it! She would go to Martha.

CHAPTER 9

Confidences

Martha was missing George. She could do nothing else at the moment. But with her husband and his brother still in the house she could do nothing about it either.

And then George appeared one morning like an apparition, walking up the drive in the snow.

She was standing in the kitchen, looking out of the window. Dumbfounded, she scuttled in panic into the pantry by the back door. She heard a ring, and she heard Alexander going to answer it, as if this visit had been expected. What had he done to get hold of George? And when?

For a few minutes Martha, silent in the pantry, listened to a murmur of conversation. Then her husband's voice, in a louder tone, was calling out her name. At that she ran mindlessly out of the back door, and down a few steps through the bushes to the greenhouse. The snow was almost gone but her feet were already soaked. She crouched panting in a corner of the greenhouse, next to a weedy white azalea, which she had put out after Christmas because it looked as if it were dying in the drawing-room heat.

After a minute or two she remembered that Alexander might bring George out into the garden – he had said something lately about the idea of the large conservatory, and where it might be put. In a fresh panic she rapidly evacuated the greenhouse, and with averted head ran through the shrubs and evergreens to the front gate. Out in the roadway she found she still had her apron on, and she took it off hastily. To be seen like that by one of the neighbours might look odd.

She had some idea of lurking, and waiting for George to come out by himself. Wild hope! – but when he did eventually appear it was with Alexander. She just got back into the shrubbery in time to see them walk out of the drive. Then Alexander returned with a smile on his face; not actually rubbing his hands together but looking as if he might have done that, were he in the habit of doing so. Watching him, as she continued to skulk in the bushes, Martha felt more out of place than she would have thought possible. That she, Mrs Alexander Grey, should be watching her own husband, as he returned from saying a cordial goodbye to her lover! Watching him from behind the bushes in her own garden!

She could have giggled. Miserably but like a maniac. And only a few days before she had been the accepted matriarch of the Christmas festivities, made much of by them all!

And here was George, evidently now become her husband's property.

She felt like a prisoner in her own house, guarded by those twin ogres, her husband and his brother. For the first time poor Martha felt really desperate to break out. She could no longer live snug at home, while enjoying the bliss of her secret relationship with George. She must do something, and yet how could she? What was there to do?

The answer came next day. Smiling his old smile at her, Bobby announced that he must be off. What a pleasant stay it had been. And Alexander, too, said it must be London again tomorrow. Christmas had softened him up: it was time to get back to work.

Martha's heart leaped up. She hadn't dared to ask him when he would be returning to his usual routines. She would have loved to pour out her heart to George in a letter, but it seemed wiser to keep it short.

My Darling My Darling My Darling Tomorrow (when you get this) at Rosamond. Eleven. Love Love Love Love. I love you.

That was all she felt she had time for. She was in a fever now to post her letter.

Everything worked out as she had hoped it might. Alexander caught the 9.05 to his office: Bobby had disappeared. Martha, in spite of her anxieties, was gripped by the intoxication of a freedom both old and new. She had always, in the old days, loved to be in the house alone. But now, in a few minutes, she would be going out to meet George!

She spent some time doing her face. George loved to examine it, she knew, bless him. He had even shown interest in how it might be made up. But she had never bothered much about it before. Now she was going to see him for the first time for what seemed so long; she wanted to look consciously nice for him. She was really in a fever, but she continued to go about things methodically, checking her purse with the keys – she would lock up carefully when she left. It would be so wonderful later on to get home to her empty house, and to think of the time she had spent with George!

At the last moment she had a sudden idea, which made her smile to herself. Running upstairs to the bedroom she took off her pants and put them under the stockings in her top drawer. She never wore tights. As she was doing that the bell rang.

Coming back down the stairs she paused. The bell rang again, and after a few moments a third time. Could it be George himself? Perhaps he had been lurking outside the house, and had seen Alexander leave? Knowing she must be alone he had not been able to wait for the hour of their meeting!

Full of a reckless joy she was suddenly sure of it. She would throw caution to the winds, fling herself into his arms on the threshold, take him straight upstairs to bed. If her husband was trying to take George from her – if he and his brother suspected her of being an adulterous woman – then very well, she would behave like one.

Rushing down the stairs she opened the front door. There stood Ginnie.

Ginnie began to cry as she blundered over the doorstep. She held out her arms to Martha who could not stop herself from recoiling. The two women stared at each other, Ginnie with a mouth that trembled, and a piteous appeal that already looked uncertain: Martha with open horror.

She had half an hour in hand. It would take her twenty minutes to get to Rosamond's Bower, as they had once christened it. The nearest of their old secret places, it lay not far off a pathway that went through one of the remaining areas of old and dense woodland on the estate, too close to the motorway to have been developed.

How was she to get rid of this woman, and be at Rosamond on time?

*

George waited at Rosamond, or rather in Rosamond, since their snuggery, in the heart of thick macrocarpa and Lawson's cypress, was saturated outside from the melting snow. The woods were dripping, but the dark interior was still nearly dry.

George was early, but he knew Martha would come as soon as she could, perhaps even before eleven. It would be right for him to wait for her. He longed for her so much that he almost wished she would be a little late. Delay would be the proper thing, as it would be for a crowd awaiting the Queen. The royal one knows that expectancy can only grow greater until she comes. The big moment will surely arrive, and the crowd have nothing to do but wait.

But Martha was not like that. His gentle queen, yes; and with a new rush of adoration he knew she always would be. But in fact she was and always had been almost obsessively punctual.

He remembered their time together by the big cedar tree, when they had been spied on by Major Grey and the Zeiss fieldglasses. Awful. But he strove to blot out the vile memory by concentrating on the happy one of Martha smiling at him in her loving way, and holding up her skirt. She would be here soon, he knew; just like she was, and with the same smile.

Rosamond, however damp, was secret and secure – had Martha chosen it for that reason? It was the closest to her house as well. But the thought of that house reminded him of her husband, and of Major Grey, whom he hoped never to have to see again. George had kept to his side of their bargain; and since Martha's note had come he felt he could be sure that the Major had kept his own side of it, too.

He was sure because of the way in which Mr Grey – Martha's husband – had behaved at their meeting. And getting Martha's note had dispelled all his post-Boxing Day fear and unhappiness: the fear that she had in some way abandoned him. With her

140

house full of people she could not in any case have met him that time in the churchyard. His lowest moment had been when his father told him Mr Grey was on the phone, and Martha's husband had asked him to come round for a chat about their conservatory project. He had dreaded seeing her with her husband, and both of them being friendly and kind to him.

His spirits lifted when she had not been there at her house, or at least not visible, as if it were a pledge that she was still faithful – silently faithful – to their old secret relationship. And then this morning her note had arrived!

None the less he was beginning to feel very cold, crouching in the bower. He looked at his watch. It was already half past eleven. What could have happened to her?

To distract himself he thought of the time he had first brought Martha here. It seemed long ago, a hot day, and she had exclaimed in a whisper at the neatness of the place, its fragrant coniferous warmth, the soft dry floor inside. It had been early in their relationship – before they had made love – but there had been no need for that. Nor would there be now. He just wanted to see her and to talk – talk, and feel they were themselves, and together again.

Besides, it was rather too wet for love. He must not allow Martha to get bedraggled before she went home. And again – he couldn't stop himself – he began wondering about Major Grey, and about Martha's husband. When Major Grey had intercepted that letter of his, and had lightly mentioned it at the Antelope .... That had been a horrible moment, but he hoped he had not shown it. He had comforted himself afterwards by feeling sure that Martha at least had never got the letter.

And yet his high spirits had quite left him now. It was so unlike Martha to be late. Had something again gone wrong?

It occurred to him that the very special kindness and friendliness which her husband had lavished on him yesterday (he had even asked George to call him Alexander) might yet be those of an entirely reasonable man who had begun to feel suspicious, for whatever reason; and so might have had a long quiet chat with his wife. No reproaches, no hard words. Could they have simply agreed together that it would be far better all round – better for him, George, especially, – if he were to become a friend of the family? The best way out for all concerned?

George had once, and not so very long ago, heard his parents talking quietly together in their bedroom about their son, and his future. He had tiptoed away, and had felt very depressed. It was dreadfully easy now to imagine Martha, and her husband, having the same kind of chat together: about him, and about his future.

As with all lovers at some point there was an uncharted depth of uncertainty in his conviction that he and Martha loved one another. Perhaps their love would turn out in the end to be nothing at all, easily dispelled by commonsense, and by a realisation of things, such as she might have had over Christmas, with her house full of relations and friends? Had it been really been her intention to come and tell him, kindly and reasonably, that all was over between them?

In that case, he thought with a sudden and illogical hope, she might suddenly have felt too upset to come? In floods of secret tears? – dithering? – or pouring it all out to her husband? Could she have written that note just to cheer and prepare him? No, she couldn't, he was quite sure! And Martha, he knew, was not a ditherer.

Whatever the cause of the failure she might yet come. He was sure she would. He would go on waiting.

Below him the endless sough and whistle of the motorway, roaring to a crescendo and falling back again, was as hypnotic as the waves breaking on a beach. George's eyes closed. He had slept very badly, if at all, for the last few nights.

*

Ginnie had not slept either. She had marks under her eyes which Martha noted, as if mechanically. But Ginnie of course entirely failed to see the look of despair on Martha's own face. Misery bestowed on her a kind of innocence, so that she did not believe that Martha at the moment had any function, or desire, except to be of use and comfort to her.

Martha could not, at least did not, disabuse her. That would have been impossible. She saw that Ginnie like a child held, for

142

whatever reason, rights to woe which could only be put aside by a passion of sympathy. Coupled of course with a bitter lament that she, Martha, must leave at once to keep an urgent and unavoidable appointment. A more glib or resourceful or simply hard-hearted woman might have managed that. Martha, alas, could not.

Almost at once she hardly wanted to. Part of her was still crying out 'I *must* get to George – I must! I must!' But the sight of her sister-in-law, and the tears she was shedding, paralysed this part of Martha totally. As the seconds went by, and she still did nothing, she came to understand that she could not, and would not be getting to George; and that there was nothing she could do about it.

She saw George waiting and waiting, leaving at last – in what state of mind? Sinking from disappointment into apathy, perhaps resentment: slipping further and further away from her.

All this she might avoid, even now, if she could only bring herself to utter loudly some forceful excuse: that she *had* to go out at once, *must* go: would be back as soon as possible. Yet she knew she could not do it. The sight of Ginnie's face made it impossible to go away and leave her. If only she had herself left home – just five minutes earlier!

She went on mechanically patting the other woman, and uttering soothing words. And Ginnie's troubles all came pouring out. How Peter was leaving her and going back to his ex-wife, the Russian; and what was she to do about Pinky, who really loved her father? And what was she to do with herself? How was she to live and carry on, now?

Martha could think of nothing to say. She could only think of George and see him in her mind's eye, crouching forlornly alone in Rosamond. She felt physically sick with longing to put her arms around him. He would go on waiting, she knew. For how long? She must pull herself together – she really must. What was Ginnie saying?

Ginnie was sobbing out that on top of everything else she seemed to be pregnant – indeed in some way she felt dreadfully sure of it. She would rather die now than tell Peter. She had been going to tell him when he came here with Pinky on Boxing Day. Just when he told her he was going to leave her.

143

What was she to do? If she did nothing she might have to have the child. She couldn't face that. She had never really wanted children anyway – it had been all because of Peter. How could she escape? – but she must, mustn't she? What else could she do? Sobbing as if her heart would break she laid her face on Martha's bosom.

Martha could think only that it should have been George's face.

It seemed so unfair, Ginnie got out between her sobs. She had never wanted anything much. Just to get on with her job and lead a quiet life. And here she was in a pickle like this.

The word 'pickle' touched Martha. It seemed so characteristic of the real Ginnie, in a way that these pathetic transports of self-pity did not. Martha felt embarrassed for her. Poor Ginnie was not really at all like this, and should not have to be behaving in such a way. She was not equipped by nature to do so.

Feeling embarrassed for her sister-in-law was not the proper reaction: but what could Martha do? Like all those who feel cut off by nature from the human race she was also a natural prey to embarrassment. She had always suffered from what to herself she thought of as 'bathroom shyness': she had endured agonies as a child if anyone saw her going into the loo. Loving George had cured all that of course, at least when she was with him. Perfect love casteth out shame no doubt. But, quite apart from her own predicament, Ginnie's troubles were now giving Martha a real attack of the old shyness in a new form. She could hardly bear to listen to what the poor thing was saying, because of the way she said it.

Martha always had a painfully acute sense of how others were feeling. But feeling for others, she now realised, was not the same as feeling with them.

She could not stop herself becoming more and more embarrassed the longer Ginnie's frantic queries and lamentations continued, although she put her arms round her and tried, in the intervals of the poor woman's sobs, to sound comforting and caring. She thought despairingly about George, while Ginnie howled harder than ever.

*

144

George was walking aimlessly along the woodland road that wound under the trees and through the estate, before joining the public road that led to shops and village. It was now after half-past one.

Late as it was, he still nourished a faint hope that he might see the figure of Martha hastening towards him, hurrying to the bower. And at that moment a figure did appear coming his way, advancing briskly beneath the dark spruce trees. But this military-looking form was not Martha. In a few seconds he realised who it was. It was Major Grey, the man whom George hoped never to have to see again.

From a few yards range Bobby Grey called out a hearty greeting, as if George were the one man in the world whom he did, urgently and ardently, wish to see again. As they came together he turned beside the younger man and began to walk with him in the same direction.

*

Ginnie could not drink the tea that Martha had made for her, in order to have something to do. In the midst of her own woe and desolation she was beginning dimly to realise that Martha was not after all to turn out to be the source of comfort she had blindly hoped for. She had got Martha wrong. And Martha, she could not but see through her tears, was becoming increasingly preoccupied.

In fact it had occurred to Martha that the only way she could both enter into and escape from Ginnie's troubles was to blurt out in return her own urgent predicament. What she wished for most was to be able to say that she *must go now*, that her lover was waiting for her; that she couldn't bear to keep him waiting any longer. Then she would rush out of the house and leave Ginnie temporarily to forget her own woes in sharing the secret of Martha's affair.

But the idea occurred to her only to be instantly dismissed. Of course she would do nothing of the kind, just as she would never confide to anyone, let alone Ginnie, what she felt about George.

Then in desperation she had another idea: at least it had the merit of being practical. She would take her sister-in-law to a

145

pub – no, better still – to the Bayleaf restaurant! A good meal and a glass of wine, even two glasses, might do both of them a power of good. It would help Ginnie to face up to things; and they could talk calmly and rationally about her troubles. What she might do: what she could do.

It was one way, too, of getting rid of her. She would take Ginnie to the station, which was no distance from the Bayleaf; and then she would rush round without shame to George's. If he wasn't there she would leave a note for him – a loving, grovelling note, full of abject apology and remorse, undying loyalty .... She would leave it if need be with his father – she wouldn't mind anything about secrecy and security now.

Ginnie was acquiescent. She was too worn out to care; and yet Martha's soothing words about a nice little place where they could have something to eat did help to revive her in some degree. Before they left the house Martha remembered to run up the stairs and put her pants back on. It seemed almost a symbolic act: she had failed and betrayed George, however little it was her own fault. By clothing herself respectably again she seemed to be closing off their own future.

Still the walk to the Bayleaf did help to calm them down; and all the emotion had made them both hungry, though neither mentioned the fact. The waitress proprietor in her leafgreen apron welcomed them at the door. It was late now, and the little place was almost empty: only two customers left at one of the tables.

These were Bobby Grey, and George.

Bobby rose to his feet at once with a welcoming smile.

'Hullo, both of you,' he said, 'and what a pleasant surprise. Come and join our little lunch party, my dears! What could be nicer!'

Was there a way in which Martha might have risen to the occasion? Had she managed to do so she would also have been the sort of a woman who could at once, and with a torrent of excuses, have left Ginnie and rushed off to her appointment with George.

As it was, she panicked. What other reaction was possible? Smiling wildly at Bobby, and at the waitress, she babbled something about not disturbing them – they had only looked in to book for lunch tomorrow. Could they do that, please?

As she pulled Ginnie away, uttering some sort of goodbye with regrets, she managed a fleeting look back at George. There seemed to be no expression of any kind on George's face, although his eyes looked in her direction. But the absence of anything she knew and loved in that look appalled her, and filled her with an immediate despair; and the sense that all was over.

Faces, and their expressions, are necessarily simpler than what is going on behind them. George's could only register his own bewilderment at her sudden appearance. Bewilderment, and amazement at the apparition of this woman (or these women, for both in some way appeared much the same to him) who themselves seemed to look at him as if they had never seen him before.

Scarcely registering how his companion had accosted them he simply sat there at the little restaurant table, and continued to do so after the women had gone, gazing apathetically at Major Grey's roguish face, or down at the cutlery and the leaf-green paper tablecloth.

The two women, who for George had represented one single conglomerate betrayal, trailed back in silence across the common. Martha was possessed not only with shock and misery but with a rage which was most unlike her. She could think only that from the exasperating accident of this woman arriving, uninvited, at her house, there had come this final tragedy of misunderstanding. She was sure now, direfully and dolefully sure, that George would want nothing to do with her ever again. Look at the way she had seemed to behave, after writing that note! She could not, and did not, blame him.

Ginnie for her part was feeling deeply ashamed of her own emotional breakdown. She felt past caring; and yet she was glumly convinced that she must be the cause of the hostility she could feel beside her in Martha. She had quite misunderstood her sister-in-law, that was clear. Her own cry for help had merely made Martha withdraw from her, into herself. Nor could she understand why Martha had dragged them out of the restaurant like that. To have sat down with the genial Bobby, and his young friend, might have been the kind of distraction they were looking for, however little it would have suited her present troubles. Why couldn't they have stayed in that friendly cheerful atmosphere, and had their lunch?

Her eyes filled again with tears as she trotted beside Martha, who was walking very fast. How unfair that she should have had even this forlorn little treat snatched away from her!

Back at Prentice Wood Martha put water on to boil with the idea of poaching eggs. Her sister-in-law, following her uncertainly about, was offered a drink which she first accepted, and then thought she wouldn't have after all. They sat down at the kitchen table, and while pretending to eat tried to talk rationally about what Ginnie should do. Martha could only think of getting rid of her.

Back at the Bayleaf George and Bobby Grey were enjoying their late lunch. George had discovered in himself an enormous hunger and thirst. The bottle of red wine, and Alfred's ham *au porto* and creamy mashed potatoes, seemed just what was wanted. He ate wolfishly. Bobby Grey watched his guest with amusement.

When they had quite done with the dish he called out his congratulations to Alfred the chef. They were by now the only customers, and when she had brought cheese for Bobby and a toffee pudding for George, Caroline the waitress came to sit down beside them. She had the sort of easy manners, as well as good looks, which made this acceptable. She smiled at George and began to take an interest in him. George found himself flattered by this, just as he had unexpectedly found himself enjoying food and wine.

Bobby Grey regarded George and the waitress benevolently. He was amused by the way the girl was making a pass at the young fellow. Would she be up to detaching him from Martha? Very possibly. Martha could hardly keep him tied to her apron-strings for ever. He recalled with further amusement that moment in the wood, when his old Zeiss glasses had fastened on the pair of them, making love. His sister-in-law's upheld skirt, and her stout white hips! How comic she had looked. And her lover too, handsome young stud as he was.

Well, such innocent pleasures were not for him any more, if indeed they ever had been. Yet time was when he wouldn't have at all minded having a stab himself at this young woman in the restaurant. He was happy now to leave her to George. Happy? Bobby Grey's miserable eyes, which like his brother Peter's looked as if they had been glazed with some substance like glycerine, always made a contrast with his really very sweet and attractive smile.

The waitress, who had introduced herself as Caroline, was struck by this smile as she turned for a moment from George. It reminded her of a delightful if thoroughly unsound man with whom she had been madly in love when she was nineteen. And here she was now, a sober divorcée of twenty-seven, sitting between two good-looking men, each of them attractive to her in a different way. It made her feel quite skittish again. It was a long time, after all, since she'd had what her disgusting husband, who liked her to be coarse with him in bed, used to call a good fuck. She was very attached to her Alfred, the chef with whom she shared a flat, but being his fag-hag, or whatever, did have its limitations.

Alfred was so gentle though; and she turned to smile affectionately, and draw him into the conversation. He stood like a nice horse, looking placidly at the company over the half-gate of his little kitchen. He seemed preoccupied, and was gazing in an enquiring way at George, to whom he had just been introduced.

'Was it your mum who passed on the other day?' he suddenly asked. 'Excuse me for wondering, but a friend of mine told me his friend George had just lost his mum. I thought it might be you? I do hope not.'

George said no, it must be some other George; and they all had a laugh.

But perhaps the fat chef had not been so far off the mark. A sob rose abruptly in George's throat, so that he turned away and coughed and took out his handkerchief. The conviction of loss suddenly horrified him. For he *had* lost a near and dear one. Not his mum – that was long ago and long out of mind – but Martha.

149

CHAPTER 10

The Cellar

Like all crooks Bobby Grey knew the value of honesty. And the value of innocence. Where young Pusey was concerned he proposed to make use of this knowledge.

He had found, which didn't surprise him, that George had been as good as his word. The cache existed all right. What was in it was just junk these days; of little or no value to anyone, even to the IRA boys who had stuck it down there. They had lashings of hardware and explosive if they wanted them again, as they no doubt would do. No real requirement for this little lot.

But there could be something else. The thing they had heard about at the interrogation. By rights of course he shouldn't have been in on that at all. But at the time he had still had good friends in the service, and one of them had suggested to him that he might like to come along. He was glad now that he had, very glad. It might make all the difference.

Seemingly, the IRA boys had wangled this thing out of the KGB, years and years back. Of course one would have expected that they were just taking poor old Paddy for a ride; that the thing they had handed over was a fraud, a bogeyman as it was known in the service, his own old service. But in the light of recent developments it didn't look that way.

It was Peter who had first alerted him to the possibilities. That brother of his was a bit of an ass, but he had his moments. Knew the language, once had a Russian wife, ex-KGB, and by all accounts a much shrewder operator than young Peter had ever been.

And so it had been a question of putting two and two together.

It didn't greatly perturb him that the Thing itself might turn out not to exist. The point was to sell it as a possibility. Iraq? Why not? All sorts of people couldn't afford not to buy it on the

151

chance. Peter would be batting for the Russians, who wanted it back. So would he himself, in theory; but in practice he proposed to bat solely for number one. A three-cornered match. The IRA boys, with a watching brief, would be out to make what they could from the Russians, and from Peter, and from yours truly as well.

It would be amusing to see young O'Connor again. Not so young now of course; nor so spry, probably, after what had been done to him. Not that Bobby Grey felt any guilt about that. The man had known what would happen if he got picked up. As a result he might well have been romancing of course: no blame to him if he had been.

The Thing could have been lifted by somebody much earlier. It might have already been sold by the Irish. It might never have existed. Take your choice. What mattered was that no one of the interested parties could afford to write it off completely. And that was where the money was, or would be if he played his cards carefully.

Which Bobby Grey now proposed to do. As they approached Manor Farm he glanced at his companion. George Pusey looked as if he neither knew nor cared what might be going to happen next. Innocent as the day; nothing at all to do with this caper. Confuse, even bemuse, O'Connor? Lose him any initiative that might be going? Thought you might like to meet the mother's boy for old times' sake. And now, what about the goods?

Since they're not down here. As you're well aware. That shouldn't surprise you, my dear young Irishman. Do you want to be taken in again, for questioning? That could happen, you know, if you don't have something to tell me.

Bobby himself was sure the Thing was nowhere. Felt quite confident about that. This Thing – chemical, biological or whatever it was – which the employees of the various services had to pretend to be so interested about, because in a sense it continued to be their bread and butter, whether it existed or not. A potential danger: that was the line of course. Had helped to keep them all in work, anyway.

After first showing his hated companion over the place George had had nothing more to say. Stood there like a stuck pig while Bobby rooted around a bit. The gilt words on the wall had amused him. FEAR GOD HONOUR THE KING. Nice jest that, by someone or other. A bit subtle for the Paddies, one would have thought, wouldn't one? But it didn't do to underestimate the Paddies.

In any event that crisp command on the wall was hardly relevant any more. Pity, really.

They picked their way now through the debris and undergrowth, and reached the black hole in the barn floor. The mess carefully strewn over it had already been cleared away. The trapdoor installed by George had been replaced, no doubt from below. So the man they were going to meet must already be down there?

He was. A short sandy-haired man, in his shirt-sleeves for some reason, scratching his left forearm thoughtfully. Probably he had given himself a slight graze on some protrusion, on his way down.

At any rate he'd got there discreetly enough, just as he and his mates must have done, four or five years ago. He'd even lit George's Tilley lamp.

'Ah Major, so you've come here safe,' the sandy-haired man courteously observed. Then, while Bobby Grey smiled at him in silence, with the mildly scornful patronage of the superior who expects a whole flood of patter to follow, the Irishman too became silent.

Quite amiably so, but he seemed to have regained the initiative. The pause that followed was decidedly awkward. 'So it's not here?' said Bobby Grey eventually, conceding victory in the game of silence.

'It is not,' said the other. His own smile was almost shy, but he seemed, at least to George, to have complete mastery of the situation. 'You shall have it if the price is right,' he added, as if reassuringly.

Bobby Grey found himself sweating slightly. Must be the Tilley lamp. The place was humid too. His eye fell on George and Martha's matrimonial bed, spread neatly in a corner and covered with a patched but clean old quilt.

George was trying not to think about Martha, and the fact that they had only slept in that bed once. Why did people say 'slept together' when they meant make love? True, he and Martha had actually slept there, at least for a short happy time. Must have

153

been the wine they'd had? Nice wine. Martha had brought it with those cold omelettes.

Full as he was of Martha's desertion and his own feelings about it, he had hardly bothered to ask himself, as they walked along, why Major Grey had wanted him here.

It was the silence of the Irishman, in contrast to those clipped comments of the Major, whose air of dominance George had always disliked so much, which made him begin in spite of himself to take an interest in what was going on. With a belated awareness of the tension in the man, it struck him now that Grey might actually have need of him, as an assistant, an underling of some kind.

Why? But then he remembered how this man Grey had spoken of his mother, and how she had been described by the young Irishman as his 'Santa Monica'. Could this be the same man?

He stared for the first time into the Irishman's face. Quite an ordinary face, with a perhaps unnaturally ruddy look about cheeks and nose, as if its owner were a drinking man. Dull blue eyes under the sandy hair. As if conscious that he was now the object of George's attention the Irishman quietly returned his gaze while at the same time taking out a small packet, as if he were going to roll himself a cigarette. What he did, however, was to take a pinch of something whitish between finger and thumb, and sniff at it delicately.

'You were looked after – nurtured I might almost say – by this young man's mother,' said Major Grey, as if mockingly. 'And yet you stand there and tell me I can have it if the price is right. Shame on you! She watched over you like a mother, did she not? But young George here has another mother now,' he went on, as if conversationally. 'Judging by your nose and your cheeks you have learnt how to hold a bottle: by the neck, don't you know? And this young man has made the discovery that a woman should be held by her waist. To begin with, at any rate.'

George found himself glancing at the Irishman, as if already aware that his own face must be screwed up with disgust at this vulgarity; and he was reassured to find that the other's face wore what could only be the same sort of expression. He felt a brotherly warmth for the Irishman, and thought again how attractive his own mother must have found the man, not all that long ago.

154

In the anger he felt for the Major, and repulsion, too, for his speech and whole manner, George found himself making a sort of growling noise in his throat. He stared at the Major, trying to convey what it was he felt about him. Then he turned again towards the Irishman, hoping to exchange another and even warmer glance of fellow-feeling.

But, to his annoyance, the Irishman ignored him. Smiling at the Major he seemed to be waiting for his next vulgar sally, with pleasurable anticipation.

The Major, it was clear, was trying to bait him, to make him lose his temper, like a toreador baiting a bull. There was something sinister in the way he remained quite unperturbed.

'So do the boy a favour then?'

The Major's tone was wheedling, almost falsetto.

George could not think what the man was about.

'Let him have it for free, don't you know? As a nice little present he'd be willing to share with his old friend.'

'Meaning you, Major?'

'Meaning me then. Why not?'

The Irishman laughed politely.

As if determined to tease his opponent into a frenzy, the Major leant forward, and made as if to tap him on the chest.

'We all know you lot want to get back to your shenanigans,' he said archly, as if putting the absurd word in inverted commas. 'No doubt the Thing will be a help with that? If you've got it,' he added, putting his head on one side.

The other man made no reply, other than a slight shrug of the shoulders and his usual smile.

An impasse had been reached; but the advantage seemed to lie with the Irishman.

The Major evidently saw that. As if abandoning the ploy of needling the other with his heavy humour he became serious, or at least affected seriousness.

'Now see here, O'Connor,' he began, with a parade-ground rasp. 'You know as well as I do what our arrangement was. Moscow let you boys have it, to put the fear of God into MI5. Moscow is in bed with us now, and if you don't play ball we can give you hell.'

155

There was a pause. 'Is that so then?' remarked the man called O'Connor, as if with mock solemnity.

He turned away and taking out his little packet had another sniff. Then he dipped his hand into the opposite pocket and brought it out holding a pistol.

'It's yourself I've been coming after,' he said.

George stared at the gun, knowing at once what it was. A Makarov 9mm, out of the little wooden box. He was conscious of an absurd and jealous indignation. How dared the man take one of his own guns from here – his own property? He was the more certain where the gun had come from because he himself had taken another and identical one from the same box. That had been on his last solitary visit to the cellar, before he had brought the Major down here. Oh why hadn't he hidden the box then, instead of leaving it out on the open floor!

But it was too late to bother about that. With a sick feeling he saw that it had been no use taking the gun, since he didn't have it with him now. Naturally he didn't. What would he have wanted it for, at Rosamond's Bower? He knew that if Martha had seen it she would have been upset – worried, too, on his behalf.

He had taken the gun almost as a gesture of defiance. Something to cheer himself up. He wanted some little secret to preserve, now that everything else had been blown and destroyed by the coming of Major Grey.

He had hidden it, carefully wrapped up, in a deep dry cavity he had once found in that old cedar-tree in the park.

Much good that did him now. Or the Major.

Perhaps the Irishman's gun wasn't loaded? He, George, had taken a packet of cartridges as well as one of the Makarovs: but was it possible that the Irishman had simply picked an unloaded gun out of the box, for purposes of display and intimidation? Or had he brought it with him? Did he always carry it, loaded and ready? A professional killer would do that. Was this man such a person? Had he come intending to kill the Major? Would he now kill them both?

It exasperated George to realise there was no way of knowing. The situation could be absurd, or it could be deadly dangerous; and from the Irishman's appearance and behaviour there was no way of finding out which. This helplessness made him feel furious rather than frightened, at least for the moment. He would love to have been able to pull out his own gun and confront the Irishman with it: to see whether that would disconcert him, and shake his calm air of knowing just what he was going to do. Of course it would be absurd; but it would be better than standing there, and wondering what would happen next.

Bobby Grey was as surprised as George to see the gun appear in the Irishman's hand, but it also amused him, even elated him. What show-offs these people were, when it came to the point! He despised O'Connor for not being able to think of anything better than this old trick. He also felt liberated: a curious, mellow sensation, as if he had just been drinking some exceptionally good malt whisky. Bobby Grey was accustomed to drink such whisky, but he had never got this kind of lift from it before.

'I fancy this is your way of saying you don't have the damned thing at all?' He tapped his head with a forefinger. Don't worry: I'm accustomed to dealing with people not quite all there, the gesture seemed to say. 'But, you know, it'll cost you if I don't get something back, something I can sell. Since I'm hoping to retire now, as soon as I can see my way.'

There was something so engagingly frank and open about the Major now, that George found himself feeling admiration; not only for the frankness but for a sort of heroism that seemed to be behind it. If he had lost, he was losing very stylishly.

The Irishman seemed to feel that too, for his own face had a look of something like admiration on it.

'Ah come now Major, you won't be retiring,' he said.

'You think not?'

'They'll not be wishing to be without you, for sure.'

Major Grey turned to George. 'Cut along now, old fellow,' he said, and his tone for the first time was warm and friendly. 'We shall have to speak of some tiresome things the public are not supposed to know about. No point in having to get you to sign the Official Secrets Act.'

To be called 'old fellow' by this man, and in such an affectionate tone of voice, gave George a sudden immense pleasure. It surprised him. He was sure too that he could be a help now. No winks from the Major, or anything of that sort, but he knew, he was sure, what he was required to do. And for once he acted quickly.

Ignoring the Irishman and not looking at his gun, he took two swift steps and with a sudden leap was on the mounting-block. That was successful enough, even elegant. But as he put his foot on the rickety ladder, up which he had twice helped Martha, the thing gave a sort of skid, twisting him round to face the way he'd come. Neither of them looked up at him. They were looking at each other: the Irishman non-committal as ever, the Major with an indulgent smile, as if decidedly bored but too courteous to show it. Behind him the gilt letters of FEAR GOD HONOUR THE KING winked from the wall.

Recovering himself, George clutched hold of the sides of the trapdoor. He felt supremely ridiculous. Was the Irishman looking up at him, perhaps surprised, or more likely with that same expression on his face, at once amiable and impenetrable? He managed to get his feet up on to the side support, and wriggled himself with a jerk up on to the floor of the barn. Terrified now that he might hear a shout or a sudden movement behind him, even the bang of the pistol, he stumbled helter-skelter over the tiles and broken glass, getting away from the place as fast as he could.

Had he run away like a coward, leaving the Major to face alone whatever was going to happen? Or was he going to be the hero, risking his own life to bring help, to effect a rescue?

But whichever he was, and probably he was neither, George knew what he had to do. As he ran down the road he was trying frantically to remember which of the big secluded houses of the neighbourhood was the nearest. That might make all the difference. The road curled round through the trees, full of its carefully preserved and cultivated potholes, and several hundred yards further on was the first house, itself at the end of a longish drive. He was out of breath and gasping when he at last reached the front door. He seized the wrought-iron bell-handle and pulled it violently.

He heard the bell's deep fluty tones somewhere far inside, as if pealing an unperturbed requiem.

The Major had looked good, standing there. George felt a surge of hero-worship, such as he used to feel, years before,

158

when reading about Hamilcar Barca or the Duke of Wellington. He was sure now, too, that the Major had set a trap for the Irishman, in which his own co-operation must in some way have been essential.

The plan had evidently misfired. But whatever happened he mustn't let the Major down now. He must instantly ring the police; and Martha's words – how long ago? – came into his head. 'Surely you ought to tell the police, darling.' He was going to do that now. As soon as he could get into this house, and on to the phone.

It struck him as he waited that the Major's air of total cynicism, making a pile out of the racket before retiring and so forth, must be a blind to confuse the Irishman. But perhaps the Irishman was deeper than he looked? Who, in that case, had been playing with whom? George felt sure – why? – that he could put his own money on the Major.

He rang the bell again as hard as he could. Was there no one at home? What was a woman of the house likely to be doing at this hour? There was a small window not far from the front door, thickly screened with the leaves and orange berries of a berberis. Must be the downstairs loo. No good knocking on the window. George none the less tried to peer through it, and got a shock when a face peered back at him, under a head of grey ironwaved hair.

With his mouth and hands George made desperate sounds and gestures of crisis. The eyes under the plucked and darkened eyebrows remained intensely suspicious. Of course – she must have dodged into the loo in order to see who was at the door.

His clothes must be covered in cellar dust; his hair in all directions. While he stepped back, and tried to look gentlemanly in spite of these things, the face vanished. There was the rattle of a chain at the front door, and then it opened a couple of inches.

'What on earth do you want?' demanded a brittle standard-English voice.

In his excitement George could hardly think what it was he wanted, or how to say it. But that did not matter. Even as the words began to come, something else happened. To the unknown lady it probably meant nothing, but her watchful look slightly changed its direction, none the less.

It was a detonation, a sharp rumble of sound: loud enough

159

and yet more or less of the sort which could occur any place and time nowadays, without anyone taking any special notice. There were lots of noises around. None the less the unknown lady paid some attention, and George paid a great deal. Because he at once knew what it was, what it could only be.

So suddenly did he know it that he also knew now there was no point in bothering this lady at all. Better not to. Much better not to. He began to back away from her, making explanatory expressions with his mouth and eyes. There was only one thing to do, and he was going to do it. Get right away. And never go back. Well of course never go back. His lair – all his lairs – were a horror. The only refuge now was out in the open. No more lairs. And no more Martha.

Muttering something and then waving a hand, he hurried back along the driveway, as fast as he could without actually running. It occurred to him, too late, that the lady of the house might remember him, and his behaviour, if the police came to make an enquiry.

Had they both been killed? Or one of them? Or neither? The Semtex, or some of it, must have gone up: he could be sure of that. But of nothing else. Nor did he ever want to be sure. Again he saw the Major's face as it had been at the end, with that look at once foxy and transfigured.

What should he have done? Should he have stayed or gone? And going as he had done, how could he have got help sooner? The little gun he had hidden in the cedar tree ... If only it had been in his pocket. Again he began to run.

He could have done nothing effective – he knew that. He did not live in the same world as those two, or as anyone else for that matter. Only, once, in a same world. With Martha.

Again he saw the Major's face, and hers. But they were soon a blur from the tears he was shedding as he ran along.

*

Ginnie went back to London. She had always lived in, or at least with, books. They were her job, even her lifestyle as people used to say; and she wanted blindly now to get back into the world they had once offered her.

160

She was not hopeful about it, and when she thought of Pinky, and her odd ways, she started to cry. But Peter and Pinky came to see her the day after she got back; and she did not cry then, but embraced Pinky, who soon wriggled civilly out of her clutches; and then she asked Peter how he was, and what he was going to do.

His replies were much as she expected. Peter said he would always be there, with her and for her, and so would Pinky. And Vera? Yes, well, Vera would be there too. She would love to meet Ginnie; but of course she respected Ginnie's wish not to meet her.

And still Ginnie said nothing about her own state. Not a word. She felt quite proud of her ability to withhold all that from her husband, this smooth polite man who came to see her, but would not be living with her; and with whom her daughter behaved more as if she herself were a wife than Ginnie could be; or had, she now felt, ever been. Pinky continued to see nothing in the least odd about her present situation: she was clearly enjoying every moment of it; and that was a relief.

Ginnie felt as if she were a close but unregarded relative, awarded an occasional family holiday in some seaside resort, perhaps to a place like Sorrento, where she had once had that holiday on her own. On the second morning of an endless fortnight it would rain, and she would be sitting in the afternoon in her hotel room, wearing the obligatory gaudy garments of a holidaymaker, and wondering how on earth she was to get through all the time that remained.

However, that nightmare premonition of the rest of her days was destined to be cut short. She had not revealed her supposed pregnancy to Peter; and her own sombre satisfaction in that secrecy blinded her to the fact that he might himself have something new to tell her. In fact he had; but he too had remained silent.

The news he might have told her, but did not, was that she would not be seeing him again, nor Pinky either, for some time to come, if ever.

Since it had to be a last meeting it would be very much better for all concerned, so her husband had decided, not to mention this fact.

161

It had all come about very suddenly. Peter had been sleeping luxuriously late at the hotel that morning when Vera, who had been on the telephone, had woken him up.

'We have got to go, my Peter,' she had said to him. 'It seems your brother is dead. Something very bad has taken place. All of them will be after us.'

He took it in at once. If Bobby had got himself killed – and how the hell had he managed it? – the operation was blown. To the members of any post-mortem enquiry it would soon be known what he and Vera had been after, and they would be picked up for questioning. Or worse. No doubt about that. Whoever Bobby had been working with must know already? And had tipped off Vera.

All that was plain enough. But as he prepared in haste to get up Peter saw the child's head at the foot of the bed, between two ranges of adult feet.

'Vera, we can't go,' he cried. 'I can't leave Pinky!'

'Then she will have to come with us,' said his wife calmly.

*

Down at Prentice Wood Alexander had been meditating how best to resume the siege of young George Pusey.

The young man's standoffishness both intrigued and provoked him. He had determined to enlist him more directly in the conservatory building project; and for that purpose to suggest that George came to live at the house, when the operation got started.

Alexander had had another stroke of luck. It looked as if the post of a new manager for the firm's building programme near Bristol would be in his gift. Mr Pusey might well be the right man for the job. How could the son then continue to resist his father's benefactor?

He mentioned casually to Martha the real possibility of George coming into residence with them. He felt some curiosity to see whether his wife would jump at the idea, or whether she would be alarmed at the thought of her lover in the house, even horrified by it; and by, as it were, the proximity of sin. He had not lived with her for more than thirty years without realising

162

how innately respectable she was, a respectability partly engrained by the neighbourhood, partly by the timidity of her own temperament. He had been all the more amazed in consequence by what Bobby had told him; and of course by Martha's own unchanged demeanour. Unchanged, that was, except for her impressive display of family hospitality over Christmas.

Martha took the suggestion soberly. She seemed a little distrait these days, which was natural enough if her lover was in any sense in two minds about her, as he might well be. How astonishing it was, none the less! Martha, of all people, of all the people in the world …! And with a chap almost young enough to be her grandson! No, let him not exaggerate: her youngest son, let him say. Born a good while after Ben and Penelope. So perhaps more natural than you might at first suppose?

Natural? Well what about his own feelings for young George? They were familiar, and delightful, and he didn't care in the slightest whether they were natural or unnatural. Had to be careful of course, even these days. No good doing a Stringham. Poor old Dick. He recalled that Martha never liked Dick Stringham. The conventionality of women: and yet Earlwood, even today, certainly did remain, as it were, a spontaneously conventional society. Unpermissive. Took very little notice of what had become the spirit of the age elsewhere.

To get his desk clear Alexander decided to go up to town for a day, possibly two. After that he could devote himself for a week or so to wooing George, or at least getting him domesticated at Prentice Wood. He noted his wife's elation at the news that her husband would be going to London. Had noted it with pleasure on her behalf. If she invited George round while he was away, and there seemed every likelihood that she would do just that, she could only be helping on her husband's schemes, doing him an involuntary service.

Alexander's prediction was correct. Martha, as we have seen, did write to George, not to ask him to her home but to the Rosamond meeting; and Ginnie's arrival fatally messed that up. After Ginnie had gone, accompanied by twinges of unspoken guilt on her sister-in-law's part, Martha opened the vodka bottle. She had three or four before Alexander got home. He noticed this on his return; but he had a bit of news, picked up at the station, which was more interesting. There had been an explosion of some kind in their midst, at the derelict Manor Farm house. Only a neglected gas-main probably, but it seemed there had been a lot of damage. The police were there, and they had cordoned the area off. The old place was clearly unsafe at the moment.

Though she was still blurry with doom and drink, Martha received the news with agitation. She prayed it had not been caused by George, in the dangerous hideout to which he had introduced her. Not for the first time she felt glumly aware of the gap between their ages and generations. George belonged, though not necessarily wishing to do so, to an era which caused and accepted and lived among violent episodes, as they lived among new expectations, new music, new drugs.

Her life could hardly move along with his, nor could he stay in hers indefinitely. Love him as she did, she had at this moment to admit that: more clearly than she had ever done before.

Where was he now? She somehow felt sure, although it gave her no relief to do so, that he had not, after all, waited for her that day in Rosamond. Why should he have done so? Because she had not been able to get there herself, she felt that the same indifference or paralysis must have worked with him too. Why otherwise had he been sitting like that with her brother-in-law, in the Bayleaf restaurant? But although she now felt sure he could not, for whatever reason, have gone to their bower, it did not in any way comfort her, or atone for her own non-arrival.

Of course when she had at last got rid of Ginnie she had not rushed round to George's father's house, as she had first planned. She had felt too hopeless and desolated, too paralysed as well, to do so. She had come home to the vodka bottle instead.

Seeing George in the Bayleaf convinced her, as she continued to brood over it, that she had literally lost him in some way to Bobby Grey, that diabolical brother-in-law. What might not Bobby have told George about her? What could he not have invented or made up? What irreparably cunning mischief had he done?

The pair of them together in the restaurant had certainly looked like conspirators. Almost as if they had been buddies (a term common in Martha's childhood.) She was sure that Bobby had not only done this because he had somehow found out

164

about her and George, but that he must have told her husband too. It would explain so much about Alexander's odd behaviour; not least his own sudden interest in George, and the way he had made up to him, for instance, at the Boxing Day party. It could only be the same interest that Alexander had, or once had, in Nigel and Fiona.

George was once her own secret darling, and now he had become everybody's open favourite. They had turned him around – wasn't that what was said in spy circles? They had spied on both of them. And they had seduced George. Taken him away from her.

Martha was not feeling yet what it meant to have lost him, though she was sure she had. In her numbed state she came near to feeling it two days later. As she was shopping in the High Street she saw her lover in conversation with the waitress from the Bayleaf. He looked a different young man from the one she knew; and she had surely better think that this was just as it should be. She didn't get very close to managing to think it, but she would just have to go on trying.

Her own home she felt she could not continue to live in for the moment. She must learn to face the way things were; and in privacy – the privacy that had always suited her. She realised that now with a sudden surge of hope. And yet she was in terror, too, that George might appear again, and, ignoring her, confabulate with Alexander. If that must happen, it should happen only when she was well away.

But not too far away. After some thought she booked a room at a small hotel about seven miles off. No one knew of her in that locality, and she could get there by bus or taxi. She had a particular reason for it too, although a melancholy one.

She told Alexander that Ginnie needed her for a few days. The poor woman was in a bad way – something about Peter – Martha was not specific. Alexander, she saw, would rather welcome her absence. It would simplify whatever plans he had laid, and improve his chances with George. For the moment Martha didn't care about that. She wanted only to get away.

Alexander missed Bobby, and wondered where he could have gone off to so suddenly. But he was too engrossed with his plans for the Pusey family to concern himself with what had

165

once seemed Bobby's exciting and mysterious doings. Bobby was a here-today-gone-tomorrow sort of chap; and he always had known how to look after himself. No one, of course, had connected his disappearance with the gas main explosion, if that was what it had been, at the old farm. The police, and men supposed to be gas board experts, men in white coats, were still poking about in there. The place remained cordoned off. But press and radio had barely reported the incident.

They were entertaining their public with the saga of a thirteen-year old who had run away from home and managed to smuggle himself on to a series of long distance flights, ending up somewhere in Malaysia. What a lot of trouble he was causing. But TV, radio, and papers were finally able to reassure their public that he had just been found, safe and well.

*

Caroline of the Bayleaf had been delighted to encounter George again, on her way back to the restaurant for the evening dinner session. George looked haggard and unkempt, but it suited him. She asked if anything was the matter, and he told her no, but in a haunted way that intrigued her. She would like to find out more, and get to know him better, so she suggested he should come back with her to the Bayleaf and have something to eat. The evening at this time of the week was usually quiet. No one was there when they arrived except Alfred, comfortably addressing himself to the saucepans simmering on his stove.

Caroline Shuldham was an impulsive girl with a chequered career already behind her, and a good capacity for enjoying herself. She had been a university student and got in a few scrapes: one of them, coincidentally, with Peter Grey, who at that time had been caretaking with his Russian wife at a house near Oxford. The pair had been engaged in various clandestine activities, and Caroline had found herself involved in them. But she had no idea that the middle-aged man who had come in with George for lunch, and whom she had rather fancied, was Peter Grey's brother; or that the eldest Grey lived in a large house at Earlwood, not so far away.

After a pleasant and quite prolonged affair with a young

university teacher, Caroline, a motherless girl, had gone home to her father's place, determined to marry and settle down. The man of her choice had been a local landowner and widower, a solid man as she believed, and indeed there would seem to have been good grounds for the impression she had of him. Her father, who disliked the man, did his best to dissuade her, but she paid no heed.

After the marriage she soon found that her father had been right; and although he was not the kind of parent to say 'I told you so', a coolness developed. But Caroline soon gave up being loyal to her spouse, who in the privacy of the home, and even outside it, was not a nice man. She found he had many involvements with women, also with men (he knew Alexander Grey's Nigel, oddly enough, and Fiona); and, which was worse, it pleased him to taunt his young wife with the manner and variety of his knowledge.

All this Caroline, who had it in her to be the most easygoing of wives, might well have tolerated if she had been able to establish a comfortably intimate relation with her husband. But this he tacitly yet wholly effectively disallowed. So then she would have children: but first came two miscarriages, and before she could achieve a third pregnancy things really bust up. She could, she felt, take no more.

About the time of the divorce her father died. It never rains but it pours. She remembered the silly old proverb as the rain came down in the village churchyard. She was miserable in every way: she had been much attached to her father, and she bitterly regretted now the coolness that had arisen between them over her marriage.

The rain had come down indeed; and not only on the day of the funeral. After he died it turned out that her father had made some very unwise investments. That was not her fault, but she herself had been very unwise too. Out of indolence and lack of proper care she had allowed her husband to control the money her father had settled on her at the time of her marriage. It proved impossible to get it back out of him. The divorce settlement too had been highly unsatisfactory.

But Caroline had come to feel a sort of pride in herself, as well as a complete contempt for her husband, which made her acquiesce in these losses.

What should she do? She did various things and had a lover or two. Unsatisfactory. She began to think she must be a basically unsatisfactory sort of girl.

Then she met Alfred. Naturally enough it was at a restaurant, a fashionable little place near Drayton Gardens, where he was the number two chef. They got on at once. He was supremely restful. Queer of course, but that was no problem. In his own way he fell for her, which made her feel maternal, and she was tired of sex. Alfred loved to rest his round head against her bosom, while she stroked his hair. He had a connection in the Earlwood locality; she had put in her remaining money, and they started the Bayleaf. If all went well, and as Alfred's skills matured, they might try something more ambitious later, up in London.

The lunch-time encounter with Bobby Grey and with George had greatly invigorated Caroline. She was delighted to meet George again that same evening; and, being the sort of masterfully but inoffensively upperclass girl that she was, she put George in the kitchen, to help Alfred and herself deal with the few dinner-time customers. After that they had a meal together. Caroline assured George that he was too tired to go home that night, and directed him to ring his father and then to make use of the spare bed at her flat. George was not to know that by a fortunate coincidence Alfred had just moved out of the flat to join a friend, on an experimental basis.

In any case George was too tired and frightened to do anything but yield with a thankful passivity to Caroline's directions. She took him back to the flat, and he did not sleep in the spare bed. It was a day or two later that Martha saw them in the street together. They were obviously getting on very well.

Naturally George was in a state of terror about what had taken place at Manor Farm. Just what had taken place? There was no way to find out. He dared not go anywhere near the area. He dared not do anything, for fear his involvement in whatever had happened should somehow be traced. In his heart he knew, or thought he knew, that the Major was dead, but what about the other man, the Irishman? Where was he now? What more might he do?

Three days after the incident two men, plainclothes policemen no doubt, came to talk to his father. They did not reveal what had happened at Manor Farm – perhaps they didn't know themselves – and all they seemed concerned about was how long Mr Pusey had owned the place. They did, however, ask him not to talk about the matter: quite a sacrifice for George's father to have to make when he and his son paid their nightly visit to the Antelope. But he remained manfully noncommittal when friends asked him what had been going on.

Alexander Grey's offer of the job was a wonderful distraction from all this, and he discussed the possibilities endlessly with George. He seemed to have regained all his old fire and enthusiasm for work; and his gratitude to Alexander was effusive. He was round at Prentice Wood every day with George, and tireless in his advice about the specifications for the new conservatory.

George went there numbly with his father; and submitted numbly to Alexander's blandishments. He was only grateful that the authorities had shown no interest in him, or asked him questions. Alexander he dealt with as best he could: Martha, it appeared, was away. That was a relief, though a relief he could hardly bear to think about. Alexander again suggested that he should come and stay. With despair in his heart he said that would be fine.

Caroline, as it happened, made him the same offer. He felt like a criminal who has to choose between two new identities, two cover stories. George was certainly attracted to Caroline, and she soothed him. To be in bed with her helped him to forget the nightmare of the cellar, and the faithlessness of Martha. He forced himself to think of Martha in that light, for his own sake, though something in him knew it couldn't be true.

There was irony in the fact that he might now move into Martha's house, and behave as if he were a natural inhabitant. He shrank from the idea. Out of the question – repulsive – even if he and Martha had still been lovers. Why? Well, it was. But guilt, fear, and concealment had given George more than his natural cunning, which itself had really been no more than a version of his innocence.

169

He waited until his father, rubbing his hands with satisfaction, told him that the deal was all stitched up, and that he'd have to be going down to Bristol in a day or two. There were so many other things too: possible sale of the house, the Manor Farm insurance – all that would take some time, and proceeds would in any case go to the creditors.

What would George himself wish to do? For the moment, of course, he must take Mr Grey's handsome offer to stay and do all he could while he was there for the Prentice Wood family. Such nice people! What a boon it had been meeting them – a real boon! And Mr Grey so fond of George! No doubt Mrs Grey would be too. They mustn't lose touch now ….

As soon as he had seen his father off to Bristol George rang Prentice Wood. He knew Martha wouldn't be there. Alexander had already said she would be away several days, and had given him a commiserating look, implying in a kindly way that he knew George would miss her presence about the house. 'We'll just have to rough it here together' was what he had said.

George hated the phone, but he shrank still more from having to talk to the man face to face. Putting a lot of upsetness and agitation into his voice he explained, when Alexander answered the phone, that the offer of a lifetime had quite unexpectedly turned up, and he really couldn't refuse it. He had always really wanted to be a chef; and now the couple at the Bayleaf had offered to take him on as a sort of apprentice – teach him all the ins and outs. They were so kind. He'd love to do it. Of course the hours there would be long, but he'd try his best to get round to Prentice Wood whenever he could manage it. The evening work was so late, especially at weekends, that Alfred the chef had offered him the use of a room in his flat.

He was so sorry to let Mr Grey down.

Alexander, to do him justice, took it rather well. Of course, of course … if George's future career was in question, that was all that mattered. But how sorry Martha would be! And he himself, naturally. They had quite set their hearts in having a young person about the house again.

Alexander was not deceived. He would hardly have given the young fellow credit for such ingenuity. Well, it was a challenge. If young George wanted to make a fight of it, he would do his best to oblige him. He would use Martha as bait, and as black-mail if need be. No doubt George thought he could ditch Martha. But there were ways of applying pressure there, unless Alexander was very much mistaken.

No sooner had George rung off than he was on his way down to the Bayleaf. He would become a different person. He would be able to forget all about the cellar, and its contents, and what had happened to it. He would be able to forget all about Major Grey. The thought of Caroline, and her kindness to him, was delightful. It was quite a different George, of course, that she had taken a fancy to; not the old George at all. But he was determined it would be his real self from now on.

He had a shock, though, as he entered the High Street. A short man with fairish hair, and not wearing a coat or hat, though it was a cold day, was just turning down towards the station. George stopped. The man's back was turned, but something reminded him suddenly of the Irishman. As if conscious of George's scrutiny the man had gone behind a parked car.

George crossed the street and went on. And then, on the other side, he saw Martha, coming slowly out of a shop. She didn't seem to see him. She was supposed to be in London, with her sister-in-law. So her husband had said.

Gazing into the shops on his own side George hurried on as fast as he could. The Bayleaf, and its personnel, seemed now to be his only refuge.

*

Martha's one idea was to keep an eye on George.

She was not jealous of Caroline – rather the reverse. She felt she only wanted George to be happy, and that was certainly true. The only thing wrong about it was that she continued to feel, deep down, that George was only likely to be happy with her. And there was a bottom of good sense in Martha's emotions, where her lover was concerned.

She visited the High Street every day. It made no difference if she met anyone she knew; she was just carrying on with normal life. Her husband never came there. Nor did she propose to try not to be seen by George himself. She wouldn't mind if he thought she was still pursuing him. All she wanted was to know that he was all right. And she was not deceiving herself. She knew at least that their love affair – that first happiness together as she preferred to think of it – was at an end. But she very much needed to need him – to stay in touch with him somehow. Even if he no longer needed her.

Of course she could have written him a letter, quite a practical one. She knew that the guns he had found in the cellar at Manor Farm must have been involved in the thing that had happened there; even though no one seemed to know just what it was. The place was still guarded and cordoned off. She knew the authorities must have the guns now; and she prayed that there was no way in which they could connect them with George. She prayed that George would not somehow give himself away.

Mercifully, no one with whom she herself had been in contact – her husband, Mrs Jones, one or two of the neighbours – seemed much interested. That sort of thing, wherever it took place, was hardly news any more, although of course Mrs Jones went on about it in her usual style, as evidence of the way things were going, or else what they were coming to. For with the authorities still very much in possession of the place it was beginning to be rumoured that something must have been going on; some kind of terrorist activity, even in Earlwood, of the kind that everyone read about in the papers.

She wanted to write, she longed to write, if only to warn George: to tell him not to lose his nerve or give himself away; to assure him that she too knew nothing, and would say nothing; and that they still had between them their own safe secret. Their love secret.

But Martha had her pride. She was not going to remind him of anything to do with her, or him and her. She had always been a poor letter-writer. The only letters she had written to him had been to express her love, and nothing else. Except where they would meet, and when.

So she would not write. But even though she had her pride, she would find nothing difficult about approaching George in the street, were she to see him on his own. Just to tell him to be as silent and as careful as he possibly could be. Of course she would not go near him if he were with the Bayleaf girl. She hated

172

the thought of spying on them; but she did long to know where George was from day to day, and if he were safe and well.

There was another reason why she wanted to warn him. Something wholly unspecific, and yet it could not help worrying her. She had noticed once or twice, during what she hoped were her ordinary comings and goings down the High Street, a little man loitering on a corner with his hands in his pockets. She had noticed him because he was not the sort of man usually seen in the locality. Martha got it into her head that he might have had something to do with what had happened at Manor Farm. Perhaps he was a government agent (Martha had heard of MI5 and 6, and Scotland Yard of course, but had little idea of the difference). Could they be keeping George under observation, suspecting he might know something of what might have gone on at Manor Farm? After all, his father did own the place, little as he had ever done about it; or would do, now.

After helping at the restaurant – he had become shopper, washer-up and occasional waiter – George had gone home to show the house, where he and his father and family had lived almost since he was born, to a prospective buyer. Then he would come back for the night to Caroline's flat. Martha caught sight of him as he hurried down the High Street. She hastened across and addressed him at once in a voice that seemed to him so unexpectedly firm as to be almost threatening.

'Do take care, George. You know about the explosion there seems to have been at Manor Farm? Don't say a word about it now, will you? I just hope they don't find out what you were doing down there.'

Feeling himself for the first time since they met a really quite different person – a person who had nothing to do with her – George murmured some sort of agreement. No difficulty there. Martha, too, found herself astonished by the ease with which she could speak to him in this new way, and in public. She felt herself to be quite different as well; and there was even a horrid relief that their old loving lairs and fantasies, their holes and corners, could be reduced to this brisk piece of advice. Meeting him like this, no doubt on his way home to the girl to whom he was very properly now attached, had acted like a cure. Perhaps she had half-consciously hoped it might, and that was really why she had spoken to him?

The love-liquid might have dried up in her, but it had left her feeling quite uncharacteristically powerful and impersonal, with what seemed a strong but rational solicitude for this young man who had once been her lover, and would always be her dearest.

Speaking to George like that had made her forget all about the man she had seen loitering on the corner.

*

When George let himself into the flat with the keys Caroline had given him, it was to see her lying face down on the floor.

He stared at her stupidly for a moment. What was she doing there? The room was nearly in darkness; a weak little lamp in the corner the only one switched on. But there was light from the doorway into the bedroom, and a man came through it towards him. It was the Irishman, whom Major Grey had called O'Connor.

Oddly enough George was not wholly unprepared for this moment.

Two days after what had happened in the cellar he had gone back to the old cedar tree in the park and retrieved the Makarov 9mm. Unhappy as he was, it had cheered him to explore the weapon. The action was not too unlike the big Kalashnikov, with which he had grown familiar in the cellar. He even ventured to fire the gun off once or twice in a secluded grove of the park, aiming it at the trunk of a silver birch, whose parchment skin showed the impact of the bullet.

Although the area was not real country, there were enough occasional reports from local shotguns to make the noise of the pistol unremarkable.

Here was Caroline, apparently dead, and here was the Irishman coming towards him with a concerned expression on his blunt reddish face, as if just about to explain how she came to be lying there. His face was hateful to George, who took a step or two backwards. He had no idea what to do, and paralysed by excitement and hatred as he was – this man had killed the Major,

174

he was sure, and now Caroline – he had even forgotten the pistol in his pocket.

But he remembered it as quickly as the Irishman raised a hand, perhaps in threat, perhaps as a token of peace, and as a preliminary to explanation.

When George pulled out the pistol the other dropped his hand, and his face took on a mean professional look.

George knew that in one second he would be suddenly and brutally disarmed: his wrist broken or his leg smashed by a rapid and expert kick. The Irishman pivoted forward on his right foot and his left went back.

George cocked the action of the Makarov – the safety was already off – and the sharp sound seemed to freeze his opponent for a moment. He hesitated, then, changing his tactics, shot out a hand towards the gun and gripped it near the end of its short barrel. He jerked it upward, and simultaneously the gun fired twice. Another split second and the shots would have gone into the ceiling, making the same dark holes which a few days before they had made in the white skin of the birch tree. The noise was deafening in the little room. In the woods it had been the merest pop, sounding quite harmless.

It seemed as if it was the racket itself that flung the Irishman over and backwards. He vanished as if a giant had casually smacked him.

*

Ginnie stood by her work-table, reading a letter. It was from her brother-in-law Bobby Grey, and it enclosed a cutting from *The Times*.

My dear Virginia,
You must be the only literary member of our family. This is the kind of obituary I should like to have had. Do you know anyone on the *Times* newspaper? I ask, because I am very keen that I should not have any obituary at all. Not one for myself you understand. Could you please let them know this, whoever the fellows are who run these things? I ask because I have no idea what the procedures are, or whether they put the things in without having asked the deceased's permission.

175

And so I repeat that I do not want any obituary.
                              Yours
                         Robert Grey.

Stupefied as she was with her own problems, Ginnie had no idea
what all this could be about. Her eye ran mechanically over the
cutting. A Polish flying officer, much decorated, whose gentle
impudent face smiled shyly over his shoulder from inside a
cockpit. Loved in the mess, and always known as Droby. Married, in 1943, Mary, daughter of Major Sibley R.E., who survives
him. They had a daughter and two sons.

What was she supposed to make of that? And what was she
supposed to make of her brother-in-law's letter? She knew nothing about how obituaries were written, or about whom, or why.
Why should she? And why should Bobby Grey be so anxious not
to have one? What was the point of the thing anyway, or rather,
if there was a point, what had he got against it? Why had he sent
her this one about the Polish airman?

There was something slightly dotty, even a bit mad, about the
letter. She shrugged her shoulders wearily. Were all the Grey
brothers, the family she had married into, quite insane?

And then a sudden thought struck her. The letter was from a
man who expected he might be killed. Why ever should he
suppose that? But she knew vaguely that he was, as Peter had
been, in the secret service, or whatever it was called now. Why
hadn't she thought of that before?

But now that she had, her own troubles seemed abruptly
diminished. The eminently dislikable Bobby, as she knew him to
be, even though Martha might have been too loyal to say so,
could be seen in a different light, almost a heroic one? She
remembered with a pang the first time she had seen and talked
to him, by the edge of the golf course at Littlestone, with the larks
singing high up in the pale-blue expanse of seaside sky. That was
before she had met Peter.

The postmark on the letter was three weeks old. It had been
addressed incorrectly, and sent from somewhere quite close to
Prentice Wood.

Reading the odd communication a second time, and looking
at the distant smiling photo of the Polish flying officer known as

176

Droby, Ginnie felt humble. She warmed in her thoughts not only to the exasperatingly enigmatic Bobby, who had sent her this impossible letter, but to his brother Peter, who was after all, or had been, her own husband. In his own peculiar way Bobby seemed to be appealing to her. She was touched by that, although his request was so outlandish that she could have done nothing about it, even if she had possessed the will, and the means.

But why hadn't she appealed herself to her own husband, even though all she could say and tell him would be equally impossible, equally incapable of solution? Martha had proved a broken reed, though she knew how unfair it was to think so; whereas her own husband had never failed her yet.

She would tell him now, over the phone, what was the matter with her. She would ask him to tell Vera: she would even ask him – why should she mind now? – to seek Vera's advice. It might be well worth having. She would appeal to them to make much of her – to love and to cherish her. She suddenly longed only to belong among them all again – Peter, Ginnie, Vera, Pinky! Even the little stranger, the newcomer!

While this impulse lasted she made quickly for the phone, and then paused a moment. Bobby wanted no obituary. A single bell seemed to be tolling, unhurriedly. She must not only tell Peter about herself; she must get news of his brother.

She grabbed the phone, which had become the normal mode of communication with her husband, or ex-husband. She dialled and asked for Captain Grey, correcting this at once to Mr Grey, suite 32. He had always been Captain Grey for her in the old days. Afterwards it had become a fond occasional pet name, to tease him.

The telephone gave out slow elegant burrs, in keeping with the smartness of the hotel. No reply. After a tense minute she got herself back to the reception desk.

'Is Mr Grey in the hotel, do you know? Has he gone out?'

'Just a moment, Madam.'

A burr and a crackle and a murmur of voices. The seconds went by. Then another voice, female this time.

'Yes, Madam. Can I help you?'

Ginnie started her inquiry over again.

177

'Just a moment, please.'

She should have asked for Vera, for Mrs Grey. Something must have stopped her, but it should stop her no longer. She would tell all to Vera, if Peter was not there.

'Mr Grey has had the account. It was paid this morning.'

'But isn't he still there?'

The voice was patient, but a little knowing now. Ginnie was a possible girlfriend, enquiring for a husband who had been borne off by his wife and family.

'No, Madam. We understand they left early this morning. The gentleman and his wife and the little girl.'

'Did they leave a message, please? Or an address?'

Another pause.

'No, Madam. Nothing at all.'

CHAPTER 11

Lost and Found

Nobody seemed to know quite what to do about George.

The police had arrested him. He had been before a magistrate. Martha, Alexander, and his father, all with their various anxieties on his behalf, did their best. But bail was not granted.

The principal difficulty, at least at first, had been to find out what had actually taken place. Not that George was silent, or withheld information – quite the contrary. To everyone who questioned him he gave the same laboriously truthful and detailed account of everything that had happened to him: from the moment he had stumbled on the weapon horde in the cellar to the arrival of the police and ambulance at Caroline's flat, summoned by George himself. He spoke carefully and accurately of Bobby Grey and the Irishman: what they had said to him, how they had behaved. The only person he did not mention was Martha.

Caroline was not dead after all; and neither, it appeared, was the Irishman. George must have pulled the trigger when his opponent seized hold of the gun. One shot had just missed the top of the Irishman's head, and the other must have ploughed through his scalp, knocking him over and inflicting a nasty flesh wound. So at least the ballistics expert conjectured, from the position of the bullet holes, and from the account given by George. There were also bloodstains on the carpet and the stairs, and round the front door.

George stated that he had been kneeling by the Irishman, thinking him to be dead, when he was pushed violently to one side. He saw the man stagger out of the door. And at almost the same moment Caroline had groaned and sat up, looking dazed.

When she was able to talk to the police, in hospital, she told them she had opened the door, expecting her boyfriend. The man who stepped in had seemed surprised to see her, but he enquired, with ominous civility, if he could have a word with George. He appeared a dangerous intruder; and Caroline, her natural pugnacity instantly aroused, had attempted first to scream and then to fight. In consequence she had been half throttled, as well as knocked out. Her face and neck were black with bruises.

That was all plain sailing; and yet things looked black for George too. He had unlawfully possessed an offensive weapon, a loaded pistol, and inflicted grievous bodily harm upon some person unknown. How could the police even be sure that this other person had not been trying to protect Caroline, when George had attacked her, in a fit of jealous rage? Before the police and ambulance arrived there had been plenty of time for the couple to concoct their story, if they had been so minded, and if Caroline had wished to exonerate her lover, for she had been perfectly frank in letting the police know that George was living with her. His own story, of Major Grey and the Irishman, might well have been made up.

True, there was no sign of a third party, except for the blood-stains. He had vanished, he might even be dead. And although this Major Grey undoubtedly existed, and was known to persons in the locality, he seemed to have vanished too.

But though the police, in their methodical way, went on with the business of tracing the wounded man and preparing possible charges against George, he was soon being quietly taken out of their hands. Other persons, in other departments, were anxious – in some cases very anxious indeed – to talk to George: to find out what he knew, and to prevent him knowing anything else, or talking too much to other people, people from whom they had every reason to conceal what they themselves had been up to.

Persons high up, who were not involved, were none the less not keen, for a variety of reasons, to find out just what had really happened. Lower down were those actually involved in the *konspiratsia*, including the ones who had supposedly tipped off Vera and Peter. They may well have felt a little uneasy, and one of them passed a bad quarter of an hour in the office of a senior official from another department.

The press got some nice pictures of Caroline, looking very heroic in hospital. A pretty girl who had tried to fight off a burglar was always good for news, and the media faded George out. Annoyed that he had been taken out of their hands by the security people, the police were also disposed to write off George.

All this took time; but when this and various other matters had been attended to, or dropped, he was at length released from custody.

Martha had written to George during this time. Since they could not be love-letters they caused her a great deal of trouble to write. She tried to be affectionate and supportive, and that was all. When this awful business was over, she and her husband would of course wish to give him all the help they could. She was aware of some irony in her full acceptance now of the pretence, once dreaded by both the lovers, that George was more than just a family friend, almost a young protégé.

She included Alexander's sympathy and good wishes, at the end of the letters. Alexander too wrote to George, giving him reassurance about costs and legal matters, and sketching out ideas for the future. He would soon be back among them, and then they must embark together on the conservatory, and other projects. Husband and wife said nothing in these letters about George's attachment to Caroline, and his employment at the Bayleaf.

Nor did George's father. He wrote fondly but distractedly from the West Country, and his letter was more full of his own good fortune than his son's mishap, although it included best wishes and sympathy from the other people in his new life. Mr Pusey explained his son's difficulty in some detail at the local pub; and there was great indignation that a young man who had fought off a burglar in defence of his girlfriend should now be suffering for it. He told the same tale to a hospitable farming family he had come to know. One of their number was a widowed daughter, in whom he was soon taking a great deal of interest.

When Caroline had recovered a bit and was back from the

hospital she too wrote to George. She did not mention that she had returned to the restaurant to find herself a local heroine. Even Alfred basked in her reflected glory. The Bayleaf was booming.

The story here was rather different from the one Mr Pusey had told his friends. Back home it was Caroline who had played the courageous role in resisting the burglar, and banging him on the head: while George had somehow made a mess of things, getting himself locked up in consequence; and fair enough no doubt. Caroline had saved the day, and, incidentally served a warning on all cowardly thugs who might be around. They would think twice now before invading local homes.

This version of events, however inaccurate, showed a certain sense of natural justice. Caroline was indeed the kind of person to take charge, the stuff from which a heroine might be made. George was not. Not the kind of man who can get good things done, or stop others doing bad ones.

It is quite possible that Caroline's attitude towards George, and to what had happened, was insensibly influenced by this popular version of the occurrence. It was nice to be a celebrity in the neighbourhood, even at the expense of someone else. She wanted George back with her, none the less; although she may have had some internal reservation about how long such an arrangement was likely to last. She may have begun to realise that it was not easy to envisage any sort of future with George; or, indeed, for him.

However that might have been, it was George himself who settled the matter for her. He evaded a meeting. On his release he told her on the phone, in his polite hesitant way, that he was going down to stay with his father. He was not sure when he would be back.

She thought he sounded different. No doubt he was different. Who wouldn't have been?

Martha understood that, at least. She had heard nothing from him. She supposed, she even hoped, that he had gone back to Caroline, but she took no steps to find out. She could and would do nothing more. George had his own life to live.

Their life together had been a secret one, an affair of lairs. She had loved it, as she had loved him, but now it was over. She still longed inexpressibly for one of their old torrents of talk; and she imagined him telling her everything, and what had happened, and how and why. She could not get out of her head that ominous rhyme they had once chanted to one another. It had been delightful then, and reassuring, as cosy and harmless as a wicked fairystory.

> As one that on a lonely road
> Does walk in fear and dread,
> And, having once looked round, goes on
> And turns no more his head ...

It sounded dreadful; but in fact the words, however misremembered by George, seemed so wonderful that they conveyed nothing of their own truth. Or perhaps they delivered that truth only afterwards, when first pleasure in the poetry was gone?

It had gone now for Martha. She wondered whether George remembered it, and if so whether he said it to himself, and thought of her. It had been a love ritual, when they had left one of their harmless lairs, where they had clung to each other and caused no one any trouble. The last time they had said it together had been when they left that cellar with the guns; and that place had not been harmless, though she still had no idea just what had happened there; and she never spoke of it to her husband.

Alexander did not speak of it either. The opacity between him and his wife, which had once been so peaceful, now seemed to her as ominous as the cellar itself. What did Alexander really intend to do about George?

He was not sure himself. Although he had never thought out his intentions, it had once been his unspoken idea to own Martha and George as he owned – or part-owned – his ex-wife Fiona and her young husband Nigel. That had always been a satisfactory arrangement for all parties, as he felt. Why should not he and Martha and George form another such unit?

Why not indeed? But somehow things were not working out that way. George's own reluctance to participate was a challenge Alexander was sure he could overcome, just as he knew that Martha too would sooner or later toe the line. The trouble that

183

had led to George's ordeal in custody was of no significance either. It should even help to speed matters up.

Then what was going wrong? It must be something to do with Martha herself. He had always assumed that he understood his wife as well as could ever be necessary. Even the news of her infidelity, astonishing as it had been, had also seemed to offer its own stimulating challenge: the prospect of getting first to know, and then to possess, her lover.

For the first time he had begun to ask himself what Martha really thought about it all. Did she secretly welcome the arrangement he thought he could bring about? Did she welcome it because she would be able to make love with George at home when he, Alexander, was away at the office? No! He was sure he knew his wife better than that.

Then what was she up to? Her manner seemed impenetrable, and it had begun to excite him, as the thought of George himself had once done. Hers was now a true secrecy; and could it, invisibly even to herself, be guarding George against him?

If that were the case he could only respect it. He perceived, however dimly and almost unconsciously, what Martha's real motive might be. Had she given up all of George except for the wish to protect him, to look after him in any way she could?

If that were so he could only feel this new kind of respect for her: and to feel respect for his own wife was as alien to him, as outside the natural order of things, as had been the astonishing news of her adultery. That had excited him, because of the fascinating prospect of her fellow adulterer. But to have to feel respect for Martha merely depressed him. It was not only alien: it was objectionable.

And George himself seemed much less exciting now. Alexander hardly knew why. But, and in a way that did him credit, he was still glad that he had contrived to get that job for George's father. He didn't care whether the son was grateful for this or not. The sight of the elder Pusey's adoring eyes and his happy deferential smiles had been enough. Never mind about the younger one; he had at least given the older man a taste of pure joy. And at a time of life when he had felt himself thrown on the scrapheap, even though it had been through his own fault.

Alexander Grey was a natural fantasist and conspirator, like

184

his younger brothers. It was in the blood no doubt. But his was a much more solid and sober instance of a family failing. His scheming itself was less conscious; his façade of respectability more genuine, more kindly even. Although Martha and her secret (for she still had one, it seemed) had begun to depress rather than to stimulate him, he would not allow his own concept of their family life to suffer.

And yet he found himself spending more and more time alone with the television. He thought how big and desolate the house seemed to be becoming now. He came later and later up to bed; and in the stillness of the bedroom, with no one to see him, or for him to imagine seeing him, he cast looks of quiet resentment at his wife's sleeping form. He wondered sometimes if she were really asleep, but he took no steps to find out.

As the days wore on Martha too became aware of a change in the way her husband spoke about George, and about the future. She had become accustomed to the point of numbness to the programme he had set out when George was still in custody: helping him, putting him on his feet, looking after him together, almost as if he were a son. The prospect Alexander had so much looked forward to had ceased to sicken her, although she could still hardly bear to think about it.

Sometimes she caught herself actually hoping, however guiltily, that George would simply thwart her husband's plans for him by disappearing altogether, and of his own accord. Life without him, with their love intact in her memory, would surely be more supportable than the future Alexander had planned for them, a future in which George would be closer to her than he had ever been, and yet absent; unreachable and untouchable. Better no George at all than George on those terms? But at other times she knew she wanted him there, on any terms.

When it had been secret her love could afford to be shameless, as she had once happily thought of it. What they got up to together, in their little nooks and corners, had been nobody's business but their own. But how could she make love with George under Alexander's eye, as if it were a part of family life? The idea revolted her. And yet – how did she know – she might yet come to it, if George were to fall in with Alexander's plans for him.

185

She knew George would not do that: and she would be proud of him for evading those plans. Better that he should stay with Caroline; or, if that did not happen, better if he found someone else, and left their lives for good.

Martha suffered during this time. Her thoughts went miserably to and fro as she strove to maintain a calm and even bright exterior, and to accept the situation. It was this that both impressed Alexander and also began to get him down.

He took to travelling to London every day, as if the future of the firm still depended on him. This, and the incessant grateful letters he still received from Pusey senior, gave an unexpected stimulus to his work in the office, which till then had hardly been more than the routines of a senior executive soon to retire. He began to take sides again in high-level office intrigues. Away from home he began to enjoy himself.

The days alone were a relief to Martha. She would settle now ever more deeply into Prentice Wood; it must become her life again. She set herself the target of getting the house in really good order; she even tried to take more interest in what Mrs Jones was talking about. She lit her woodfires, like fragrant offerings, in every room. It was quite unnecessary, and it made dirt and smoke; but such achievements helped her to feel a little bit as she had done at Christmastime, when she had known a modest success in her own style.

Her new regime worked well; and she combined it with conscientious reading and needlework. She listened to talking books and the concerts on Radio 3. She got through *War and Peace* at last and started on *Anna Karenina*. *Madame Bovary*, in an old translation, she soon gave up because it depressed her, and did not go with the sensible new life she was going to live. Her affair with George had not been a mistake, she concluded. She must think of it as a bonus offered by fate and added to her life, but it was over now. Only in church did he still seem with her. She turned her head to look over her shoulder at least once during each service, to see the place where she had once seen George, standing there at the back on Christmas morning.

And then one day when she was at the hall window, polishing the woodwork, she saw him walking up the drive. It was a little after twelve o'clock, and Mrs Jones had just gone home.

186

Three hours later a taxi came to the door. Martha and George got in with a bag or two. They held on to each other's knees as they went up the drive, out of the sight of the taxi-driver. Martha did not look back at the house.

Nor had she left a note. But at seven that evening she rang Alexander and told him what had happened. He was just home from the office, as she had calculated. She did not want him to be alarmed and wonder what had become of her. Because she was in a callbox, and with limited change, they had only a brief conversation.

CHAPTER 12

Home

With his old butterfly can-opener George beheaded another massive tin of baked beans. He was in a small kitchen, smaller even that the kitchen at the Bayleaf, and less professionally fitted out. Through the partition Martha could be heard talking to a solitary customer in the café, and there was a chink of crockery as she put down his pot of tea and cake.

George poured most of the beans into a saucepan, to be heated up later and added to sausages and fried eggs. He and Martha drew the line at cooking chips. To the rest of the beans he added some chopped chives and mint, a little crushed garlic, lemon juice and oil, and a pinch or two of curry powder. This was a recipe of Martha's, and he was preparing it for the occasional evening regular who liked it, or a chance comer who might show curiosity. On the slate where she wrote the daily menu Martha described it as Arabian Salad.

No one could really accuse George of making a mess of things, even of baked beans. In any case making a mess of things, particularly of their lives, is the best that some people can do.

While George was stirring the bean mixture he felt as happy as he ever did these days, and reassured by the sound of Martha's voice. Next moment she came in, and gave him a quick kiss as she refilled the kettle. A couple had just come in and ordered a cream tea.

Most of these things had been brought to pass by Mr Pusey's new wife.

She was called Phoebe-Ann, and had been widowed for a few years. She was the daughter of a farmer, like the first Mrs Pusey. She and Martha Grey had become best friends, as they might have said had they been eleven or twelve again, and at school together.

She had entirely taken over her new husband, and she had made herself responsible for George and Martha as well. She was also about to have a child, her first.

Martha was in a state of ecstasy about this. Her new friend, masterful as she was, had found Martha a great source of reassurance and encouragement. She also looked forward to making use of Martha as a nursemaid and babysitter.

It happened that a small and rather run-down café had been for sale, in the village where Phoebe-Ann and her relations lived, and where she had brought her husband to live after they had got married. Phoebe-Ann had decided this might be just the thing for George and Martha. She had got it cheap, and between the three of them it had become quite a success. True, when she became pregnant Phoebe-Ann had decided she might have to make some other arrangement about the café, for with the baby she would be needing Martha's services. But that was still in the future.

Martha had no time now for church on Sunday mornings. It was their busiest day. She sometimes went early, and then George always accompanied her. The parson assumed at first he was her son.

George's father commuted daily to his work on the new building project, ten miles off. Things were going well for him there. He fitted beautifully into the close circle of Phoebe-Ann's family. It was like a business. Her father and mother, still hale and hearty, married sister, older brother on the farm, younger running the local garage. A strong family; and they all recognised Phoebe-Ann to be the most dynamic and resourceful among them.

She had helped manage her former husband's business concerns, and her only sorrow had been lack of children. Now that she was over forty and pregnant for the first time, and had got not only a new husband but a new stepson and daughter-in-law, all ideal for her needs, she was able once again to fill her circle with the satisfactions she was born to receive, and to give.

Ideal for her needs? In a peculiar way, yes. She, and all her kin, had accepted Martha and George, and their quaint relationship, without a second's hesitation or difficulty. So indeed had George's father, as he accepted everything that had been proc-

190

essed or sanctified by his new wife. Seeing the four of them together, the two pairs, an outside spectator would take it for granted that Martha and Mr Pusey senior were a comfortable couple, about the same age. George and Phoebe-Ann might have been their son and daughter, or Phoebe-Ann might have been their daughter-in-law. The actual pattern of their relationship would hardly have been suspected; and yet the four of them had quickly come to take it so much for granted that they would have felt surprised, in their turn, at its being thought unusual.

Indisputably the four of them, soon to become five, made up a family group. Martha and George still had their secret. But it had become invisible. It was both cherished and ignored.

They had their old privacy too, though in a different form: a bungalow close to the café. George painted and decorated it, doing the doors and shelves in different colours. Lovingly absorbed in this work he would chatter to Martha by the hour, as in the old days, although now his tones sounded more subdued. Nor did Martha listen very closely: she did not always catch what he said. After a heavy day he sometimes tired her a little; but she knew he was still happy with her, and that she reassured him.

There were moments, perhaps more often than before, when she too needed the voice of reassurance. For him to call her by her old pet name for instance. But when at a moment of love she referred to herself as his Dulcie, she was chagrined to see him turn away his head, looking as if he were biting a lemon.

In the course of nature she and George would have gone their separate ways. That had not happened. But they were no longer lovers. There was a price to pay for living happily ever after. George's visible expression, when the old pet name was uttered, suggested what it invisibly was.

Relations with her new family were often a relief to Martha now. In their presence George was much quieter. But he was always polite and diligent, and full of a slightly anxious helpfulness. Phoebe-Ann was kind to him, bossing him a little. He looked as grateful for that as his father did, and Martha never minded the hint of patronage in her new family's treatment of her loved one.

She did not trouble herself with illusions. George had come

191

back to her because he had found there was nowhere else to go, no refuge as proper to him as the old lair. She felt she could keep him now with a clear conscience.

They had changed roles: it was George, and not Martha, who was now in the seat of obligation. He was grateful as she had once been to all human beings, just for letting him be. He was grateful now to everyone but Martha; and the rest of the family neither knew or bothered about how he behaved when alone with her.

Martha's conscience was all the clearer because of the manner in which she herself had conducted affairs with Alexander. There had been no suggestion of a divorce. Alexander did not want one; and in this matter at least she had still been happy to oblige him. He had offered a generous settlement; she had stoutly refused to take a penny of his money. With whatever motives, he had already done them the best of good turns; and she was more grateful for this than many beneficiaries would have been. She and George owed everything, as she was well aware, to the excellent job that her husband had found for the elder Mr Pusey.

And so Martha remained firm; and, naturally enough, without consulting George. She had brought nothing to her marriage, and she would take nothing away, now that the marriage had apparently come to an end. (Even about that there seemed to be no certainty, just as there could never be any certainty, for her, about George's future.)

Was it possible that she could keep George closer to her by not having very much money, and by not always sharing with him what they had? Yes, it was possible.

Martha was greatly cheered by the equability, or the indifference, which her own children had shown about her present arrangements. Penelope was intrigued by what she heard of her mother's lover; and she paid a visit once in order to view him. She was nice, if a little queenly, to them all; and her appearance was a success, the more so because she herself had got engaged at last, to a fellow merchant banker. They were all invited to her wedding. Martha would have loved to have gone, leaving George to mind the café; but she decided against it in the end: she did not really feel equal to facing Alexander. At least not yet.

Later on perhaps, when she hoped to see as much of her daughter, and the new husband, as could be managed.

Martha's sudden disappearance from Earlwood had naturally occasioned a good deal of talk. Where had she gone off to, and with whom? Alexander made no comment: nor did he give, as he could have done, the local equivalent of a news conference. Media-wise however, as things turned out, that might have been the sounder move.

For local opinion at Earlwood soon began insensibly and mysteriously to go against him. Unlike Mrs Stringham, at the exciting time of the scandal about her husband and the public lavatory, Alexander came somehow to be thought to have behaved rather less than splendidly. Highly unfair of course; but there it was. It began to be thought, on the other hand, that it was Martha who had done in some way the right and proper thing, even the splendid one.

Quite what she had done, however, her former acquaintance remained uncertain. Naturally, the Earlwooders had known of George, but they knew nothing of the previous role he had played in Martha's life. And so the story got about that Martha, always in her own way mildly popular in the area, had gallantly if inadvertently sacrificed her own solid marriage in order to redeem and sustain young George Pusey, and to rescue him from the consequences of his own folly, though it never became clear just what that had been.

*

Bobby Grey's domestic circumstances at this time were also unusual, but they were much less harmonious. Nor in any quarter in which he was known was he thought to have behaved splendidly. Quite the reverse.

He had hoped to have been thought dead. His death would have had a certain convenience for some people; but it had been easier to arrange to be killed than to keep that fact of his demise alive. Some who heard of it were not the sort of people who left such news alone. It was soon evident that the rumour he had set going had been exaggerated.

But his actual whereabouts remained obscure. Officials and

interested parties, who were anxious to pursue his present and in some cases his previous misdemeanours, received routine reports of sightings, but nothing positive had been established, and such indications as occurred were not necessarily followed up with zeal. Some persons would have liked to have found him, but others preferred not to. Those familiar with his temperament and his old habits assumed he was abroad somewhere. Probably leading the life of Riley on a beach in South America. Even his brother Peter thought that.

The real thing, as regards dying, might have been the better bet?

That sometimes did occur to him. It remained a fact, however, that the Irishman hadn't obliged. And Bobby did occasionally wish that he hadn't tried so damned hard to discourage him. Done his damnedest, when it came to the point. Even so it might have been a close call if he hadn't told young George Pusey to hop it and had not the young fellow so promptly obliged. That had made all the difference. Bobby knew that O'Connor was hardly likely to shoot the son of his former benefactor, his Santa Monica. And after George's exit it was clear both to Bobby and to his potential murderer that the cellar must be blown before the police got to know about it. It had not been difficult to persuade O'Connor of that. A hefty explosion in this respectable spot could only be good publicity for the IRA boys, however the authorities explained it.

Quite a neat feat of co-operation. And yet he had known O'Connor would be after him again. Perhaps after George too? – that had to be considered. What with one thing and another he himself needed to lie low, hide himself away. Not that it would do him much good in the long run. As for the money, he hadn't made any. That Thing, whether it existed or not, had been a total failure on the Futures Market.

And that was why he was not enjoying the tropic twilight at the moment, with a glass of rum punch beside him. His digs, as it happened, did face the seafront; but it was that of a grim little resort in the north of England. The sea was not visible from his bedsit, and that was one slight relief. There was a fish and chip shop instead, over the way.

Landlord was an ex-sergeant. Fine upstanding chap; or had

been when they had first met. Served together in the Middle East. The sergeant had come to show great aptitude there in the procurement and sale of illegal substances.

Quite a bit of money in that, until they'd been rumbled. So he'd had to resign his commission, and Staff-Sergeant Corke had been busted. But he was a loyal sort of chap, and always an admirer for some reason, although his wife had taken against Major Bobby. As a lot of women did, if they didn't fall for him. Corke might yet be a help though, if O'Connor happened to be around.

And that might well be the next thing. It was always on his mind. Very persistent fellows those Irish, or at least these IRA types. Never let up, or so it seemed. So this time it might really be curtains for Major Bobby. And yet you never knew. He and O'Connor might become bosom pals in the local. It was a cat and mouse situation. Bobby had once been the cat himself. But no longer.

Up in his room he spent his time listening to the wireless. He liked radio-plays, full of the bogus northern voices of those BBC actors, whom he called to himself the Scargill shits. For amusement he toiled away on his own imaginary obituary. There was a casual reference in it, near the end, to the hazardous destruction of an IRA arms dump. Stiff upper lip. A job that had to be done.

But however many versions he produced it never sounded quite right. He sat there for hours with a bitten Bic pen in his hand, staring at the haze that hovered above the fish shop chimney.

*

Martha was not concerned with obituaries, her own or anyone else's, but on the day she left Prentice Wood she had taken a talisman with her. She had been hastening about upstairs, sweeping clothes into a bag. George was sitting huddled in the drawing-room, where she had momentarily left him. She looked for the last time into her kitchen, and her eye caught that of the woman on a big Christmas card. When the other cards came down she had put this one up high on the dresser.

195

It was well presented: an expensive affair sent by some firm with which Alexander had connections. A chaste gold inscription, low down on the back, explained it as a funerary picture from Fayoum, in Roman Egypt. Getting on for two thousand years old the original must have been; and it was in the British Museum. Martha had taken to communing with this woman, whose long face and round dark eyes gazed straight at her.

Martha had felt impelled every day to greet the woman, and to get to know who she was. She felt she could do that. So before she left the kitchen she took the card and tucked it carefully into her bag.

Now when George was absent from the bedroom she sometimes got it out for a look. George had never seen it. It was the one thing she kept from him. She fancied the woman in the picture would understand why that was.

She could not help wondering sometimes if George had anything he kept from her. She need not have wondered: George had. It was also a picture, which he put away as soon as it occurred to him. It was of her, as he first saw her; and before (like all women, as he supposed) she turned into something that might just as well have been a man. Caroline had always been like that for him, he remembered. But Martha at least remained in his mind's eye; and the picture he had there made no difference to the way in which he now lived with her.

Most days he thought of her as she had once been for him; and most days Martha had a look at the woman on the card, noticing how the unknown artist had made the eyes so huge and dark and round by putting a tiny spot of pure white near the top of each.

Just after Martha's daughter got married she wrote to her mother to say that Alexander had sold Prentice Wood. He had kept it on so long really for her sake she said – the reception and all that – and for Ben of course, who had so many local friends. She was sorry her mother had not come to the wedding, but she had quite understood. George was sweet, she added.

Alexander had gone to live somewhere near Haywards Heath. Penelope did not think it necessary to mention that was where Fiona and Nigel were living. She knew her mother knew that.

Martha had made it her business to get to know Caroline, in the days when George was in custody. Now she heard from her – an exuberant letter. She was going to be married to a really nice man who managed some National Trust properties, and she was expecting a baby. Martha felt very glad for her.

Ginnie had also written to Martha. It was a dull sympathetic letter, hoping that everything was turning out happily. About her own difficulties she said nothing at all, although she thanked Martha for her advice and support, that time after Christmas. She did mention that Peter was still away.

Martha knew Ginnie would never be close to her now. This made her sad, after the letter had come. She could not help wondering whether Ginnie had realised that the doomed appointment with George had been the reason for the lack of sympathy the poor woman had found, when she had blundered over Martha's doorstep.

Martha thought of that with a little shame and a good deal of regret. Could she really have been in such a fever that day about George, so determined to have and to hug him at Rosamond? Nowadays as she bustled about she was often absent with him; concerned with and thinking of other things, and answering him as one answers a child.

But George was not a child, nor was he like one. He was not growing and demanding and changing. He was, on the contrary, as calm and secure as a husband. For yes, to her now he *was* a husband. She still found his presence in the bed the best thing in her new life. And she forgot there that he should have a proper job; or that he should be studying, or learning how to be a builder, or an architect, or something like that.

She sometimes felt, and really quite guiltily, that she should speak seriously to his father about it all. But Mr Pusey (as she still always thought of him) was so taken up with his own job, his wife, and the joyful prospect of paternity, that she hadn't the heart to bother him. Nor did she really want to. She perceived that Mr Pusey, who had more experience of his son than she had, realised in his own way that nothing much need or could be done about George. And she was happy to acquiesce in that.

Martha had been doing her best for so long to oblige the human race that plain selfishness, when it arrived for her at last, came as a natural benison, like true love. She, like George, had done all the wrong things. Yet the right things, for her and perhaps even for him, seemed to have come out of them.

*

Perhaps they had for Ginnie too. All she had said in her letter to Martha was that Peter was away. That was true. He was. And so was Pinky.

Neither of them seemed likely to return in the foreseeable future.

Of the Grey brothers it was Peter who was having the worst of the deal, however much he had brought it upon himself. All the insouciant pleasures of an English life, on which he had always so much depended, had run out on him at last.

His depressions, most unusual for him, made Vera quite concerned, although he depended on her more and more, and strove to remain cheerful for her sake. Yet today his heart, once abnormally buoyant, was often heavy within him. He missed Ginnie, far more that he would have expected. He even missed his brother Bobby, now gone to ground and incommunicado. Above all he missed England.

He had derided the place; made hay with it; let it down whenever possible. But now he missed it sorely. Exiled from that happy home he felt as hopeless as a boy on his first day at school. He loved and clung to the past; he hated the present; and he dreaded the future. So many of the Russians all around him seemed to feel the same way.

His one great solace was Pinky. As they strolled along the handsome granite bank of the Neva they communed together as they had always done. He was coming to depend on her more and more, and she herself was growing almost by the day. Was she going to be a little Russian girl, or would she remain an English one? Peter often thought, and with a remorse that was most unusual for him, what a strange fate he had brought upon her. Fortunately she seemed to be enjoying it no end.

And Vera, who had begun by putting up with her step-daughter – Vera would have endured anything for Peter's sake – had become first fond of her, and then doting. They chattered together in Russian, which, thanks to Vera, Pinky already knew well. It amused her father that Pinky, the one-time paedophobe, loved her Russian school-mates, among whom she was highly popular. She boasted to them about England.

In her new life she hardly mentioned her mother, although Peter spoke of Ginnie to her every day (it was a secret way of saying how much he missed his other wife). He told Pinky she would soon be visiting her mother over there back in England. (But would she?) He encouraged the sending of frequent post-cards to the flat in South Kensington, with pictures of ice and snow and fir-trees, palaces and witches and water-maidens from Pushkin's poems. Also postcards with the portrait photo of Lenin. Pinky had conceived a great admiration for the founder of the Soviet state.

CHAPTER 13

With Loved Ones Far Away ...

Ginnie put a neat squiggle in the margin of the MS, and added a questionmark with her red ballpoint. The author would use the word 'horrendous': this was the third time in what was not in other respects a bad thriller. Its message was: stay private.

She was going over it like this in order not to have to go back to the labour of wrestling with a blurb. Her boss has asked her to jot down ideas for one, if at all possible, for a novel called *Away from Somewhere*. She was gratified he had asked her, but was finding it something of a trial. Its author had decided that *Away from Somewhere* was about 'the politics of belonging'. That phrase at least Ginnie could cling to, as she turned 'angry', 'powerful', and 'passionate' round and about. 'Anger' could go with 'sex' and 'familial' with 'protest' perhaps? Actually she had rather enjoyed the novel, powerful as it undoubtedly was; and she had grown quite absorbed by the two sisters' struggle to find out who they really were. When the novel came to a halt they were still undecided, but Decla was helping on a broadsheet.

She must get new glasses, Ginnie decided; she was beginning to peer over the top of her present ones. She felt humble about Decla, the leading character in the novel, and wondered what she was doing now; for it was Ginnie's habit to go on with novels in her own head, if they had appealed to her at all.

Her own story was, as it were, resting for the moment; and she was by now fairly certain who she was. No doubt she would be a different person if she hadn't had the abortion, nearly two years ago it must be. So all that was somewhere behind her.

Pinky, now getting on for eight, still seemed not particularly to care who she was, or might be. Though always restless she was as nearly noiseless as ever, and her company was not un-soothing. She still had the habit of murmuring under her breath as she wandered about. Ginnie did not presume to ask what stories she had lately taken to telling herself; but she identified with her daughter's daydreaming faculty, and even took a sort of pride in it.

This was Pinky's second visit to England since she had set off for Russia with her father and step-mother. Ginnie had no idea how these trips had been arranged. She had been rung by Peter, who had always phoned or written regularly, and asked if she could come and collect Pinky for a holiday in London. Ginnie had gone at once: the publishers for whom she worked proving sympathetic.

So it had been a second time. She had barely encountered Peter and his wife, nor had she seen anything of the town of St Petersburg. Peter had simply brought their daughter to the airport. Ginnie thought she herself preferred it that way, and it was clear that he did. Pinky still seemed to find it natural too.

Ginnie missed her husband more intermittently than she had expected. Chiefly, she sometimes thought, she missed his lying to her. That had become and been so cosy, so much a part of their relationship. It went with his flattering awareness of her, which had always been total; and delightful. It had occurred to her as she reflected in her grasswidowhood, or whatever it should be called, that the natural possession of honesty often made the possessor indifferent to the feelings of others. Liars were much more in touch: no doubt they had to be. Perfect sympathy went with constant wariness, unending dissimulation.

Well, all that was over anyway. She knew Peter would have liked to spend some time with her still: in England, as husband and wife. But Vera stood in the way. She would not have let him sleep with Ginnie, and Ginnie knew quite well that Vera would know if he had. Vera was the one person to whom he could not lie, and had never done so. Perhaps that was why she had got him in the end.

They could not themselves visit England. Too dangerous. At least that was what Peter said, and though she disbelieved him, as she disbelieved everything he had told her, it looked as if something – apart from Vera – did indeed stand in the way. But perhaps that too, the danger of arrest or some other trouble, was something Vera herself had fixed up? Who could say? It seemed

202

quite possible. Ginnie admired her predecessor and successor with detachment. Vera could do anything.

She had certainly proved a good stepmother to Pinky. The child continued to flourish in her new environment. Recently she had taken up ballet; although, as she airily told her mother, it was just for amusement. Tomorrow Ginnie would be taking her home again. Home was St Petersburg now.

The phone rang. Pinky strolled across to answer it. She liked phones. She knew from her visit how few calls her mother got.

She listened gravely, and then made a noise of assent and turned to her mother.

'Your old friend Alice,' she announced, looking at Ginnie with a new kind of respect.

Ginnie picked up the receiver. It couldn't be *that* Alice, surely? And even when she heard the voice she was still sure it couldn't be. There was no trace of those warm and lazy tones, synthetically and yet somehow comfortingly Australian, which had been so much a part of love in the hotel bedroom at Sorrento, and down in the little bungalow on Romney Marsh.

'Gin?'

No one else had ever called her that, but she was still bewildered.

'That isn't you, Alice?'

'Oh yes it is, Gin.'

The voice sounded cultured and dynamic, with the vowels touched up a little, American-style, and a hint of the old bossiness in a new form. It was a voice that was still happy to take Ginnie's cluelessness benevolently for granted.

'And you're just the same as ever, my love? Sitting reading away in that little flat of yours?'

Alice didn't pause for an answer of course. Her voice, still disconcertingly unfamiliar, sped on. She had been in America for years, had a high-powered job. A penthouse flat in New York. A cottage at the end of Long Island. Over on business, as she sometimes was. Suddenly got it into her head to give a ring to her old Ginnie. Just the same as ever she knew she'd find her.

'Well come and see me, Alice – do!' What else could she say? And yet she couldn't help adding, 'I shall always remember

203

those bonks that weren't. And are you still doing any smuggling?'

Alice in the old days would have been delighted by such mock-humorous queries, and have laughed, as she would have put it, like a drain. Long ago, in the lumpy bed at 'Silver Spray', Alice had confessed that the tales she had told Ginnie of her exploits with cruise passengers at Sorrento, and the money she had made out of them, had all been made up. The real Alice, if there were such a thing, had been as virginal as Ginnie.

The smuggling had been real enough however. Ginnie was not likely to forget the day the 'Boys' had visited the cottage, when that Irishman, Pat O'Connor, had nearly raped her.

Pinky beside her was jumping up and down with excitement. 'Bonk' was a term she was still unfamiliar with, and it would no doubt have vanished from circulation before she was much older. But that her mother should have known a female smuggler she found wildly exciting. And the smuggler was coming to see them! Pinky on her visits secretly found London a rather boring place, and this sudden turn of events promised new and unexpected thrills.

Ginnie saw that Alice, like 'Muz Paybody' and Vera herself, might well become one of those celebrities before whom her daughter used to prostrate herself in silent adoration.

Alice's new voice seemed less heartily amused by Ginnie's queries than it would once have been. She too had been an inveterate liar, like Peter. It occurred to Ginnie that the only two people she had loved had both been liars. But Alice had seemed to tell her lies as a favour. They conferred an obligation almost, as part of her charm. Certainly they had enabled her to possess and manipulate Ginnie.

Alice was asking now about 'Silver Spray'. Wouldn't it be fun to run down there together and see the old place? It was clear that, like many donors in munificence, Alice still felt possessive about the bungalow she had bestowed on her friend.

'Well Alice, what a pity! This really is sad. I'm just going away.'

'You are, Gin?' The voice sounded definitely disapproving now. It was not for Ginnie to rush about the place. She should be

204

sitting reading in her little room, waiting for her friend to re-appear. After what was now getting on for a ten-year absence.

'Well I'll drop in right now, Gin. You got a friend there by the way?'

That, Alice's voice made clear, was not the way things should be either.

'It's my daughter, Alice.'

'What was that you said, Gin?'

'My daughter. We're off back tomorrow to my husband in St Petersburg. He's working out there.'

Ginnie, as she said this, gave her daughter a most uncharacteristic wink. What she was saying was strictly true. She always told the truth, so far as she could.

Pinky looked uncertain for a moment and then smiled broadly at her mother, with a happy air of joining the little conspiracy.

After hearing of this outrage on her old friend's part it was clear that Alice wanted to hear no more. But Ginnie decided to tell her anyway.

'My little girl's got the same name as you, Alice. Pinky we call her. Isn't that nice?'

That Ginnie should have presumed to become two people was bad enough; and Ginnie knew that only brute curiosity could have forced out of Alice a disdainful 'Who's we then?'

'Well, me and my husband. The funny thing is that you knew his brother, down at Littlestone. Bobby Grey – remember him? This is his brother, Peter.'

Bobby, who had bewitched her briefly when she met him, all that time ago, on the golf links, had stolen Alice's suitcase, with the drug haul that turned out to be worthless. Alice had hoped to run away with him.

Ginnie had gone well beyond the limit now. It was the first time she had reduced the other to silence. That she, whose sole function had been attendance on her patroness, should have become Mrs Grey, sister-in-law of Alice's Bobby! – No, this was too much!

It was all too clear from her silence that Alice thought so. But Ginnie's own moment of triumph was over in a second, and instead she felt ashamed of herself. What a mean thing to do!

205

And it would leave her afterwards more desolate than ever. She couldn't help looking at Pinky for a little reassurance, and was relieved to see her still enjoying the joke.

As their eyes met, Ginnie remembered that last talk in bed with Alice, with the lighthouse beam coming and going on the ceiling. They had slept then; and later Alice had woken her, and taken her down to the sea's edge. The faintly phosphorescent foam ran over their bare feet as they stood there in the dawn with their arms round each other.

She found her own eyes swimming. Pinky saw it too, and looked away with a slightly contemptuous expression.

'But do come and see me, Alice – you must!' – and she found herself wondering if her old friend was really so much on top of the world after all. Had she rung up in search of help and support? Even money?

'Can I do anything?' But again she had gone too far. Alice had regained all her old poise, and her new voice, tailor-made for her role as high-powered executive.

'Not a thing, Gin, not a thing. Just thought I'd look you up for the sake of our old times. But to tell you the truth I'm going to be that busy till I fly back I don't know when I'll have a moment. I'll ring again,' she went on, choosing to ignore Ginnie's own imminent departure, 'when I see how things turn out. 'Bye now.'

And Alice was gone.

Barely was the receiver down before the phone rang again. Pinky looked as if she could hardly believe it. Ginnie picked it up this time.

'Hello?'

'Hello. I am talking to Ginnie Thornton?'

'Well, yes.' It had been her maiden name.

'Mark Brassey.'

No 'you remember me, don't you?' or anything of that sort. But of course she remembered him. It never rains but it pours. First Alice, and now Alice's old suitor, for here was another relic from those bygone days: the bland capable solicitor whom Ginnie had met in the Sorrento hotel, and who had wanted to marry Alice. Alice had then shown every sign of wanting to marry him, too. There had been an engagement, but Alice had 'chucked' him in the end. So Mark had told Ginnie at the time. How long ago it seemed. She had not seen Mark after she met Peter.

But he had taken her out to dinner in Sorrento – she could still recall those delicious *cervelli fritti* – and in his own way had seemed to enjoy her society. In a pleasant almost invisible fashion, he had wondered about her experience of sex. She had none at the time: but, as it happened, Alice had knocked on her door that night, taken her to bed and made love to her. Not much fun, she remembered, and a good deal of embarrassment; but after a sleepless and uncomfortable night she had enjoyed snuggling up to the big girl in the early morning, and dozing off at last.

Quite submerged in these memories Ginnie stood holding the phone in silence. Mark had taken her out to dinner once or twice in London too. She was still a virgin she told him cheerfully, on one such occasion. He had always seemed mildly curious to know, with no intention of doing anything about it.

'Are you there?' said his voice impatiently.

'Oh yes, Mark, – so sorry. How nice to hear you.'

'Are you free for dinner tomorrow?' It was not really a question, because the voice had total confidence that she would be free.

'Law Society dinner,' he went on. 'The lady I invited has had to cry off at the last minute.'

She knew that Mark was bestowing a singular favour.

'Oh I am sorry, Mark. But I'm afraid I can't. Not tomorrow.'

Pinky was all ears again.

'I'm flying to St Petersburg with my daughter. My husband is out there.'

Perfect truth again. And perfect stupefaction the other end. But at least it was simple amazement, not the outrage displayed by Alice.

'Oh. Well, I must look elsewhere then. Goodbye.'

'And some other time I hope,' Ginnie was beginning to say, but the line was already dead. So she smiled at Pinky and began to tell her about Mark Brassey, whom Pinky had not heard about before.

Alice and Mark had both been right, really, in their sense of the proper fitness of things. She would not be disappointing them much longer. She could hardly wait to get back to the life that everyone seemed to think she should live, and always would live. It would be a life that was finally her own.